Squaring the Circle was made possible by a generous grant from the Pokolenie Foundation. A humanitarian foundation, Pokolenie was created in 1996 by Andrei Skoch, a teacher turned State Duma Deputy. Skoch's original intention was to help children with heart problems. Pokolenie's long list of beneficiaries has since expanded to include pensioners, disabled, war veterans, Chernobyl liquidators, and many others in need.

Today Pokolenie continues to supply modern medical equipment and ambulances to provincial Russian clinics. It also equips rural schools with computers, training tractors and combines. It builds and restores churches, helps orphanages and sponsors numerous other good works.

In addition to the Debut Prize for young writers, Pokolenie has instituted two prestigious prizes in the field of medicine: the Academicians Alexander Bakulev and Vladimir Burakovsky Prize for heart surgeons and the Healthy Childhood Prize for specialists at the Children's Clinical Hospital in Moscow where children from all over Russia come for treatment.

GLAS NEW RUSSIAN WRITING

CONTEMPORARY RUSSIAN LITERATURE

IN ENGLISH TRANSLATION

VOLUME 47

Squaring the Circle

Short Stories by Winners of the Debut Prize

**Compiled by
Olga Slavnikova**

glas
MOSCOW

GLAS PUBLISHERS
tel/fax: +7(495)441-9157
perova@glas.msk.su
www.glas.msk.su

DISTRIBUTION

in North America
Northwestern University Press
Chicago Distribution Center
tel: 1-800-621-2736 or (773) 702-7000
fax: 1-800-621-8476 or (773) 702-7212
pubnet@202-5280
www.nupress.northwestern.edu

in the UK
CENTRAL BOOKS
orders@centralbooks.com
www.centralbooks.com

Direct orders: INPRESS
Tel: 0191 229 9555
customerservices@inpressbooks.co.uk
www.inpressbooks.co.uk

Within Russia
Jupiter-Impex
www.jupiterbooks.ru

The series' editors: Natasha Perova and Joanne Turnbull
Camera-ready copy: Tatiana Shaposhnikova
Front cover: Yulia Panteleeva of Sever Publishing House

ISBN 978-5-7172-0086-8

CONTENTS

INTRODUCTION

This book presents Russian prose by a new generation. The authors never lived in the Soviet Union — or were very young when the USSR collapsed. They are new people, and entirely new writers. They are free of the Soviet legacy in all senses. They have no nostalgia and do not resonate to the sort of art that attempts to turn everything Soviet into vintage chic. And unlike many older writers, they are not fighting the Soviet past.

These new writers are simply living their lives and simply writing about them. That "simply" is of great value and importance. Only this newest generation of Russian prose writers has at last been able to see the present moment in its entirety. One may say without exaggeration that this is the most ingenuous and honest literature in Russia since 1917, the year of the deplorable October coup.

Why the title *Squaring the Circle*? The authors of this book and their young readers live in a system of multiple uncertainties. The problems that life poses them often have no solution. To solve what is insoluble, to do what is undoable: that is the demand made of a young person today by unpredictable Russian reality. Young people have no algorithms for building their lives and careers. No one can promise that a particular effort will lead to a particular result. Just the opposite may be true. There are no guarantees, but anything is possible. It is this system of uncertainties — that so abruptly replaced the Soviet man's "confidence in tomorrow" — which taxed the parents of these young writers during the turbulent 1990s. But the children have adapted surprisingly well and cannot imagine living according to a plan or knowing their entire life in advance. Theirs is a fundamentally new way of thinking, a new way of seeing the world.

Literature, as a form of activity with no guaranteed results, suits this generation. Although you would think: in Russia, as elsewhere, people are reading fewer and fewer books. Literature as an art form cannot compete with the entertainment industry. The new generation is a computer generation: computer games and the blogosphere cut into a book's readership. In Russia this situation is compounded by the fact that the old (Soviet) system of book distribution has fallen apart, while a new one has yet to be built. Russia's vast expanses are impassable for literature. Large wholesale book dealers send commercial books to the provinces, while new intellectual titles are often confined to Moscow and St. Petersburg alone.

Nevertheless a new generation is declaring itself with increasing confidence in poetry, prose, and plays. In Russia it is known as the Debut generation.

In the early 1990s the Booker Prize, brought to Russia from Britain thanks to the kind offices of Sir Michael Caine, gave new impetus to the Russian novel. A decade later came a prize for young authors, a prize that helped engender a new literature, an example of which you now hold in your hands.

The Debut Prize was instituted in 2000 by State Duma Deputy Andrei Skoch, creator of the humanitarian foundation Pokolenie (Generation). Skoch originally conceived of Pokolenie as a medical charity to help provincial Russian clinics, sick children and pensioners. The Debut, Pokolenie's only cultural project to date, has become a prize of national renown.

The Debut has a strict age limit: entrants may not be over the age of 25. Members of the Russian literary establishment were skeptical at first. They doubted that writers so young would have something to say to readers. Young writers might try their hand at poetry, they argued, but they didn't have enough life experience to write a story or a novel.

However, the Debut has shown that a person's life

experience at any age is complete in and of itself. What a person knows about the world at 20 has been forgotten by the time he is 30. What he could have written at 20 he will no longer write at 30. He will write something else. Strangely enough, most writers live without their first book: it remains in their minds, in drafts. The Debut inspires young Russian writers to complete that first book. The Debut prompts them to commit to literature their unique experience, what might be described as the shock of their first encounter with grown-up life. Not just their new existential status, but daily events. Suddenly a person is faced with bank applications, having to pay rent and buy insurance; no one will fill out the forms for him, no one will answer for him. And he suddenly feels horribly alone in the world. This sort of loneliness, like any other, has a huge creative potential. The Debut brings in the first literary harvest of the writing generation — and it does so every year.

Every year, the Debut receives from 30,000 to 50,000 entries from every region of Russia, former Soviet republics and around the world. These are reviewed by a large board of experts: critics, literary journalists, writers. Since 2005 the board has also included Debut "graduates". Entries compete in different categories: prose, poetry, essay, drama, fantasy, children's literature. The short list totals 100 authors. The semi-finalists are judged by a jury. The jury generally consists of the biggest names in contemporary Russian literature. The Debut finalists (20 to 25 in all) are brought to Moscow in early December for what is known as Debut Week — lectures, master classes, talks at writers' clubs and the awards ceremony, a highlight of the literary season. The winners in the various categories each receive 200,000 rubles (approximately £4000). Pokolenie then publishes the works of the finalists and the winners in anthologies or as separate books.

2010 marks the first year of Debut's international program. Funded by Pokolenie, the program aims to present the works of

Debut finalists and winners to the foreign reader. Collections of these works will be translated and their authors will be sent to international book fairs and festivals. This year's collection appears in English and Chinese. Future collections will be brought out in French, German, Italian, Spanish, Japanese, and so on. Since the number of Debut finalists and winners is only increasing, as is their level and mastery, publication of their works in English will continue.

Today an unusually gifted generation is entering Russian literature: not only the tens of thousands of competitors for the Debut Prize but, above all, the ones who remain when all the sifting through all those reams of Cyrillic is done. Literature has not seen such an influx of energy in a long time. Perhaps this change is an anthropological response to the difficult position of culture and literature. This new generation writing in Russian — both the individual writers and the phenomenon as a whole — deserves great attention.

Olga Slavnikova
Writer, winner of the Russian Booker Prize
Director of the Debut Prize

Squaring the Circle

Для Мэри от Кузнеца,
19. 11. 2010
Лук

ALEKSEI LUKYANOV

High Pressure

Translated by Marian Schwartz

Make yourself comfortable.
We're glad you chose our toilet paper.
Have a nice time.

1.

The crisis caught the RailTrans management with its pants down. The southern switching zone had just met its freight quota, for which the workers had been given a bonus, and literally a day later they screwed up a shaft on a locomotive. It might have been okay. Put it in the roundhouse, nose to the grindstone, and repair the damn engine, but the spare parts were a little pricey — nearly five million. Before the general — that's what they called the general manager — could get angry at his negligent subordinates, the world financial crisis broke.

True, there was a slight delay finding out about it.

First Lyokha the smith came to work in a pretty foul mood.

"What's your beef?" the welder asked.

"The Internet's out!" Lyokha flung open his locker and started changing. "It worked 'til twelve, the bastard, and then bam! Nothing."

"I had my TV set stop working," Mitya joined the conversation.

"Me, too," Andryukha chimed in. "I was watching Oskar and De La Hoya duke it out. He'd just nailed him!"

At the height of the sports commentary the mechanic popped into the changing room.

"Gomarjoba!' he greeted them.

"Oskar, did you really nail De La Hoya last night like they say?" Lyokha asked him.

"Me and my left!" the mechanic agreed. "Busted him up so bad the TV went out and still isn't working."

"You, too?"

Later it turned out the radio wasn't working either, on any frequency, their cell phones were silent, and even the land lines had gone haywire.

"Radio Moscow is whacked! All the radio stations of the Soviet Union are dead!" the smith declared solemnly when even the radio in the factory kitchen responded with the silence of the grave.

Until further notice, as it turned out.

Two days later a telegram arrived, saying the government of our Russian capitalist federation regrets to inform you that the radio, television, and Internet, as well as cellular and cable communications, are done for. Basically, there's no beer now or for the foreseeable future. Our means of mass communication now are the mails and the papers will be coming out more often.

The newspapers did start to pile up, coming out morning and evening and sometimes even at lunchtime. Naturally, no one much felt like working. The men started comparing what was being written in which paper, what the financial crisis was all about, and where the catch was. On this the newspapers were quite unanimous. *Pravda, Komsomolka,* and *Speed-Info* chorused that the Dow Jones was plummeting from the Empire State Building, the dollar was about to go up in flames, and basically you're on the right track, comrades!

To which Lyokha said it was all a crock. Igor told Lyokha to go to hell and said the West didn't get our rocks off anymore and now the Chinese were our brothers!

Then Gardin walked in and said, "The general told me to

tell you that due to the financial crisis China is turning back our fertilizer shipments."

"Which means what?" Andryukha asked.

"Which means, sonny boy, you're going to be eating less," Mitya joked.

In less than a week RailTrans had cut the work week by four hours and canceled several bonuses and special allowances.

"We've got some shit about to hit the fan," Lyokha commented one day when he and Igor were holding the ladder for Andryukha coming down from the trestle.

Igor looked up.

"Yeah, definitely some shit," he agreed.

Then they laid off everyone coming up on retirement, cut the work week to three days, and made nearly all workers take unpaid leave until they got some work. There was the smell of global cutbacks in the air, and that was when everyone realized the shit had already hit.

True, no one on the crew liked or respected Gardin, but they had to admit he wasn't a total ass. He had one good quality: he always had money and was always good for a loan. Of course, it would have been much better if they didn't have to pay him back, but you can't ask too much of some people.

In less than two short weeks he called in the whole crew, even the foreman, who'd been pensioned off.

"Do you read the papers?" he asked.

"What the hell for?" the crew answered in chorus.

"I'd rather have a beer myself," the foreman made his position clear.

"Well, you're wrong," Gardin reproached them. "Okay, sit down, I'll read to you."

He opened up a central newspaper and started droning: "...the academy of sciences has developed a revolutionary new technology that will replace outdated telecommunications..."

In short, the public wasn't reading the newspapers. First, they cost too much, second, the guys at the top hadn't taken into account that young people prefer fluff and don't like to read anyway, and everyone over thirty just uses papers to wipe their ass. So they'd decided to find some alternative to TV and radio for getting propaganda into every home. The best they could come up with was using steam heating as a system of mass telecommunications. Some eggheads did some figuring and designed a clever device – a steam broadcasting generator – that could receive and transmit information using steam. Now the crisis was irrelevant because we were going to start producing and installing high-pressure steam communications all over the country: HP. For ourselves and the whole world.

Indeed, the jobs started pouring in immediately. There weren't that many steam communications specialists in town, so the minute the men installed a generator and network pipes in the admin building they were sent straight to other sites for the same purpose. The only question was, where was the money coming from? Yesterday the country had no money, there was a crisis raging, and businesses were cutting jobs everywhere! You went to bed and everything was bad; you woke up and all of a sudden everything was fine. Well, not totally fine, but like it was before.

They raised this question during a smoke break.

"They had the money, no argument there," the welder stated authoritatively. "So did our general. Look over there. They sent all the working stiffs off to tighten their belts, but they haven't sacked a single admin geezer. What's up with them, are they clocking more hours or something?"

"It's not whether they have the money, it's what they're spending it on," the smith cut in. "Look, the general bought a new SUV to replace his old one. Nearly fifty grand. The old one just had three years on it. Good as new. Why this fucking new SUV when he could have repaired a locomotive?"

"We just aren't doing our own work," Mitya was a little hysterical. He had nowhere to blow off steam and had to slog away with everyone else. "We're responsible for water and heating and maybe repairing equipment. What are we doing here?"

"There isn't any work there, though," Vovka said.

"Exactly. There's no work there, so we're doing this dirty work here."

"On the other hand, they pay," Vovka said.

"What is it with you and money? It's a matter of principle!"

"Stop bitching," the foreman interrupted the discussion. "I'm done busting ass by myself."

Of course they went to work. What choice was there? But it left a nasty taste. All production in the country was at a standstill and the electricity was sometimes on, sometimes off. The welders had switched from arc to acetylene torches long ago, the smith was busting ass forging clamps for joints, the mechanic had made dozens and dozens of rivets and bolts for the clamps. Work was hopping. But there was no satisfaction. It felt like constructing a gallows for their own hanging.

Still, the fear of being broke and not paying off loans receded. Not only that, but they were able to make some good money on the side.

One day, after they'd been given their assignments and the boss had gone off on his own business, Igor said, "There's this moonlighting gig... We've got to hustle or someone else is going to get it."

The offer was surprising, to say the least. Usually the welder only offered under-the-table jobs to Vovka, his partner, and the foreman. Well, and Lyokha, occasionally, when he needed forged parts for a fence or railing. But now, the whole crew...

"What, you mean there's work for everyone?" Andryukha was surprised. "Me, too?"

"Well, someone has to pass the wrenches." Igor shrugged.

Everyone started to laugh but Mitya broke in.

"What are they paying?"

"Depends on how you go at it. The cash they're promising — blow your mind."

"So how much?" Mitya wouldn't relent.

"Three hundred for five sites."

"Apiece?"

"For everyone."

"That's stupid," Oskar commented in the voice of a veteran moonlighter.

"It was all stolen long before us!" the smith parried.

Everyone roared with laughter again.

"Three hundred *thousand*," Igor clarified.

"Wow!" Lyokha's eyes bugged out.

"Das ist fantastische!" the mechanic agreed.

"Tell us what to do," the foreman, who had been puffing away silently in a corner, exhaled. "Don't beat around the bush."

"We have to make them an illegal steam broadcasting line. But it's a secret, and if anyone spills the beans I'll shoot him myself."

Silence hung over the smoking room. The smith was jotting something feverishly in the margins of yesterday's paper.

"That's a little better than forty thou each. Say we're a month or so working on this, it's not too shabby. Only if we get caught we're all going to jail. I'm not so wild about jail time for forty."

Igor said no one was going to jail for these jobs. There were five buildings and each needed a steam broadcasting generator installed, besides heating.

"Is there a chance in hell of getting those generators going?" the foreman asked. "They've got to be hooked up to the main network."

"That's just the point!" the welder answered. "They want an illegal hookup to the network."

"What about materials?" Mitya asked.

"Their materials. But just try and lift so much as a bolt, you little bastard."

"When have I ever lifted anything?"

"I wasn't counting, I was warning: no making off with the goods."

Right then Gardin came back.

"I don't get it! The boss leaves and they make themselves comfortable. All right, back to work. Now!"

The men dispersed to their jobs reluctantly, not failing, of course, to tell each other under their breath where their boss had come from and where he could go. Gardin doubtless heard but he couldn't exactly object. There's no arguing with the truth.

2.

Disaster hit the next day. The crew was extending a segment of the overpass to connect the northern and southern parts of town, the clients were rushing the general, the general was hounding Gardin, and he was putting on the pressure. He came by every hour to see how many meters they'd done.

"That motherfucking piece of shit! If he shows up one more time, I'm gonna stick it up his you-know-what!" Igor spat under his mask. "The bastard's gonna come and breathe down our necks... Fuck, Andryukha, can't you see we're out of wire? Get me a new spool!"

Andryukha rocked back and forth like Roly-Poly, so you had to be really lazy not to swear at him, but the laziest of all was Andryukha himself.

"Knock out one more joint and then a smoke," the foreman promised.

So they knocked it out. But when they sat down for a

smoke, they found they'd suddenly forgotten certain words.

"Hey, wait." After a minute's silence the smith jumped down off the pipe and started walking alongside it. "We used to have really strong words... You know, starting with... with... first letter 'f' last letter 'k' with a 'u' in the middle," Mitya said.

"Well, how many letters? Does anyone remember?"

"What is this, a crossword or something?" the foreman asked, almost weeping with frustration.

He had a sinking feeling in the pit of his stomach. As if he'd looked away and had something stolen. The work immediately slacked off. The men were crawling, like tortoises, picking up and then abandoning the next pipe, and their lips were moving constantly, as if articulating could restore their memory. But no. It was like a morning dream, when you feel as though you've just dreamed something important, but the more awake you get, the less you remember.

In a fury the smith grabbed a crowbar and started beating on the pipe. After a few blows the crowbar bent, Lyokha was out of breath, and on top of it all Gardin showed up.

"What's this? Not working again? I'm" — at this the boss choked — "really fed up with you! A whole hour and they've just done one joint."

You could tell Gardin's emotions were tearing him apart, his face reflected a full range of them, and the boss's operational memory was feverishly and very obviously scanning the dictionary of general usage in search of the words he needed to fully reflect the moment's expression.

"It's no good!" the boss finally said.

The men exchanged looks.

"No good?" the smith checked to make sure.

"You think it's good?" Gardin hollered.

"It's okay," the foreman said, "we're on schedule."

Gardin took a deep breath... exhaled... took another... exhaled again... muttered, "You guys here are I don't even know what," and fled to the duty room in disgust. Before long they heard his car pull out.

"I remember for sure there was something about close relatives. Either a sister or a mother," Andryukha said. "Igor just said it."

"Should have written it down," the welder snarled.

What was left of the workday was spent in complete silence. A few interjections rent the air, of course, and the foreman's brief orders to pull, push, jerk, and so on, but can you call that conversation?

They did without jokes and jibes in the shower room, too. Everyone felt naked and tried to keep their backs turned. Mitya didn't get even one slap in the face, though Igor had always liked to give him a couple while his eyes were soapy.

Oskar said that while the men were laying line, there'd been two fights. First the trackmen had mixed it up with each other, and then with the builders, and somehow it all came out stupidly. They should have tried to talk it out... not just reached straight for the cudgels! Luckily, there weren't any injuries.

Who could have known that this was just the beginning of great turmoil?

Igor and Vovka did most of their moonlighting right in the workshop. Which made sense. They had the angle grinder right at hand, and the shears for cutting sheet metal, and the lathe, and the welding station. So the prep was done in the building, and on site the welders just installed what they'd prepared, whether it was heating, a screen, or a porch.

For use of the means of production, Gardin had to be paid an equal share. Of course, when they could manage the job without the boss knowing, Igor and Vovka didn't mind, just like anybody else, but that was pretty rare. And ever since they'd put in security, even rarer.

The smith didn't want to fork anything over to the bosses

for protection, so he wrapped up all his moonlighting. Why should he? Sure, the materials belonged to the factory, but it wasn't as though they belonged to Gardin. Gardin didn't pay for the rods or sheet metal out of his own pocket, and to be frank, he was known to use them for his own needs.

Oskar's approach to moonlighting was simpler. He characterized his business with a famous joke: "You see that bearing there? It used to cost a bottle of vodka and it still does." Although, of course, it wasn't all as easy as they made out. They did have to line Gardin's pockets to look the other way when customers showed up.

The others pilfered on a small scale, whatever fit in a pocket, or at most a bag. This wasn't considered theft, though, because every so often someone from admin – the head bookkeeper, job scheduler, even the general himself – would summon the men to his house to replace a radiator, plumbing, or a toilet, or just to move things from one apartment to another. How many times they had to fix the garage door at the general's suburban house or install a new stove in his bathhouse goes without saying.

The funniest story happened just before the electricity disappeared. Gardin was inspecting his team before assigning jobs. There was something about his men's look he didn't like.

He shook his head and said, "Epishin, Mitya, Tsarapov, and..." – he tried to remember Lyokha's last name but obviously couldn't – "...and the smith." You're going to be... you know... volunteers. You're going to put a stove in for the chief."

The general's bathhouse stove had started smoking all of a sudden. The foreman and Igor had welded and installed that stove the year before last. There'd been no complaints at first. Now there were.

In principle it wasn't hard to remove the wretched piece of iron and stainless tank. The only problem was that the flue happened to be attached to the stove itself, not the ceiling. This meant they had to prop up the flue, pull out the fool thing, drag in and install a new one, and reattach the flue. And if you consider the fact that the RailTrans men had brought the old stove into the bathhouse empty and then, on the general's orders, lined it with brick... A total pain in the butt.

True, they did transport the Sondercommando in style — in the general's SUV.

Somehow they got the old stove taken apart by lunch and started carrying it out. But as soon as they started dragging it out the ash pan turned out to be filled to the top, all the way to the grate.

"What's this?" The foreman was puzzled. "How's that?"

Vovka roared with laughter. "The ashtray's chock-full, better buy a new car."

The foreman let fly such choice invective that even old hands like Mitya, Tsarapov, and the smith gaped. Standing next to the sooty iron, the men stared at the general's vegetable garden. A standard garden, six hundred square meters: raspberry and currant bushes covered in plastic for the winter, a glassed-in hothouse, and beds for greens.

"What I'd like to know" — the smith breathed steam — "is whether the general works in his garden himself or drags in the trackmen?"

"You bet," Vovka joined the game. "In the morning the track foreman assigns some guys to sling sledgehammers and crowbars and the slackers to weed strawberries and dig potatoes."

Then the general arrived, was speechless over the reason for the clouds of dust, and the men went back to the workshop. No thank you or any other inducements did the general use on the volunteers. Fine, thanks for not making them work as bathhouse attendants.

In short, the men were sick of moonlighting for vague gains and dubious bonuses. They'd prefer honest labor (if only in the sense of a job commission). So the whole crew applied themselves to moonlighting.

While they were assembling and adjusting the HP broadcasting systems, they didn't feel like talking. The complex machinery and murderous drawings forced them to focus on the job's technical aspect. But when it came to the final push — laying the route as such — the men were drawn back to the larger questions of being.

They jerked the pipe onto the concrete blocks, clamped it roughly to its neighbor, then moved on and repeated the action. It was in the intervals between pipes that the conversations began.

"What's the point of this broadcasting anyway?" Vovka muttered. "How do they mean to remove the static? When the system heats up the condensate is sure to shoot off."

"Vovka, quit muttering." During dull and exhausting work Igor got nervous and irritable. "They're paying cash so that's it, no questions."

"No, really. Look how long we've gone without television and radio. First it was pretty tough, but now it's okay, we got over it. We aren't even reading newspapers. I stopped into a museum a while ago —"

"Shut up, will you?" the foreman snapped, and the men, stiff from snow and wind, grabbed the end of the pipe and dragged it onto the support. Then Andryukha was left holding onto that end, and the men moved off six meters or so to lift the other.

"What if we don't need the sacred words after all?" the smith asked at that moment.

That was the term Lyokha got from a magazine that linguists had given to the linguistic lacuna created by the absence of swear words.

The men groaned. No work or conversation was worth a

damn without the sacred words, and sometimes it was even hard to think without them. Andryukha was left at a loss again and again, the foreman didn't go through the drawings quite as efficiently, and Mitya, who was always trying to rationalize the work using labor-intensive operations, had definitely cooled to invention.

Lyokha remembered he had a book at home where everything was written in sacred words. But he came in the next morning in a nasty mood, angrily threw the book on the table, and said he couldn't make head or tail of any of it.

They sat down to read.

Listen up. I know it's not going to be boring. But if you get bored, then you're a complete hole-butt and can't tell your ass from your elbow in molecular biology or the story of my life for that matter. Here I am before you. A good-looking guy, cool clothes, mustache moving sweetly. My ride may be old, but I don't give a cuff. It runs. I've got an apartment, not a co-op, and my wife's nearly got her doctorate. I've got to say, my wife's a puzzle. A puzzle of the highest puzzlement and deepest depths. That Sphinx the Arabs have — I saw a short about it — that's got nothing on her. Once you pull it apart, there's nothing to it. Well, getting back to my wife. Don't pour too much, just half. It's smarter to take it that way, then you don't go cross-eyed. Take a bite of something or you'll get smashed and won't understand a tish.

"Quit jabbering," the foreman interrupted Lyokha. "I couldn't make out half of what you said."

"Me neither," the smith said.

"What are you, foreigners or something?" Mitya got angry. "Give it over!"

Mitya grabbed the book — by some Yuz Aleshkovsky — from Lyokha and started reading for himself:

...you're a complete hole-butt...

"What kind of book is this? The letters keep swimming around."

I don't give a tish...

"Where'd you see 'tish'?" Andryukha took a look at the book.

"Andryukha, sit still and don't make me mad." The smith pushed Andryukha aside and himself loomed over Mitya. "It's not 'tish,' it's 'shirt'!"

The experiment failed. Mostly it was all understandable, but there were a few words... obviously the very ones they'd forgot... in short, the letters didn't go together right. The smith said there was this disease, dyslexia, when you can't read a word the right way. Apparently everyone had come down with dyslexia at the same time.

"Got it on!" Oskar clapped. "Igor, you're a Kazakh polyglot!"

"A polyglot in one language?" Mitya wondered. "How's that?

"It means he knows a lot of words," Lyokha explained. "Igor, is it true, do you really know how to talk like them?"

Igor frowned.

"Zhon zhibek matadan, kara burysh, kichkintai bola... Oy!"

Everyone looked at the welder, who was staring into the distance.

"I guess Kazakh's missing a few words, too."

Lyokha thought about it and agreed.

"Yeah. English, too."

Oskar turned pale.

"And German."

It turned out that no language had the words to... well, they did serve some purpose, didn't they?

Vovka wouldn't give up, though.

"If we needed them, we wouldn't have forgotten them."

He went on in that vein, that really, if you thought about it, you didn't need steam communication, or newspapers, or museums, all you needed was grub.

Igor listened and listened to these decadent discussions and then grabbed a crowbar and started chasing Vovka down the line. Silently, not even promising to kill him.

"He'll kill him," Mitya said.

"No, he won't." But Oskar was doubtful.

"One of the two." The smith twisted a finger at his temple.

The foreman looked at this mess, waited for the right moment, and tripped Igor, who fell and nearly hit himself with the crowbar. But he did seem to cool off. Vovka stood a little off to the side, saw that blood and thunder had been averted, and went back to work, too. The foreman was about to give him a smack in the face and knock the junior welder, well, on his... what was the word?.. backside.

"Nothing better to do?" the foreman asked the welders.

Vovka tried to object but the foreman gave him a crack across the mouth.

"Okay, Mr. Big, stop the manhandling," the mechanic broke in. "It'll be dark soon and we've only laid four pipes."

No one said another word the rest of the day, and they laid two more pipes than usual.

3.

It's widely known that in wartime the tangent of a right angle equals one. All joking aside, except that the phenomenon of the sacred words was not the only one of its kind. In some places — Frankfurt, Uganda, and Kiev — two times two now equaled approximately three and fourteen hundredths, and they even came up with a sacred name for that number, the fuk (from the first letters of the places where it was found). Since communications were maintained only by mail, there could have been dozens of similar phenomena, hundreds of times more, it's just no one had picked up on them yet.

Despite the crisis and the resulting problems (due to

the fuk factor, mistakes crept into lots of blueprints, and the thinking slowed by the absence of sacred words made it hard to find the mistakes), HP broadcasting was launched even before the New Year.

The crew illegally welded pipe on the Perm-Syktyvkar-Vorkuta stretch, and no one even noticed. The system's centralized pressure test went off without a hitch. Evidently the designers had raised the pressure tolerance a good twenty points, so the small loss of pressure on the main line went undetected.

It all seemed too good to be true. But as soon as HP broadcasting was installed in the city and environs, they found the catch. The crisis hadn't really gone anywhere: they'd just been too busy to notice it

There was a requirement that they supply a pressure gauge — a very pricey one, by the way — for the heating pipe. Naturally. What if you secretly tapped into the radiator and started using steam for free?

State services popped up to service and install the gauges, and if you wanted an autonomous heating system and didn't plan to hook into the HP broadcasting network, you started getting pestered by all kinds of services and departments whose demands made it less expensive to hook up. Hydrocarbon prices soared to an unprecedented high and the cost of food rose, too.

But there still wasn't any work.

Gardin said that since everything was done and there still wasn't any freight everyone would be put on unpaid leave. The money cleared from moonlighting was barely enough to last till spring, and then only if you didn't pay your bills. Spring, of course, promised a little relief. The sowing season began then, fertilizer was in demand, and there would be freight to move. And in the summer you could switch over to grazing: mushrooms, berries, fishing, petty theft. But what then?

"We'll go to the countryside and live there," Mitya said.

"Uh huh," the foreman grunted. "I haven't noticed many people rushing off to live there."

Igor had lived in the country and agreed entirely with the foreman: no one was going to let them spread out there.

It was in these "days of doubt and dreary musings" about the fate of his homeland that Andryukha offered his bright idea.

"Let's take a tour to Sweden and request political asylum."

"Who needs you in Sweden?" Mitya asked.

"How can you ask for asylum there when you can barely make yourself understood in your own language?" The foreman shook his head.

"Where are you going to get money for a tour?" The smith sniffed.

"What do you need Europe for anyway?" Igor sang his familiar tune. "I hate them. We keep looking to them and their civilization. They can stick their civilization where the sun doesn't shine."

"You should have thought of this before, Andryukha," Oskar said, ignoring the welder's harping. "When we had the Internet. You could have met some rich Swedish girl on a website and organized something with her."

"A Swedish family!" The smith guffawed.

The volume shot up as they all discussed this once promising idea. After all, the crisis hadn't hit Europe as hard as us, for some reason. Why was that? What cretins did we have sitting in the Kremlin and what kind of lunacy had they dreamed up with this HP broadcasting?

"I've got an aunt living outside Petersburg," Lyokha suddenly remembered. "Pretty close to the Estonian border."

"I've got one in Petersburg," Igor said.

"And Mitya's got a granny in the sticks," Andryukha joked.

Oskar was modestly silent, although his brother lived in Germany.

"It's like this," Lyokha said. "We could go visit my aunt and cross the border."

"What for?" his colleagues wondered.

Lyokha explained a little disjointedly that the demographic situation in Europe was no good, Europe was getting old. And it was also being mobbed by Arabs. "And rightly so," Igor parried the smith, but Oskar stopped him, saying that Kazakhs had no say in this. "We're so close in culture. There's more European in us than in Arabs. We're much more desirable immigrants for Germany and France," the smith continued. "What if we up and go to Dusseldorf!"

At this everyone looked at Oskar. What would he say to that?

Oskar said he liked the idea in general, but who was going to let them in? "Even if they did, they'd drive us out eventually anyway. Though... by the time they caught us, and sorted things out, and sent a note to the embassy, and the embassy figured out who these fugitive bumpkins were and what province they were from... we could drag out half a year, and just you see, we'd get a foothold somehow."

"And you" — Lyokha poked Igor in the chest — "you could go back to your Kzyl-Orda. And from there it's just a stone's throw to China. If you can squeeze in."

"But how are we going to cross the border?" Andryukha asked.

"Cross the ice on the Gulf of Finland!" Mitya suggested. "A tried and true method. Lenin did it."

"Go ahead, but I'm not following Lenin, and I won't take my kids that way, either," Lyokha refused. "It can only lead to no good."

Mitya and the foreman took umbrage for Lenin and tried to prove that under the Soviets life was marvelous. Education and health care, equality and brotherhood, vodka and sausage. People had a conscience. Lyokha had indeed lived pretty damn well under the Soviets: the Soviet Union fell apart while he was still in school. But he wasn't giving up. He asked flat out, If we lived so well, why did everything get demolished? And to the traditional answer, that it was all the shitocrats and Gorbachev, he asked, So where did the shitocrats come from? Weren't they the Communists, weren't they from the top? As a rule, this was where the dispute faded out.

"Well, what do you suggest? Which way?" Mitya asked.

"Which way what?" the smith didn't understand. Since the conversation had now turned to the whole country, he couldn't answer right off.

"Which way are we going to cross the border?"

"Legally."

To say that this approach to the problem struck the men as untraditional would be putting it mildly. No one had anticipated that kind of rejection of stereotypes. Lyokha tried to explain.

"Can you imagine us trying to slip across the border illegally? The border guards would shoot us. And they'd be right."

The men doubted they'd shoot. "You mean they'd fire at children?" "Well, no," the smith conceded. "On the other hand, they'd catch us, tan our hides, dishonor our wives, and take our money. And they still wouldn't let us cross the border."

"What do you mean take our money?" Andryukha was indignant.

"Read *The Golden Calf*," Lyokha advised. "They'll say, 'Give us your gold,' slit your fur coat, and take all your money. Not only that," Lyokha added, "there'll be the disgrace. As if we were trying to cross the front lines and were turned back. No, the only way to go is the honest way. Buy a ticket. I did some figuring. It won't cost more than forty thou, if you take your wife and kids. And half that much for Andryukha."

The men let out a whistle.

"Then what?" Vovka asked.

"We get to Finland... or, well, Sweden there... or Dusseldorf... and we run to the local authorities and ask for political asylum."

"How are you going to ask them?" The foreman was still angry over the Communists and Lenin.

"What don't you like about life here?" the smith asked.

There was a lot the foreman didn't like, if not the whole business. He was just about to give them a rundown of all his grievances when Lyokha cut him off.

"Look, everything you don't like is the reason you're trying to enter the fraternal bosom of the European Union."

"Brothers don't have bosoms," Andryukha commented.

Everyone gave that serious thought but let it drop. Evidently, this had something to do with the sacred words.

"Only" — the smith pointed to the ceiling — "we've got to do this deal together. I mean, show up all together at the police and make sure the females are howling and the children begging for food, and say, 'Either you take us, or we're done for and Putin personally is going to whack us at the border.' "

The country had already crossed into the next year, and with a bang, too, cutting off the gas to our brother Slavs and, consequently, all of Europe. HP broadcasting fizzled there right off and the frosts had been a really nasty business, but we didn't give a crap because humanism was humanism but the Ukes were freeloading off our gas, something we simply could not allow!

"I have an idea!" Igor perked up. "How about exporting gas to Europe? Why not?"

"Are you going to carry the gas in your pockets?"

"We could siphon off a couple of tanker cars and then

we wouldn't have to go anywhere, it'd be enough money for a year."

"Who's going to give it to you? You think there are a bunch of idiots sitting around at Gazprom?" the foreman grinned.

They explained to Igor that if honest citizens were allowed to sell gas freely, that would be communism, and there's not one single... well, you know... in short, no one would work and everyone would sell gas.

"They'd just pay blacks to drill wells," Mitya concluded his lecture on political economy.

"I guess there's just no making a living, is that it?" Igor was furious.

Everyone looked at the welder.

"What have we been telling you?" Oskar was amazed. "Get out, we've got to get the hell out!"

"China," Vovka added.

Fortunately, Igor's tea was already cold so Vovka wasn't burned.

4.

Rescue came from unexpected quarters — abroad.

Lyokha, who'd been put on half time, now went to the smithy when he felt like it — to work his allotted number of shifts. All his free time he hung out at his HP terminal.

After one session he ran to work like a bat out of hell and said, "That's it, we're out of here!"

"You mean you won another prize?" Mitya asked.

Three years before, the smith had been incredibly lucky. He'd won a literary prize for a lampoon of his, and in a fit of joy Lyokha had given everyone a ride down the Kama on a boat rented especially for a drinking party. True, he hadn't supplied the vodka, and he didn't get to go, so they had to make merry without him, but that didn't exactly break their hearts. Thanks for the boat.

Now the owners had sold the boat because they'd been losing money. It was wintertime anyway. Where could they go? And what was the prize for?

"It's not a prize, you dimwit!" The smith waved a document with some writing on it. "They're inviting us to Paris!"

The document said that some Gallo-Slavic Literary Legion was inviting the smith to Paris to participate in a public celebration in honor of Gogol.

"Why Paris?" Oskar wondered.

"For a binge?" Andryukha asked.

"Are they inviting you as a Dead Soul or something?" Igor showed off his erudition.

"Don't you get it?" Lyokha gave his colleagues a pitying look. "This is our chance!"

The foreman observed the general chaos — or rather, celebration — silently and then noted with perfect reason, "So if they invited you, what good does that do us?"

Good or not, it was still worth serious thought. In the next letter they asked the smith to recommend other talented writers from the provinces they wouldn't be embarrassed to show to the discriminating Parisian audience. Then the smith had a wild idea.

"What? A writer? Me? Me! When I was your age I was carrying cast iron bathtubs to the sixth floor on my back! I jumped from forty up! I started working when I was fourteen!" There was no limit to his fury. "And you want to make me into a writer?"

Everyone looked at Lyokha reproachfully.

"Well, Lyokha, think again." Oskar shook his head. "We've got our principles, too, even if we're not your aristocrats."

"I'm not going to write anything," Vovka retreated.

"Or sign any papers," Igor added.

"Look, you're not going to have to write anything."

Lyokha shrugged. "I've already written everything for all of you and sent it off."

If someone had passed wind during a meal it would have set off a less stormy reaction than the smith's statement. The welder promised to slit Lyokha's throat, the foreman wished that Stalin was still around, Mitya said he was going to sue that minute and even took out his useless mobile.

"How will we ever look people in the eye?" Oskar asked. "You know they'll be pointing at us, 'Look, there go the writers.'"

"What are you talking about?" That caught the smith by surprise. "They're French, and they don't care whether you're writers or asphalt spreaders."

"What do the French have to do with this?" Oskar wondered. "It's here they're going to call us writers."

Lyokha hadn't thought of that, but he had no intention of ceding the point.

"Well, we won't say we're going as writers."

"What are we going as?" Vovka grinned.

Lyokha's eyes roamed around the kitchen for a while, he looked out the window, looked down – and then slapped himself on the forehead so hard that if he'd had any brains left they would have flown out his ears.

"We're going as specialists in installing and repairing steam broadcasting equipment."

The men exchanged looks.

Every Russian – or more exactly, every person who thinks in Russian – is at heart a bit of a con man. Lyokha had written a few stories, signed them with his colleagues' names, and sent them to France on the off-chance. He was by no means certain that the style of the stories differed very much from each other or, even worse, his own. Lyokha wasn't entirely sure he even had a style of his own.

But they made it through. Maybe because the general level of their writers wasn't very high, or because they weren't read very carefully, but in less than a week the answer came from France: we're inviting everyone.

Of course, there were still lots of minor issues to work out. For instance, getting a foreign passport, and fast. They had at best a month and the Passport Office took a lot longer. Lyokha wrote and told the legion just that: you see, we've got our papers together, but they won't issue our passports fast enough. The next day the provincial migration service directorate got busy on their foreign passports. And all it took was one call over steam link from Paris!

But if the delay with the bureaucratic machinery was merely boring and long, the battle with their families was exhausting. The wives, children, and others the men wanted to take abroad with them wouldn't even hear of leaving for good. Even Igor's wife, who, according to him, he ruled with a heavy hand, flatly refused to sell the house and her belongings, to say nothing of abandoning her homeland, and she threatened not to let their daughters go.

"I'll murder you," the welder raged.

There was a risk, and not an inconsiderable one. Say the men sold their apartments, cars, houses, gardens, and furniture here. Say they each got an average of a million or a million and a half... and say they exchanged that for European currency. That only came to twenty or twenty-five thousand in their money, and what kind of shack could you rent for that money and how long could you hang on? Not only that, but real estate prices in town had just dropped drastically. Everyone was trying to sell an apartment, cheaply, quickly, as if everyone were planning to go to Paris.

Eventually the men decided not to sell anything. Who knew? What if they had to come back? Then another problem arose. Where could they borrow some money? They didn't have very long to make arrangements in France's capital. In those three days, while Lyokha was representing the Ural writers' delegation, the men had to find work and submit a request for political asylum. Roaming around an unfamiliar city, without a coin in your pocket, and knowing you had a hungry wife and children waiting for you back in the room somehow wasn't all that inviting.

Meanwhile, Gardin noticed the general unease in the crew.

"What are you whispering about in corners?" the boss asked.

"Well, see, we're getting ready to go to Paris," Andryukha blurted out.

"Where?" Gardin was not expecting that.

Lyokha muddled through an explanation about how he'd put out information over the steam link about what they were doing... their crew, and they'd... we'd been invited to Paris for a conference of steam technicians from all over the world.

"Why you?" Gardin asked the smith. "You're no mechanic."

"But I'm their... our producer," Lyokha answered cheekily.

"Look at him, a 'producer,'" the boss taunted him. "I'm the producer. You're nothing but a PR man."

"What?" everyone asked.

"Where do you plan to get the money? I don't imagine you're going alone. You're taking your wives and girlfriends, right?" Gardin winked at Igor, and everyone realized the welder was going to slit someone's throat. "Look, I'll take care of the money. And you" — he poked Lyokha in the chest — "take care of a letter from Paris to show the general."

The men didn't know what to think about Gardin after that statement. Sure, he was a lout, the epitome of every earthly sin, and look at him: now he wanted to be a producer. Everyone knew Gardin was pushy and it was stupid and short-sighted to reject his help. But it would be ill advised to tell him about the trip's real purpose. Therefore Lyokha registered a new steam address on one of the French boilers, and from there he sent an exact copy of his own invitation addressed to the general director, only instead of the Gogol anniversary and all that other literary crap he inserted a conference on the development of HP technologies and steam program security.

Gardin went to the general and said, you see, he had to send the crew on a trip. After all, not just anyone got asked, only the best, and to Paris!

"Who's going to look after the heating? Who's going to repair the equipment?" The general scowled.

Gardin said there was no point pretending anyone needed their installations right now, and the boiler men would manage the heating perfectly well. They weren't children, were they?

Of course, at that moment RailTrans was not experiencing the best of times, but a letter from abroad, and with the deepest bow to the general... if you overlooked the details, then they gave the travelers ten thousand each, which came out to fifty Euros each per day. No great shakes, but it was a free ride, and they might not have given them that.

Gardin was geared up to go as well.

This news put the crew on its guard.

"You mean you wrote a story for him, too?" Igor asked Lyokha.

"Not a word," the smith swore.

"How's he going to go then?"

"That's his business."

"After all, he's... what's that..."

"A lout?"

"You're a lout yourself. He's a producer!"

"Same thing. If he wants to go, let him buy his own ticket.

They don't need producers there, they're asking for writers. I mean, HP specialists," Lyokha immediately corrected himself. "Tickets aren't our problem."

Here the smith's eye focused on a point behind the welder.

"In fact, we have a different problem right now," he muttered.

"What?"

"Lenka."

Igor looked around. Lenka, the repair shops' long-time laundress, was standing by the smoking room.

In Lenka's arms was a chirping baby wrapped in a blanket.

At first, long before the crisis, Lenka had wanted to adopt a little orphan girl, one of those abandoned at the maternity hospital by sad excuses for mamas. The desire was simple and perfectly understandable. Her only son was finishing up school, and Lenka had given serious thought to what would happen if he went to college in another town. Lenka was not quite thirty-five, young and healthy, and had no desire to marry. Her first marriage had soured her on that, but she also didn't want to get old alone. So she gathered all the necessary papers and went to choose herself a daughter.

She chose the little girl right away. Also called Lenka, which the laundress thought symbolic. For a few months Lenka visited her future daughter, played with her, and spent time with her in the hospital when the child came down with a viral infection; at the same time, she attended classes for adoptive parents given at the orphanage by lady specialists from the provincial capital.

It was at these classes that Lenka learned she wasn't going to be able to adopt her namesake. Moreover, she heard it not from one of the lady specialists but from a young woman like herself who had dreamed of adopting a child.

The moment the point was made in the lecture about how foreigners were only allowed to adopt sick children, the woman sitting next to Lenka said, "Then why did they take Vitka away from me and give him to Canadians?"

The specialist was flustered.

"How's that?"

It turned out that the future mother had darkened every door for a whole year hoping to adopt young Vitka. Everything was moving along toward formal adoption when it suddenly turned out that Vitka had a sister a year older, and brothers and sisters could not be separated at adoption. The mother grunted but decided not to give up and started the paperwork for adopting the girl, too. She went into debt, exchanged her two-room apartment for a three-room, and found herself a second job, and the bureaucratic machinery quietly began to yield. The double adoption loomed on the horizon. Then a married couple from Canada showed up, and they did Vitka's paperwork to go abroad so fast the woman barely had a chance to catch her breath. Over a weekend, basically.

"That's impossible!" the lady specialist objected.

"I said the same thing. But they told me if I was going to get angry they would take his sister Vika away, too."

Unimaginable chaos ensued. Some mamas hissed at the foolhardy adopter, saying now they were all going to be cut off at the knees; others, on the contrary, attacked the specialist from the provincial capital, saying, Look at the mess you've made! Lenka opted out of the scandal and slipped away.

As her seat neighbor had predicted, nothing came of the adoption. There got to be these stupid bureaucratic obstacles, and she had to collect a stack of new certificates. The men advised her to go to the general; he was a city council deputy now and could fix everything in a jiffy. But Lenka already had her doubts and was hesitant, and eventually she gave up on adopting.

She got herself a child the old-fashioned way: by giving birth.

And in the nick of time. She had just gone on maternity leave, given birth, and received her one-time birth subsidy when the crisis broke out. God knows the money wasn't much, but she couldn't be fired for three years and was getting maternity benefits.

When Lenka went on maternity leave the men forgot all about her. That is, of course, they remembered in theory, but in the light of the whole economic and energy mess somehow she wasn't in their thoughts. And when they were getting geared up for France, she flew out of their minds altogether.

But Lenka followed factory life closely, and when she learned the men were planning to go abroad she figured they weren't being invited for a glass of Veuve Cliquot.

"Take me with you or I'll sue," Lenka said.

"What?" They were all stunned.

"You heard me. I'll say the child is one of yours and sue for child support."

"I don't have anything to do with it!" Andryukha flapped his arms.

"No one thinks you do," Lyokha brushed Andryukha aside. "It's just that while they're investigating they won't let us go."

"Why are you doing this to us, Lenka?" Oskar asked.

"Why did you plan to go without me?" Lenka sobbed.

The men were thrown. How could you explain this? To say nothing of the fact that they'd basically forgotten about their plucky friend.

"We just... forgot," Andryukha blurted.

Hurt, Lenka howled.

"Here's the thing," Igor took the bull by the horns. "Lyokha won't have time to write another story for Lenka, naturally. We'll all pitch in and buy her the foreign passport and ticket ourselves."

"I don't need the passport." Lenka sniffed. "I have one."
And she started howling again, but this time for joy.

5.

They decided not to take steam aviation. The railroad was dearer to their hearts, and it was a shorter fall if anything happened. Gardin got the enterprise to fork out not only for a bus to the train but a little for the "specialists'" families, so they set out for the station en masse. In the four hours it took to get to the station in Perm, the families had time to make friends, the children to fight and make up, and even the men, who had tied one on before their departure for foreign lands, to sober up.

There was no pushing your way through at the station. Lyokha, who before the crisis had traveled to Moscow and back fairly often, had never seen anything like it. It wasn't just overcrowded. There wasn't room to swing a cat!

There wasn't any room left in the waiting room; people were sitting on the floor wherever and on whatever they could.

They decided to wait outside, especially since an hour wasn't so much. The women kept close to their husbands, and Gardin organized an all-round defense against the beggars, gypsies, and other marginal types besieging the delegation on all sides. Lyokha and Igor wrested Lenka's wheeled suitcase away from some lush.

"Just where are they all off to? Not the seaside surely?" the foreman fretted. "It's two months till summer, there's still snow, and they —"

At that moment the Beijing-Moscow express pulled in, and our travelers lost the gift of speech altogether.

It was like a movie about the Russian Civil War. Passengers were hanging from the steps, sticking their heads out windows, and perching on the roofs. There wasn't a conductor in sight, and the few brave souls standing by the cars with their tickets and documents kept looking around in dismay.

"You think you're getting on our train?" the passengers asked them out the windows. "You don't have a prayer. No one's getting off before Moscow."

"We have tickets!"

"And we have seats."

But the people of Perm were evidently no feebler than the Siberians. They boldly went on the attack, stormed the cars, and after some swearing, weeping, and manhandling won their rightful seats. Of course, maybe not everyone got berths there, a compartment or reserved seat, but evidently places were found because everyone left.

"I don't get it." Gardin gaped.

"I can just imagine what's going to happen in Moscow," Lyokha shook his head.

When their train arrived the men boarded it while maintaining their all-round defense. Igor, Lyokha, the foreman, and Oskar pushed away any overly frisky passengers, and Gardin directed the loading. Finally the train started to move, the passengers settled down, and they started making themselves comfortable. From snatches of other people's conversations, conductors, and a drunken conversation with a passenger in the next compartment, the men learned what was going on basically.

People were getting the hell out of the country.

In the Far East and Siberia, they said, entire villages were clearing out. Kamchatka, Kolyma, and Chukotka were going across the Baring Strait to the States, followed by the Maritimes and Khabarovsk. The Chinese were helping them, of course, buying up their apartments and property at incredible prices so our people wouldn't have second thoughts. Even offering free transportation.

It was harder for the Siberians, of course. Where were they supposed to go? Here, too, China extended a friendly hand, and a stack of trains, planes, and old automobiles crawled toward the eastern and western borders of what was once the largest state in the world.

The men exchanged looks. Everyone remembered how uncrowded the Perm streets had become. Very few cars, no traffic jams, and even in their hometown there seemed to be lots fewer people.

When Gardin went to the lavatory, Igor gave Lyokha an expressive look.

"I guess we're not the only smart guys, huh?"

"What, did you think you were some kind of genius?" the smith replied. "The people are wise. They figured out there was nothing to do here, so they've been slinking off a few at a time."

"What do you mean a few? There aren't enough seats in the car and people are traveling on the third berth!"

"Be grateful we got on at all."

"Grateful to you?"

At this Oskar said that at the next station he was going to put off everyone who was dissatisfied, and he took out a bottle. After his second shot Igor eased up, started spinning tales, Gardin joined in, and soon the whole car was listening with bated breath to how and where the welder and his boss had boozed it up and worked.

The writer-mechanics got to Moscow on jokes and tall tales, but there were as many people there as in Perm. Mostly European-looking people, which really surprised Lyokha, who the last time in the capital had seen lots of Asians, as well as natives of the Caucasus.

"I guess they're better off at home now than here with us," Mitya barked.

"I told you we don't need Europe," Igor, who had a bad hangover, grumbled. "Where to now?"

Gardin took the lead again, took them all to the Leningrad station, and bought the children ice cream, the women cold drinks, and the men beer. Basically, Gardin did his best to charm them all, and it was working. At least Andryukha gladly drank his beer and laughed at the old chestnuts his boss was dispensing nonstop. The men, too, finally realized this wasn't work but a real vacation, and they condescendingly accepted this idyll. Then boarding was announced and...

The men couldn't get on the train.

That is, Gardin was borne into a car on the general wave, but most of the delegation, with their wives, children, and Andryukha, who had a death grip on a bottle, were left on the platform.

"Hey you, come on... let go," a guy two meters tall told Andryukha.

Andryukha looked up at his left hand holding a bottle.

Someone else's.

He had his own in his right.

They went home without pomp.

Sure, they went to the zoo, the circus, and the theater, and they visited the Tretyakov Gallery, so the trip to Moscow wasn't a total waste. But the whole time the men avoided looking each other in the eye.

At first they decided that since things had turned out this way they'd leave on the next train. It was actually a good thing Gardin had been separated from the group so successfully. For a while he was even the butt of their jokes.

But then each one talked it over with his family (and Vovka and Andryukha with each other), skipped off to the ticket office without a word, and bought return tickets, especially since the trains were going empty on the return and tickets cost next to nothing.

So each of them headed home with just his own household, splitting off from their colleagues like cowards — at the circus, theater, zoo, and, of course, the Tretyakov.

The farther east they went, the more depopulated the stations and halts. Chimneys smoked feebly, as if reluctantly, and it was the rare Zhiguli or minivan they saw on the road, at best hitched up to horses and at worst, dogs. True, there weren't many Chinese yet either. Evidently they weren't in any hurry to cross the Urals and were busy populating Siberia.

For a while the men didn't go to work. They were ashamed of their faint-heartedness. But later they started drifting in, one by one. First the foreman, then Oskar and Vovka, who lived in the same dorm, then Igor came in, only to find Lyokha already there, and Andryukha, who even dragged out Mitya.

"What did we lose on that foreign scheme?" he said. "No one needs us here, either, but who did we have waiting for us there?"

The tea had just boiled, the men were sitting in the kitchen of their own shop, and they readily gave the welder every point.

Almost no one was left at work, by the way. All the office workers had gone, salaries had evaporated, locomotives had stopped, the trackmen and depot workers had scattered to points unknown, and all that remained were those who had nowhere else to go. The town as a whole became quieter and emptier, and crime went down, too. All the gangsters and thieves had left for Europe and America.

The snow melted, and the people, or at least all those left, were drawn to the land. To their vegetable gardens for now, but some of the old men had their eye on broader empty fields. The tax service was still in force, though. Maybe not consistently, and maybe creakily, but it was still too soon to turn the virgin soil. Once they left though...

The state apparatus fell apart, the corrupt cops left, following the swindlers and gangsters, the corrupt officials followed the cops, and it got easier and easier to breathe, though money was tight. Once again the world turned green, and a few distribution facilities fast going out of business sold their goods off dirt cheap, so no one went hungry.

Only the government and steam broadcasting held on. To each other. Every day the HP brought news: everything's fine, they said, life is returning to normal, and preparations for the Winter Olympics are proceeding full steam ahead.

One day – this was in May, as a storm was raging – a miracle happened. The prime minister broadcast from the steam screen. He said the people were unworthy of a government like ours, the men of state were all leaving for Germany, or at least Trinidad and Tobago, and you, that is, we, who remain, could go to hell, for all he cared. At that moment, whether for good or ill, the foreman had a bottle of liquor in his hands, pure alcohol. He smashed it on the screen so the safety valve got solidly stuck.

"We're fucked," the foreman said.

"What?" the men were taken aback.

"We're fucked," the foreman repeated, himself not believing it, and tears glittered in his eyes.

They remembered! They remembered all the sacred words! The men dashed out into the downpour, laughing and swearing gleefully, like children home alone.

Evidently, the pressure in the steam network really had been very high. And maybe people remembered the sacred words in other underpopulated parts of the country then, too, and a foremen there had struck the pipe with a wrench the exact same way, in a fit of rage. Whatever it was, the entire steam broadcast system, from the Far East to Kaliningrad, hesitated for a couple of minutes and then blew up. The government never did get to Germany or Trinidad and Tobago.

The men stood there, wet, sooty, and drenched in mud, in the middle of the huge virgin land the country had become.

"Thank God," Mitya said.

> *Thank you for using our roll to the end.*
> *Don't forget to flush.*

IGOR SAVELYEV

Modern-Day Pastoral

Translated by Amanda Love Darragh

1.

On 17th April 2005 the Minister of Communications issued a decree, grudgingly passed by the Ministry of Justice, allowing people to travel on the 'third shelf' – that is, the luggage rack – of communal train carriages. Liberal-minded citizens were up in arms, as they were about most things that year, but you couldn't argue with the facts: people simply couldn't afford full-price rail tickets – the alternative would be going by foot along the rail track. The third shelf was hard and uncomfortable, right up under the ceiling, with no bed linen, no handrail, nothing... and tickets cost next to nothing too.

"Would you be prepared to travel like that yourself?" journalists asked the Minister, a typical hog-like bureaucrat. They seemed to have it in for everyone that year. But he was a down-to-earth sort and just laughed it off.

"No. But I don't need to! Our young people don't have any money, though – they can't afford to go anywhere... And they shouldn't have a problem getting up and down, should they?"

2.

Three days before the trip Elina experienced her first kiss – her girlish innocence was well and truly shaken and stirred. What about the train journey? No big deal, she would cope. The thing was, Elle didn't like trains: the stuffiness, the threadbare sheets, the obligatory sweaty travelling companions... Last summer she had gone to the seaside with her parents (now you see how old-fashioned she still was!) It was torture. What she had found particularly repellent was all those naked legs hanging down from the upper bunks, dangling in the aisles. They were ugly, old and calloused. You had to look where you were walking or you might find someone's foot in your face... ugh, disgusting. But on the way back — testimony to the miracles of sea water! — the same legs were beautiful, clean and youthful.

This time there was no sea and the summer was essentially over. But it was still an adventure! Elle was trembling with happiness, although she kept telling herself "it might fall through, it might fall through". She had told her parents — her doting, touchingly clueless parents — the first lie that came into her head. Something about a friend in Samara. Which friend is that, then? Oh Dad, you know, we met at the seaside last year!

His name was Martin — officially Marat, but that wasn't nearly as interesting. When a boy lets his hair grow rather than messing about with it, it's just... gorgeous. His striking features and wide-set eyes... It was the first time it had happened to Elle, and she was totally smitten.

He was into live action role-playing games and spent about two hours 'hard-selling' the techniques of the movement to her, stressing the emotional involvement and how it was more than just 'waving wooden sticks about'. She didn't need convincing — she would have readily bought into any interest he might have had. Would she go with him to a role-players' convention in the far-off town of Velsk? In a heartbeat. To be honest, she would have done anything for him. Anything. But hang on, don't get carried away. You're not his girlfriend yet. And anyway, he believes in free love, he already said so.

"Have you ever travelled on the third shelf?" he asked.

"No. You're not supposed to, are you?"

"Well, they've just changed the rules so you can now. It's really cheap. We've already done it a couple of times. You just need to learn how to hold on. It's easy, I'll show you. Look..."

"Aagh!"

Calm down, it can't be that bad... and she smiled a pale smile to herself. Whatever it takes.

3.

Her mother had packed her off 'to Samara' with such an obscene amount of provisions that as soon as she was out of sight of her parents' house Elina, kind-hearted as she was, emptied most of it out by the rubbish bins for the stray cats and dogs. She was embarrassed by the way they fussed over her. She regretted it later, of course. Martin and Lyokha, his friend and trusty sidekick, had brought with them a jar of sugar and that was about it.

"Come on, we're going to miss it!" Elle was panicking. The Ufa train terminal – a squat glass block from the Brezhnev era – was ugly, and dirty. They ran, colliding with the grubby, sullen tide spilling out of a suburban commuter train. They must have missed it, surely... but no, their train was waiting patiently for them. With his shaven head bare – he usually wore the childish panama stuffed in his pocket – Lyokha even had time for a quick smoke on the platform. He was a handsome guy, Lyokha. He only managed half a cigarette, but he made it look so stylish.

"Here. Go on, Lyokha," Martin held out the tickets to the carriage attendant.

Her name turned out to be Verka – the same as the flamboyant female alter ego created by a popular Ukrainian comedian at the time, who also happened to be a train attendant. This Verka was ample-bosomed and vivacious like her namesake and even had a Ukrainian accent, which none of the passengers could get out of their heads the following day.

"My, oh my! What have we here?! Look at them! More scroungers wanting to travel on the third shelf! I ask you! What's the world coming to?!"

"One has to put up with a certain amount of rudeness from the staff. Didn't Martin warn you?" Lyokha spoke very aristocratically to Elle, as though Verka's outburst had nothing to do with them and he was more bothered about finishing his cigarette.

"You have to let us on, you know, whether you like it or not."

"They have no shame, these cheeky upstarts!"

Verka and her ample bosom led them like prisoners through the carriage along the worn-out cloth runner on the floor, calling them all the names under the sun, and Elle burned with shame as the other passengers gawked.

They stopped at a row of bunks.

"Congratulations, dear passengers! This lot will be joining you. You'll have to find another home for your bags and mattresses! How should I know where you're supposed to put them? The powers that be didn't think this one through..."

Elle was mortified. And while the old women were expressing their indignation only one passenger, a young man, pulled his bag down straight away without making a song and dance about it. He was wearing Adidas trainers, the brand name endearingly misspelt as was the case with all Vietnamese knock-offs.

"You can jump up there, can't you? No? You're kidding. Martin, didn't you tell your lady-friend what to expect?"

"*My* lady-friend?!"

Meanwhile the boys demonstrated how she should jump up — they were showing off a little bit, if truth be told, so that even the old women passengers quietened down. Elle decided to give it a go. Slooooowly does it... Don't look down. Don't just hang there in mid-air like a noodle, you could die like that.

When she'd finally lain down on the hard, dusty shelf, without any bedding, without anything at all, right up against the ceiling under the long, yellowish lamp... there was no way she would ever get down again. Elle knew this for certain as soon as she looked at the little table way, way down below. Her hands began scrabbling about in a panic, searching for something – anything – to hold on to, but the walls and ceiling were smooth and... She couldn't bear it up here. The height was unbearable. She felt sick with the fear of falling.

What was she doing on this train? And why? Somebody, help! Elle sobbed silently, her mouth wide open in an ugly grimace.

And then Verka's voice throughout the carriage:

"Ha! You're after some hot water now, are you? No way! You're not entitled to any hot water, you layabouts!"

4.

Everyone knew that Kostya from 9-D was in love with her – they were just waiting for him to admit it. Elle had caught him looking at her, briefly enough for it to mean something, and was also waiting. Finally he said woodenly, "Let's go for a walk after school."

Her heart melted with pleasure!

Elle ran home to drop off her bag, shed her drab schoolgirl exterior and grab something to eat. And to make sure she looked her best, without making *too* much effort, of course. Which skirt? This one. She rummaged about amongst her sister's make-up. Oh, would it really be like the other girls said? There was something in the expression 'he'll eat your lipstick' that... made her heart want to jump. She painted her lips pink. No, that wasn't right. Maybe she should go for red?

It was an Indian summer and a beautiful, grown-up darkness was falling. Kostya was chattering away, waving his hands about. They reached a twelve-story apartment block and he suggested they go in. "I want to show you something," he said. Elina wasn't keen on the idea. But for some reason she went in anyway.

They were in the lift for what felt like an eternity, stupidly staring at a gob of saliva on the floor.

"Here we are!"

The ceiling hatch on the top floor was unlocked, and a wobbly ladder led up to it.

"I found this place myself. There's a stunning view over the city — you'll love it! Come on, let's go!"

Elle obediently began to climb and her whole body felt the fragility of the structure. Everything in her tensed up. She imagined herself slipping down into the stairwell. She clambered through the hatch...

The roof was an open space covered in strips of waterproof asphalt membrane, featuring enclosed lift shafts like the one that Karlsson-on-the-Roof is supposed to live in, or so every Russian child imagined — one Karlsson for every block of flats. In summer, the intense heat of the sun probably melted the asphalt.

Over the edge... better not to look. Elle's insides plummeted and smashed into little pieces. It was windy up there too and she sat down immediately, clinging onto the asphalt plating. She was terrified of falling. The Height pushed all other thoughts and feelings into the background.

"Look how beautiful it is!!!"

Kostya was jubilant, ecstatic — he almost jumped over the edge in his excitement. And he was completely oblivious to the look of terror on his companion's face.

"Let's go a bit closer... Elina, there's something I want to tell you, something important..."

And no doubt he told her whatever it was, pulling her hand towards him, looking into her eyes and pouring his heart out. But Elle didn't hear a word of it. The Height stuck in her throat, preventing her from breathing. Funny how they're both words of one syllable, but Height is like falling from a tower, wailing — it seems to last forever, whereas Death is as short as a gunshot.

Kostya was so wrapped up in his own delight that he didn't even notice. This place, this secret place that was his alone, this view, the horizon, the yellow September sunset — trembling impotently down there and struggling to even penetrate the windows, but up here so free... Kostya could barely contain himself. He skipped about and ran to the edge of the abyss, charmed with the sense of freedom and his own bravery. But there was a fine line between bravery and dicing with death. Elle sank silently down by the lift shaft, choking, trying to cough up the terrible, deadly Height that had lodged itself in her throat and was pressing on her heart.

5.

Elle was too scared to sleep. They passed some nameless villages and the rocking of the train was particularly noticeable up here; the lights of the railway junctures ran across the little table way down below and back up the walls, and then there was nothing again. Her body was completely numb from lying on the cold, hard shelf and her neck was so stiff... she wanted to adjust her bag, which she was using as a pillow, but she couldn't bring herself to move. One hand grasped spasmodically at a hook on the ceiling. She was already past the point of crying, but her eyes would not stop weeping like a festering wound. Oh, God. What was she doing here? She hated Velsk already.

Now and again she drifted off only to wake with a start, and then she would grip the hook more tightly in her sweaty fist; her delirium was interrupted periodically by the lights and the clanking of the crossings, which sounded like machine-gun fire.

The reason she was here was breathing darkly and evenly

on the adjacent bunk. He was fast asleep, of course, not the slightest bit perturbed. "Where did you dig him up?" her sister had asked, when they'd bumped into her in the street.

Where they'd met, what difference did it make? It wasn't a particularly interesting story: Elle had met Marat/Martin at a concert. Just to clarify, this wasn't exactly something she made a habit of... Elle wasn't used to going out. They had only let her go to the concert because it was such a momentous occasion the whole of Ufa was going: after a long time away the pop star Zemfira had come back to perform a gig in her home town.

Elina wasn't actually that into Z, but... Once close to her fans, over the years and with each successive album Z had retreated further and further from the public eye into her own hazy world and didn't care about them any more. But they followed her anyway in spite of her indifference, and maybe because of it.

Suddenly a boy turned round and asked, "Do you want a lift up?" His light-brown hair was long and a bit greasy, and there was something slightly equine and very masculine about him.

The beer must have gone to her head, she shouldn't have finished the bottle off like that, but... oh well, these things happen!

Sitting up there on the stranger's broad shoulders she swayed giddily from a combination of the height and the... instability? – no, the flexibility! – of her supporting structure, from the beer, the wind in her face, the way the electric guitars made the air move like magic...

Elle fidgeted deliriously on the shelf. She was half-crazed with a mixture of fear, excitement and sheer exhaustion, and each cluster of lights, fleeting and furtive, went through her like bullets.

Then Verka's shrill voice exploded into her head like an express train:

"Next stop Syzran! Come and get your bedding! Who wants a cup of tea?"

6.

Once, a long, long time ago, Marat had opened the front door to find his friends on the doorstep.

"It's party time! Are you coming, or what?"

They were already off their heads.

"You haven't forgotten, have you? It's Saturday! So, are you coming?"

Ah, yes. Damn, the bastards. They'd invented a new game, like they were back in primary school or something. Saturdays were always busy at the *Stormy Petrel* swimming pool, lots of different clubs and teams had their training sessions... including the girls' team. And there just so happened to be a particularly convenient fir-tree growing opposite the female changing room. They scrambled up as though they'd never seen a naked woman before and sat amongst the branches, feasting their eyes. "Getting stuck in," as they called it. It was a purely aesthetic pleasure. And then they would go to the park to drink beer — that was their Saturday ritual. Marat used to laugh at them, but this time he let himself be drunkenly persuaded to go along with it.

"No way, you can't go like that! You'll get fir-tree resin all over you. You're supposed to wear your scruffiest old clothes on Saturday... Look at us — we're like a load of old tramps!"

Approving guffaws.

They drank cheap port on the way there to put themselves in a good mood.

It was growing dark in a typically autumnal way, and the city was full of headlights swarming feverishly in the twilight. The birds were equally frenetic above the park where people sat lazily swigging from bottles, waiting for it to get completely dark.

The *Stormy Petrel* swimming pool: a misty yellow light, steam escaping from the windows and that distinctive, chemical smell of chlorine, strong enough to burn your sinuses.

He could still remember how to climb trees. What a bunch of clowns. They would climb the fir-tree two at a time while the others stood casually drinking (they already had beer) below. Happy times...

Sevka was the first up, followed by Marat. God, it was insane. The tree trunk was scratchy, sticky and big enough to fell a brontosaurus. They spent a long time getting into position.

There they were, some naked girls, no big deal. You could just about see their breasts. God, how boring... And Sevka stared so earnestly, so diligently, it was hilarious...

"Run for it! Hey, Marat!"

And before those up in the tree knew what was happening their friends on the ground had grabbed the bottles and scattered in all directions, illuminated by a pair of headlights. It was a police car! It had appeared from out of nowhere, the screech of its brakes striking fear into their hearts.

They fell silent.

"Shit. Now we're in trouble."

"Sit still and shut up! Maybe they won't notice us... They might be after someone else."

They froze, peering nervously down onto the roof of the jeep, white as the palm of a hand. It gave no sign of life. What was it doing there? Why was it sitting there waiting, with its engine running?

Shh-hh. Careful not to snap a twig. Breathe slooooowly.

He was so tense and nervous up there — a biting autumn wind had begun to blow, howling through the branches and making the old fir-tree shake, although it wasn't noticeable from ground level. With his cheek almost pressed up against the horrible dinosaur trunk, Marat could literally feel the tree creaking and straining. God, it was so uncomfortable... When you're on the ground the proximity of the Earth's solid surface is somehow reassuring, but when you're looking down at it from a distance the overwhelming apprehension is enough to drive you mad.

Huge flocks of birds were wheeling and soaring in the black sky; in those days they used to circle restlessly above the town, whole blankets of them, making complex, agitated formations in the sky. Their melancholy calling, the wind, the silent jeep, the sudden fear, and the Height, the Height, the Height...

7.

There is a certain kind of boredom unique to long train journeys that just make you want to die. The symptoms: a tattered crossword covered in greasy fingerprints, time stretching like elastic, a grey railway morning outside the window, endless cups of tea tanning your insides.

Martin and Lyokha woke up and yawned, sweetly and shamelessly. Elle stared vacantly out of the window opposite with heavy eyes, watching the tall wooden posts fly past as apathetically as a fly might regard the first snow of the year.

"Would you like me to bring you breakfast in bed? Oi! Globetrotters!" Holding a flat broom to her ample bosom, Verka was attending to the shabby cloth runner and was evidently in a humorous kind of mood.

Several women murmured feebly and discordantly in support, their faces still bearing the impression of the worn bed-linen. The morning was just beginning. The other passengers still hadn't forgiven the impudent offenders for forcing them to get their bags down, for paying a pittance for their wretched tickets, or for their wretched youth.

"It's alright for you two to be roughing it like this, but why should she have to put up with it?" It was the boy in the Adidas who had spoken up. "She's a girl, not a monkey – she shouldn't have to be jumping about all over the place! Do you think I didn't notice her tossing and turning all night?" (Elle blushed in torment.) "No, I dare say you were fast asleep... Come down, miss! Seriously, come on, come down, you can have a sleep on my bunk... I don't like lying around during the day anyway... Come on. Easy does it..."

Witnessing such a display of altruism, the women who had previously been nodding and voicing their support suddenly lost interest.

Adidas made room for Elle on his bunk, while she blushed helplessly. There. Now they feel sorry for you. You're a charity case. The shame of it. What was she doing here anyway? Why had she got mixed up in all this? What was in it for her?

Lyokha and Martin looked on with mocking curiosity.

"Maybe Verka will make us nice and cosy in her bunk, eh?"

They roared with laughter and Verka joined in, standing on tiptoe to swipe at Martin's forehead with her broom, right on his centre parting (which used to drive Elle crazy). Just like that. And he didn't even flinch. These guys would put up with anything. As they used to say, if you're too squeamish to eat off the floor you can starve all you like.

They had once told her about how one time in Moscow when they'd run out of money Martin and a friend had killed a dog and... but Elle was no longer paying attention. She had drifted off the second her head had touched a normal pillow, the second she had stretched out on the lower bunk, so welcoming, so close to the ground...

The train kept on moving through her consciousness, shaking up the silence. With the part of her brain that was still involuntarily alert, Elle kept trying to understand whether it was just the noise of the wheels or whether someone really was whispering — was it Adidas, or Martin? And what were they saying? School... her literature class... chalk... An unassuming straight-A student, Elle had been blown away by one of Chekhov's stories – the one where they sledged down a hill and the young heroine heard whispered words of love but didn't know whether they came from the wind or from him, sitting behind her... She never did find out... But it was the happiest...

The snow doesn't look real. It's white and crunchy and doesn't melt, like foam rubber. A hill outside the town. On the way there in her stiff felt boots.... Ugh! Butterflies in her stomach. The Height, the glittering Height of Happiness... And as they rush down from the Height, her breath caught in her throat, his lips whisper to her, "I love you"... They're at the bottom of the hill. Her elation settles with the snow. It's Adidas. But the way he's looking at her! No one has ever looked at Elle with such love in their eyes. This cinematic snow doesn't look like it would ever melt, even if you caught it with your tongue.

She woke up when the sun was already subjecting the carriage to maximum discomfort. By all indications she had been deeply, feverishly disconnected from the world for several hours. Adidas sat next to her, stirring the rusty tea-bag in his cup. He turned his head, and the way he looked at her...

"Well!" he laughed. "Good morning to you!"

Elle couldn't speak.

"Do you want an apple?"

A nod.

An apple.

"Save some for me!" he laughs and takes it back...

Martin and Lyokha climbed down from their lofty bunks and sat on the cloth runner in the passage, playing cards. They observed this exchange with great interest.

8.

"...And the security staff at the supermarket called the police, can you believe it? So the police turned up, and they tried to arrest me! Can you imagine what would have happened?! Mum and Dad would have gone out of their minds. They wouldn't even let me go to Samara. But thank God, they managed to sort out the bar-codes..."

Martin laughed condescendingly, although the story had not been for his ears. Charming! What a baby!

But Elle didn't care! She didn't see or hear anyone but... She and Adidas were getting on brilliantly − they'd been chatting for most of the day, talking easily about their lives and happily swapping stories, one after the other. Employing guerrilla tactics, Adidas advanced down the cloth runner to the boiler with two pots of instant noodles... He had to do it secretly because the previous day Verka had barked at no one in particular: "The boiler isn't managing to heat up properly, you're bleeding it dry!" and tried to put a lock on it. Never mind, they ate gleefully as though sharing an illicit feast. The way he looked at her...

"I'm going for a cigarette. Are you coming?"

Elle followed Adidas onto the draughty, rumbling, blue-grey platform.

He had an attractive way of inhaling. He grinned and tossed another likely story into the furnace of their conversation.

"And one time the cops caught us up a tree! You don't believe me? It was a stupid situation, of course... That was a long time ago. Some idiots persuaded me to climb up a fir-tree and look into the girls' changing-rooms. Just for a laugh, you know... So we climbed up, me and Sevka... He... used to be a friend of mine. He drowned. Later." (Two drags on his cigarette.) "Where was I? So anyway, then I hear shouting from below: 'Run for it, Marat!'"

Elle was stunned.

"Marat? So your name's Marat too?"

"What do you mean, 'too'?"

What a coincidence! Although come to think of it it's not really that surprising. Every third male in Ufa is called either

Marat or Rinat. No, what's strange is that we've been pouring our hearts out to one another all day, and I didn't even ask his name!

"My name's Elina, by the way."

He laughed.

"So that's the introductions out of the way, then!"

He pulled her towards him and...

Kissed her.

Somewhere in the region of her heart something came loose and plunged into her stomach — she could feel it!

They kissed for so long it felt like forever, and it was so passionate, so perfect, that... They kissed and kissed. Someone walked between the carriages and banged the metal doors, enveloping them in the noise of the train. But they were oblivious! Soaring and falling, soaring and falling, a million heart-stopping, magic moments... This Height was beautiful and such...

"Oh," was all that Martin said when the lovers returned, and he put his side of the headphones back in. He and Lyokha shared their music — they were saving the batteries. Elle didn't understand that "Oh" straight away, only later, when Adidas said, "Oops!" and pointed her towards the mirror... A little bruise, a love-bite to the right of her upper lip. She burst out laughing, looked at her reflection again and collapsed once more in a fit of giggles. This thing on her lip — the height of impropriety for a good girl — made her feel... free, happy... everything all at once.

9.

"You're sleeping in my bunk tonight."

The sunset was spreading through the carriage.

"No, I mean, I'll sleep up there on the third shelf if you like," added Adidas, seeing Elle's reaction. "But there's no way I'm letting you go back up there!"

She paused for a moment, lost for words. Eventually, she said:

"We'll see. It's not time for bed yet anyway. Look, we're just coming into another station."

The train did indeed pull into a station. The women all ran about, fumbling with their slippers and rummaging under their pillows for their handbags. Verka yelled from somewhere in the region of the boiler:

"We're only stopping here for seven minutes! ... We're running late! ... Only seven minutes!"

"Do you want anything? Some beer and salted fish? Corn on the cob, maybe?"

Elle shook her head.

"Well, I'll get you some apples," said Adidas, and he picked up his cigarettes.

On the platform, waving away the mad old women with their trays and sacks, he bought a bag of crisp green apples — so nice, they were, she'd grown them herself — a bit of rust-coloured fish and a slippery, wet beer out of a bucket of cold water. The sun was setting and it was so warm and pleasant here, he just wanted to enjoy stretching his legs and...

"Let's go," Lyokha and Martin grabbed hold of him, one on each side.

"What are you doing? Hey!"

"Come on, let's go. We want a word with you."

"What the..."

The boys hustled Adidas over to the far end of the platform, which was deserted — no mad saleswomen darting about and no other passengers, who all wanted to stay close to the train. There were some railings and three or four metres down some bushes, weeds, the black ring of a tyre and the sound of water gently trickling.

"Put the bag down."

Adidas didn't even have time to move before Martin

grabbed his arms and Lyokha pulled his passport out of his pocket, its belly swollen with folded banknotes. The loudspeaker announced the train's imminent departure...

"What the hell are you doing?! I..."

"One, two, three, hup!"

Lifting Adidas under the arms, they threw him over the railings... A thud and a groan. No big deal, it wasn't that high. At worst he'd have broken something. Stunned, he started to get up...

"Hurry up! Get the bag, the bag!"

Baring their teeth with the exertion they ran as fast as they could towards the train, which was already picking up speed.

"Oh, my Lord! Sweet Jesus!!! Come on, come on... Oh, my Lord..."

Verka helped them climb aboard.

When everything started clanking and moving Elle began to dart about between the bunks in a panic. She wanted to pull the emergency stop lever — what was going on? They weren't back yet. Oh God, what should she do... Phew! There they were, walking down the passage. It took her a moment to realise that only two of them had come back.

Martin stared back as she looked at him and went over to Adidas's bunk, emptying the bag onto it. Apples tumbled out and rolled in all directions, concealing themselves in the folds of the grey railway sheets.

10.

The train kept going and the night beyond it was impenetrable, with occasional lights in the distance like moonlight. For some reason at night the view from the window was always the same — black fields followed by black walls of forests, some closer, some further away. Elle thought about the trip with her parents the previous summer. It had been raining, the air was fresh, and they had let her lean out of the window. The dark, desolate fields stretched on for ever. But she had been surprised by the strange platforms leading off into these fields. She realised that they were breakwaters, and only then did she understand that the fields were not fields at all... Thus her acquaintance with the Sea began, prosaically, through logical reasoning.

Once she understood what she was looking at, she could make out the white foam tips of the waves too, raging right up to the wheels of the train (the sea was rough). After they'd arrived in Sochi it occurred to her that the endless white crests in the sea, even when it was calm, were like nails, like the white crescent tips of human fingers... And sometimes the sea would bare its claws.

This time there was no sea.

By the general standards of long-distance train travel it was already late – people were idly leafing through their newspapers, waiting for Verka, who ruled supreme on this train, to declare authoritatively that it was night-time and to turn out the carriage lights. It didn't really make any difference – half the passengers would carry on drinking regardless of the time.

Martin and Lyokha were drinking too: let us not forget that there was a bottle of beer amongst their ill-gotten gains. That's simply the way of the world. The winner gets the bed, the grub and the girl. So they sat on Adidas's lower bunk, quietly discussing boys' stuff, chasing their drinks with the instant noodles they had discovered, which left traces of ultra-yellow fat on the spoons.

"Come down!" they shouted up to Elle.

"OK..."

They had already explained the sleeping arrangements to her. No more torture on the third shelf. She and Martin would sleep together on Adidas's bunk. No arguments! As for Lyokha, what a laugh: Verka finally took pity on him and offered to let him sleep in her compartment. She'd already dragged his rucksack in there (so that he couldn't run away). That's that!

Martin laughed loudly and slapped him on the shoulder. "If you're too squeamish to eat off the floor, you can starve..."

But until Verka retired for the night Elle would lie there. On the third shelf. Her last few minutes. Strangely enough she was no longer frightened of falling – it was as if she had made her peace with the Height. The daylight lamp was right above her face, a mechanical "eh-eh-eh" was audible in the tapping of the wheels, and when you closed your eyes it was red, not dark at all. "At least I'm getting a free sun-bed session!" The merest shadow of a smile, without even moving her lips.

Elle caught snatches of the boys' conversation – the usual male banter, with a self-righteous, complacent edge to it. They had even started reminiscing about their childhood.

"Do you remember the prank phone calls we used to make? 'Hello, is that the morgue?' 'Yes.' 'Could you put me through to Vasya on the third shelf?'"

They roared with laughter, and Elle jolted as though she'd had an electric shock. Yes. She saw herself: stiff, cold and on that third shelf. Stretched out motionless on her back. All her muscles relaxed. A lamp shining into her face, a buzzing sound, the light giving her lips a purple hue. And just to the right above her upper lip, a bruise, just like...

The train flew through fields, past forests and bushes, a source of light in its own right. The reflections from the carriage windows scorched the world and then left it alone once more in the darkness.

DENIS OSOKIN

Angels & Revolution: Vyatka 1923

Translated by Anna Gunin

A Word or Two from the Lord

At the time of the book's printing, the author was 22 years old. He considers himself a decent writer in the primitivist style and currently works in the Vyatka Cheka.

The Young Worker

A hot-blooded, hulking fiend of a young worker will break all of Papa's windows, knock over Mama's canapé, whack Brother round the ear, frighten the life out of Sister, who — ah! — will remember it for the rest of her life, he'll flatten the eunuch cat, find me in my room, shove me in the stomach, tear my lace, hoist me up, plant me like a nut on a bolt and carry me away from here — Lord, oh Lord, make it happen! He is a furious Red hammer. Yes, yes — I'm a Socialist. Long live the proletariat. And Papa is a swine. I hate him, the bourgeois. So thought Valya, the daughter of the chief engineer, in her room at 11 o'clock in the morning.

Dogs with Wings

We were walking across the bridge and imagining excitedly what kind of wings each breed of dog would have:

A German shepherd has eagle wings;

A dachshund has small wings; it flaps them often like a duck (the dachshund is the duck of the dog world);

The poodle is assisted in flight by its ears; on its sides it has an extra pair of wings, just as tousled and silly;

A fox terrier has the wings of a beetle, and during flight it is the only dog not to bark, but to emit a distinctive hum;

A pug has wings like ladies' fans;

A pointer has elastic elegant ovals;

Bichons have small pink tongues and their eyes are hidden from view; the wings of a bichon are two neat little curd cheese pastries;

When greyhounds fly the girls go crazy; a greyhound's wings are like those of the archangels on the canvases of the Italian renaissance;

Huskies and spitz dogs have invisible wings – they have lived too long among sorcerers;

It is not hard to imagine how a bulldog flies: desperately waving its negligible round winglets and itching to push off from some other dog flying nearby. The other dogs won't grumble though, they all love bulldogs. We decided that a bulldog would need a propeller;

And a spaniel flips through the air from stomach to back. He is his own propeller, and has no need of wings.

The bridge was long, warmed throughout the day, and the dogs with our wings flew over it.

The Girl and the Woman

Angel Dima told me this story.

General Krushilov, who lived in Kiev, had a daughter called Mashenka. She was an adorable elf of a girl with shining eyes and a heart as pure as a white begonia. Mashenka was barely seventeen, and her parents only ever called her mouseykins, squirrel-wirrel, and Minkie, and for Christmas and Easter they gave her long knitted socks filled with nuts. Mashenka would live in the city in the winter, then in the summer they would send her to the dacha of an old lady-cousin of Papa's for the holidays.

This was how it had always been, and so it was this summer. Only this time Second Lieutenant Knysh, a real cockroach, who was recuperating after being wounded, took lodgings near our dacha ladies. He took Mashenka for walks in the meadow and invited her to his orchard to help pick the cherries.

Mashenka left Kiev a charming and modest girl, and returned a fiery and strident woman, gawping crazily from side to side. She'd walk about the house like a bulldog on its hind legs, bedecking herself in shawls and poking her father in the stomach, saying, "Aye-aye!" while flaring her nostrils and winking. For days on end, the general and his wife dashed from room to room, clutching their heads and crying, "Dearie me!" Or shut themselves away in their bedroom, gazing into each other's eyes, holding hands and listening through the window as Mashenka stamped her feet and laughed hoarsely, explaining something to the coachman.

Big Saturday Love

On Saturday, no matter where we've been invited, and whatever the weather, Anya and I know that today our big Saturday love is to take place. What's that? It is five hours between the sheets in the middle of an empty house on a day of rest. Ah, is it really five hours? Well, we don't keep an eye on our watches like those Englishmen.

We work hard, and our life is a series of long, cold days, but the moment we got married, we decided firmly that our number one family tradition would be big Saturday love. Everything is always rather dreary, and the winter here is not getting any milder — God forbid, we wouldn't want it to. We just tell our friends not to visit us on Saturdays — after all, they have no way of telling when our big Saturday love might start and end.

Nelly

The dear thing, she hasn't worn glasses since that incident. They shattered to dust on the step of a tram. It's common knowledge that horseless trams are powered by the devil, and Nelly got on one without crossing herself.

Nelly did indeed have a ticket; she wanted to get off at the corner of the Evangelists Church. "Two cakes at the bakery, to be sure, I'll get two, not one", thought Nelly, placing her foot on the step when, a millimetre from her ear boomed a deafening, bear-like roar: "Show us your ticket, Miss." Here's what happened next: with bells ringing in her ears, Nelly saw the devil in the form of the tram driver. He stood within a hair's breadth of her and blocked her path with his arm, he was missing a tooth, his forehead was burnt and peeling, and he had only one eye, bang in the middle of that burnt forehead, I believe. The devil smiled sneeringly. "A-a-ah, too stingy to buy a ticket!" hissed his flunkies all round him. At that moment Nelly's glasses cracked once for all — the devil dimmed into a blur, the lenses shattered, and the frame slipped from her little nose and tumbled after. It seems Nelly did show the devil her ticket, because soon she was standing in the street, having forgotten about the bakery, without her glasses, unable to move because a horseless tram is powered by the devil, and you have to cross yourself, or better still, spit on the rails and say "begone", and then there are those airyplanes and watch out one might fall on your head, and there's also a black quail roaming the city stealing children.

The Bread Proletariat

Of all the proletariat the best is the bread proletariat. It is made up of people sprinkled in flour and smelling of the happiest truth that comes out of the earth. Their life is not so sweet as their cheeks and hands might be, but you must admit, a bread factory is better than an iron foundry or a coal pit. Of course, man's exploitation of man is to be found everywhere, and our floury toilers often have the eyes of beguiled children. But that's why the enthusiasm and special dedication of a man who can make a tasty twisted bread ring in the revolutionary ranks make the bread proletariat the most sweet-smelling column of all.

Aunties

How I loved them — my mother's adorable sisters and Auntie Sasha, the sister of my father. They played with me, took me for walks and told me all sorts of silly things. Now I know that they were my childhood sexual experiences. But in fact I was a sexual experience for them too. It is no accident that they sometimes changed in front of me, though it's true, they would turn away or tell me to turn around. They went bathing with me, in swimsuits, of course, but oh how they used to catch me in the water, throw me in the air, teach me to swim! I learnt to swim from most tender teachers, but I also remember how my arm or leg would unexpectedly knock against something unmentionable.

Who asked, "Do you love me?" And who said, "Give your auntie a kiss"? Who picked berries with me in grandmother's garden in loose-fitting smock dresses and, bending to reach the lower branches, revealed their breasts and dark nipples? They took me around the little town on a bicycle and suddenly played up: "Time for you to pedal." And I pedalled with all the steamy spirit of my six, or nine, or twelve years, and then they all went and got married. Perhaps I was heartbroken, perhaps not − after all, I'm not a girl. In any case, I lived in a different town. I was taken to my aunties by my parents for one of the summer months, and then brought home again.

Gangstress Lena

How many Red heroes she slayed! How she'd whistle and spit in the face of the next martyr. She could shake her curls and whip off her belt with its huge buckle. Her trousers would slip − whoops! − the rabble would guffaw.

How skinny and slight she was, Lena's thugs carried her everywhere: to her horse, to church, to the bushes when nature called. Lena would sit in the bushes, with her gangsters in a semicircle, swords drawn in salute to her.

She yelled and didn't wash properly, but they loved her all the same. She used to execute the Red heroes herself. She'd whistle and spit, she'd say, "What starts with a 'd' belongs to me." Then bang in the forehead from her Mauser! "What starts with a 'd' belongs to me" − that was her favourite saying.

Engineer Slavyanov

Nikolai Gavrilovich Slavyanov, head of the Perm state gun factories, sailed on the *S.S. France* to the World's Fair in Chicago to receive a diploma and gold medal for inventing the electric-arc welding of metals using metal electrodes. The year was 1893. The ocean was quiet, and the sea monsters rocked lazily on its surface without a thought of gobbling up the Russian inventor. *The middle of the ocean*, thought Slavyanov, chuckling into his beard. He recalled how in Perm his wife had said to him, "Kolya, bring me a white parrot from America, we'll name it Anton."

In Russia, no doubt, it was now the dead of night. Slavyanov couldn't sleep; up on deck, he wondered: *Why is she so keen on the name Anton?*

Lina's Affair

Oh, those trams in our dreary capital! What eye or heart could bear to gaze at them for long?

Every day we went home from work by tram; there were five of us, we'd known each other for years, and we knew the route like a very old photo album. Lina went with us, an unhappy girl, though clearly an optimist; at office festivities she sang and danced more enthusiastically than anyone else; yet she remained alone, always alone. We knew about that. Lina always got off at the same stop as us, it was where she lived. We also knew that full well.

One time in September when we were going home together, Lina got off not at her stop, but much earlier. Her confident composure betrayed a joy and impatience. *Lina's having an affair*, we all thought.

We flew through the streets along with the autumn. We had not yet tired of work or life. We had grown used to Lina's new stop and, when we neared it, would start saying goodbye; however, one day in November, or was it December, Lina didn't get off there, she got off at her old stop, along with the rest of us. *Lina's affair has ended*, we decided that evening, gazing into our glasses of tea.

We were right. Lina now travels her former route, and we all love her dearly. Yet we still cannot look calmly at the capital's trams: we start to cry, and we generally try to go into town less often.

Denisov the Chekist

Of course, his work was difficult. But even so, you cannot drink like that at any party and shout songs at the piano. You cannot flit before everyone's eyes, tirelessly inviting the pretty ladies to smoke, dance, and try out your revolver in the long, dark corridor. If he happens to be an educated man, well, what of it? We are all educated here. As though only he knows the early history of the Vologda Province, only he speaks French and knows the words to the song "The Blizzard". The ladies rustle their dresses and gladly listen to him. Denisov pulls the ladies' fine tresses, despite being barely acquainted; he smiles into their eyes and gesticulates sincerely. Below his left collar bone he has a tattoo of a star, but the ladies will learn of that later.

Poignant singing

We know that's how they sing in Serbia and in certain deadly corners of the Balkans. But the term is ours, and we are delighted to donate it to our native musicologists.

Such singing sounds as though, instead of the usual words, nothing was being sung but "oy, oy-oy, oy-oy-oy!" Or "aye-aye, aye, ayya-yay!" And all the words, ripped hot and bloody out of the body by the teeth, are flung in the faces of the audience who are drowning in tears. And, indeed, those very shouts of "oy!" and "aye!" with their terrible power, grief and joy, frame practically every word sobbed out.

We know, we've heard it: that's how people sing in Romania and in Bosnia, that's how the gypsies sing, that's how everyone with dark eyes sings, those whose life is endless knives in the heart, sun glaring in their eyes and wine from grapes — rather than ice, medicines and water.

We want to live until our whole body is covered in burns, we want to die of pain and ecstasy, our teeth have cracked the kernel from the apricot orchards, the pip from the vineyards of life, and we have understood all of life's hollering and all of its poison gripping the throat — that's what poignant singing communicates to everyone who hears it.

Poignant singing means the limits of human knowledge. The person who sings like that, sitting under a pear tree and crying, has understood everything and is now infinitely happy; no matter what happens to him, he is happy forever.

Poignant singing is madly close to us; here in Russia we say "yes" to it! We are jealous, we desperately envy the people who sing poignantly.

Drinking Companion

My drinking companion, Isaiah Markulan, buried his head in his collar and quietly smoked. We were both frozen, sitting on a bench in a park — it was an extremely cold evening in April. We were tired and in no hurry to go home because at home there was nothing but sleep, and we wanted to unwind, not to sleep.

A burly white cat sprang out at us from who knows where, rubbed its face against our dirty shoes then crept under the bench.

I am no lover of cats, so I am always rude about them in my stories.

Markulan and I stretched out our legs and sat gazing at the dark trees for what felt like an eternity. Few words were said and countless cigarettes smoked. Markulan did tell me, though, about his sister Vera in Mogilev and the story somehow ended with the words "Marry her".

As we got up to go, we saw the cat was still sitting under our bench staring up at us through the damp slats.

"Right, you're coming with me," Markulan said, and picked the parasite up by the scruff of its next.

I laughed and suggested he name the cat Fat Pig. Markulan looked at the cat and said, "I'll call him Puss, anyone can see he's a fat pig as it is."

The three of us walked from the park to the place where the streetlamps shone

The Only Joy

Alexander Pavlovich Buravtsev was forty-eight, and worked God knows where. His hair twisted like wire and did not think of turning grey. Alexander Pavlovich spoke in a piercing voice that always quavered and, when need be, could curse so filthily we had better not go into it.

Alexander Pavlovich was somewhat sullen with his wife, Tamara Yurevna, but now and again, lying side by side with her on the daybed, he would suddenly grab her — you know, as one does — with his fingers between her ribs.

Tamara Yurevna would scream ten deaths, while Alexander Pavlovich, his face shining, went into gales of happy, positively angelic laughter.

His wife, who was ticklish, would shriek with shrill mirth, but it was clear she would prefer these capers to stop. She would shout out, gasping: "Stop it, stop it!"

To which Alexander Pavlovich, unappeased, would rollick, "You're my accordion, you are!"

"Stop it, stop it!" poor Tamara Yurevna would cry, thrashing her legs.

Finally Alexander Pavlovich would release his wife, sigh, grow glum and, with an air of grim seriousness that is hard to doubt, say: "Shut up, woman! It might be my only joy in life."

Glimmers of this only joy flickered across his face for a long time. There is much we do not know, but we do know that Alexander Pavlovich and Tamara Yurevna have gotten along fine for many years now. Even so, we suspect that Alexander

Pavlovich is having us on about its being his only joy in life, although he could, of course, be telling the truth.

They are always together, whenever they get a free moment.

Drinking Girlfriend

Xenia would hardly wish to be called a drinking girlfriend, any woman would prefer to be called a wife, especially if she is dead.

But things are as they are, and I will tell the entire Russian Soviet Federal Socialist Republic how Xenia and I bathed at the jetties surrounded by townspeople dazed by the heat. The scraggy willow shrubs provided us a meagre screen and, with the fire-lookout towers behind our backs, I think we must have been fairly visible.

But the firemen were drunk and they all sat down below anyway, while for us the thing was to get into and out of the water in four seconds — that's what I explained to Xenia when she was still in her skirt with all the buttons on her chintz blouse fastened.

There she was, standing about in indecision, having taken off only her old sandals. "Come on, Xenia," I say, "even from close up your two little grapes couldn't be mistaken for breasts." Then Xenia turns pink, shakes a finger at me and drops her skirt onto the hot sand.

The Power under a Blouse

Power comes in all varieties. There once was a tsar, and his power was unjust, for the benefit of the bourgeoisie alone. Then there is this cannibal king, clad entirely in speckled shells, who lives on a coral atoll somewhere in the Pacific Ocean, but his power is rather odd, because in all matters he obeys a nervous sorcerer who makes a great racket and wears no trousers. And then there is Soviet power, the very best sort, which we have all done so much to bring about.

But our story will be about women.

Women are a gentle and most amusing race. They shake their pretty heads and pretend to nothing other than love. Even reading is not for every woman. Women do not enter into questions of power, but merely shout vociferously when any power stands in the way of their love. Then again, women do exercise it – power, that is – and in no small way.

Here is Inga, our neighbour, a lazy woman who wishes summer would last twelve months of every year;

Here is Marina, a fair-haired smoker of twenty; through the wall we hear her singing and banging out entirely serious, utterly awful papers on her typewriter;

Here is Polina, our Moscow friend; she is very clever, but would gladly swap all her smarts for a wild sailor with an anchor tattoo on his stomach and traces of syphilis on his mug.

Each has under her blouse, let it be known, no trifling power, especially when they walk or get up suddenly. Aah, how they stick out! It is simply marvellous.

This, admittedly, is a rather daft power. But what is to be done if even Soviet power, with all its historical tribulations and heroic glory, with its Red Army, all heart, blood and steel, can at times be feebler than the power under a blouse? Women should not feel overconfident, however: responsible Soviet workers have a surefire means of resisting the tumultuous power of the female, barely held in check by those frivolous buttons. That means is to smoke and work plenty. Fortunately, we have no shortage of either work or cigarettes.

Poppies

Aglaya and Aurel, that's what my friends were called. They lived in Moldova and they didn't know Russian too well, especially Aglaya. But poppies, there were poppies all around their house, and everywhere in that land — in the fields and on the slopes of the green mountains, poppies in a slender bottle on the table in my room left by the owners who looked after me diligently; poppies are a sign and a splash of colour, the fullness of life, they are the soul, they are love — poppies united the three of us inseparably. The Revolution is the poppies that have vanished from my eyes.

The Lavatory

The ladies' lavatory, the cause of all the trouble, had long given Vadik Vronsky no peace. As he told us himself, he'd always wanted to slip in there, hide in one of the stalls, and then — well, wait and see.

Vadik was a clever chap, a fine and courageous man, free of intolerable vices, who had never lacked for female attention. The first time he mentioned it, he infected us with his idea, and we each managed to eavesdrop at least once through the flimsy partition on a peeing female from among our co-workers, and then look at each one of those ladies with overwhelming passion and tenderness, wondering if it had been her.

Our women, proud and beautiful, strong and willful even, couldn't have imagined what rascals we were.

Vadik, however, was found out:: the next stall happened to contain Ilsa, a flaxen-haired belle from the Latgalian farmlands, who only ever wore a soldier's tunic, a woman of twenty-seven, a heavy smoker with long, firm legs. She ruined our scheme, and its mastermind, Vadik, to boot.

We were of the opinion that such a woman simply needed to be smothered in love, five or six times a day — only then would she finally be able to take her mind off her troublesome, obsessive thoughts, forget about her own legs and abdomen and cook some delicious soup, say, or make some white sausage using an old traditional recipe.

Having relieved herself, Ilsa creaked open the stall door, but rather than leave, she decided to stay and have a smoke. A few moments later — well, hello there! — she was face to face with sly old Vadik, who had come out of hiding. What can you do, it was a risk we all faced!

Vadik swore us to secrecy and recounted how Ilsa had simply moaned in admiration, cursed in Latvian, and told him he was the man of her dreams, exactly what she needed, then darted with Vadik into the stall, bent over straightaway and died resolutely on the spot, while Vadik at the instant of Ilsa's death proposed to her. They made a good pair, only Lord, do not be wrathful — we are not bad people.

Naturally, Ilsa demanded that Vadik put an end to his disgraceful behaviour. Vadik did not give us away, but as it was, we'd already had it with the female lavatory.

At the wedding table, sozzled Vadik tried to tell the whole group the story of his affair with Ilsa, but nobody would believe him.

The Appeal of the Kamchatka Revolutionary Committee

Citizens of Soviet Kamchatka!

As volcanoes spew fire from out of our earth, so too must we now spew our fury onto the heads of the enemies of the Revolution. Then they will all burn to death, or, fleeing the fire, drown in the ocean. Each one of us must become a volcano. A volcano that has awoken, not a sleepy or dead one.

Czechs

Here's the lowdown: the Czechs are occupying the towns along the Volga. In Kazan, Samara and Syzran, on the trees and two-storey houses (brick below, wooden above) they put up posters written in the Czech language.

For that, guys, no one will pour you slivovitz or play "The Goose Flew Over the Blue Morava" on their fiddles: we'll fire from the guns of the Volga Flotilla steamships.

Grapes

Grape: it is hard to imagine a more erotically charged word. We remember it from the Song of Songs, with its erotic grape allegories. The levels of eroticism pulsing through this word are not to be found even in the most youthful and ardent of matrimonial beds.

The grape: its form and breath. The grape hides behind no clothes. The grape is little islands of joy beneath my girlfriend's pyjamas, and her darkest death beneath my palm, and her voice which rang out in a grapevine idiom even before my arrival. And I did not hear how it started: the colour and rustle of clothing, the rain of buttons released from their choke. I rang the little bells, I swam, I drowned, I whirled in other vineyards.

North-South
(Walks in the city of Vyatka)

When I walk down the street, I think about the fact that I am walking North, through the forests of Komi, passing chipmunks and skunk bears, crossing the Pinega and the Mezen, to the Arctic Ocean, at the edge of which Samoyeds celebrate glacial weddings in the dark. But at this point, I want the South – and

I turn back and head down the street in the opposite direction: I walk and see a different sun, which takes up half the sky, and houses of white stone, and poppies, and basil; I walk and hear beetles humming instead of mosquitoes, and accordions and violins playing instead of creaking pines; I walk and smell spices in the air around me.

When I need Moldova, Bukovina, or Kiev, where there is such love, I take streets heading in a south-westerly direction. I walk East whenever I want to hide or punish myself.

Lilitsa

Once upon a time our Lilitsa was young: she used to sing a song about a yellow anemone, pray to Saint George and drink rakia. The rakia was strong, but Lilitsa too stood strong on her feet, danced to the roar of the bucium, and shouted, "Haide, haide!"

Now everything is different. Hedgerows, ravines, bogs and clay are disagreeable to Lilitsa. We present her with a plate of soup with mushrooms floating in it but Lilitsa sneers – she doesn't eat mushrooms.

"Russians are just like mushrooms," she pronounces. "They eat this slimy muck, sown by the Lord for worms, hedgehogs and werewolves, they fill themselves up on the stuff. They bake it in bread and serve it to their guests as a great delicacy. Russians have eyes and hair of a murky colour. Russians are like mushrooms themselves, they each have a mealy mushroom in place of a heart."

We wait patiently; we do not gloat when, after the same old words each time, Lilitsa tucks into her mushroom soup. Our Lilitsa is old, terribly old and she wipes her mouth with the tip of her black headscarf. She does not understand very well where she is and what year we are in.

We respect her contempt for mushrooms well enough, we

know that Lilitsa has lived her entire life in a place where they eat meat sprinkled with paprika and basil.

The Amur Forest Cat

The Amur forest cat, *felis bengalensis*, is a rather grouchy animal. Three times the size of your usual stray moggie, it prowls the dense mountain forests and scrubland, devouring any creature it can make short work of. Fat and ugly, it will drop clumsily from a tree onto a baby hare or a young roe deer, tickle its prey with its whiskers and growl in pleasure. It can drop onto a human too, a hunter, for instance, if a strong wind is blowing and the cat is sleeping on a branch. It laps the clear water of the rapid, cold rivers; it will splash a paw at the spot where a trout has just flashed past and shake it dry in a huff: it hasn't a chance of catching a trout. In the winter it walks around with a ridge of snow between its ears. In March it fights and fills the entire forest with its screams.

The Chinese are not frightened of them, whereas Kolchak's army, especially the men from Tambov and Voronezh, told us time and again during interrogations about how the Amur forest cat had filled them with dread.

Principle Soloist

She sang solos and delighted everyone, including the priest, while the choirmaster was just crazy about her. But the Revolution came, and the choirmaster fled to Estonia, the priest left for the village, and she sailed down the Vyatka on a steamship, moving to the district town of Mamadysh. She had wanted to go to Kazan where she started playing the piano. But in Mamadysh her trail turned cold. Old barges and mountains of river sand stood at the empty Mamadysh quays. She is not in Mamadysh, of this we are certain; we chase away the thought that perhaps she is no longer with us.

The Organist

In this city there is no work for him.

"I am not a parasite − I am an organist," he smiles, and suggests that someone deliver an organ to Vyatka.

"Granddad," we smile, "write to Lenin about it."

Scenes with a Perch

We hurled curses at that stupid perch when back home, in the kitchen sink, it took it into its head to regain its senses and start a frantic dance, frightening the mistress of the house to death. We all came running, the moment we heard her screams.

We fishermen looked in astonishment at the revived perch, thrashing in the heap of dead fish, and we talked about how it had spent two hours lying under the bench in the boat and then been kept in a grimy plastic bag at the bottom of a rucksack for an hour on the way home. The mistress of the house shouted that the perch would not let her scale it and had already pierced her finger. Little Valentina shouted louder still: "Poor fishie, give it to me!"

Woken up thanks to the perch, we stared grimly and reflected on the fact that this was a fish about the size of your average log − without a doubt, the pride of our catch. To hell with the size − it's not that easy to go to sleep at ten in the morning, even if you've just come off a boat and didn't sleep a wink the day before.

The next scene. We are not asleep: we are rushing about the yard, hauling buckets of water and filling up the only tub in the house, the one we usually wash in, and Valentina calls from the window: "Quick, quick!" The perch lives in the bathtub − for one day, then a second, a third, and a fifth; its scales brighten, its stripes gleam, it is given the name Denis in honour of the man who caught it, we feed it worms from the kitchen garden, and by week's end grandfather says that he will pour copper sulphate on the perch as he, grandfather, would like to bathe at some point and that the perch has overstayed its welcome, in a word – fry it or take it back to the river.

I carry the bucket with the perch, Valentina trots along beside me and says, "Farewell, little Denis." It is a long way to the river, but we are in no hurry.

Liepu Lapu Laipa

A path of lime leaves is a gentle image from Latvian folklore. To travel this magical path is easy and not frightening: walk along it and you will always find your heart's desire. We were told of this by Joachim Vacietis, who brought the Latvians into the Revolution – the first commander of the Latvian Riflemen, and in 1918 and '19 commander of the Eastern Front, commander-in-chief of the republic's Red Army.

"May each one of you find in Russia your Liepu Lapu Laipa," he said to his soldiers as he rode up and down the silent lines formed beside the army train, one rugged and windy day at noon.

Ivanovskoye

My sister and I found this village. It has a church halfway up a large hill; there's a bend in the river, whose current cascades down a natural slope, which is why it's so rapid. "The place of our dreams," we decided. We went there often. We spent the night in a shelter of branches at the waterside; early in the morning we washed in the river, set the soap box drifting between us. We crawled about the shallow riverbed on all fours

− it was hard to keep our balance on two feet, we ate bread and potatoes in their jackets, drank plenty of water. On the southern wall of the church, the brickwork was collapsing − on each visit we took away a stone.

This Month of August

When I think of August, I feel a twinge in my heart. In August the world fills up like a basket of mushrooms − everything that exists in it becomes manifest, visible. A little more time will pass and the basket will topple over. Much of what has accumulated in the world by August and become so intense, pronounced and scented will start to vanish. In late autumn and winter the world is empty. I love this emptiness. In winter's emptiness there is nothing to stop you from seeing a person. Here he is, alone, walking, crunching through the snow. Then there is architecture, although that too is a person.

But in August! It sends a shiver through your entire body. It is the most powerful spring in your legs. Springs for legs, rowan berries for cheeks, pools for eyes. It is the city of Gorokhovets, where the birds have started squawking, and the water in the river has turned blue. It seems if you buy an apple from an elderly woman or pick one up from under an apple tree and roll it hard, it won't stop rolling, and you can follow its path. Even if the apple is slightly worm-eaten, picked up off the ground.

Somewhere the sea is lapping, and in August its splashes can be heard even in Gorokhovets. Perhaps the apple will lead you to the sea. Only in August can you depend on it.

Angels & Revolution

Angels lived In Natasha Pikeyeva's house. It should come as no surprise − girls of her kind always have homes filled with angels. After the Revolution, the number of angels in Natasha's house grew, while Bolsheviks with Red bands flew in the sky. Natasha even had a favourite Bolshevik, he flew past her windows and swore lustily, but Natasha knew he was a good person. The angels, of course, were a little afraid of the Bolsheviks, but this one, Natasha's, they grew fond of, and kept watch for him at the window and whenever he appeared, they would run and fetch Natasha. And the Bolshevik beheld the house and window, and in the window the girl, the best in the world, surrounded by hovering angels. Then the window faded and vanished from sight, and in the house everyone's spirits lifted. Natasha and the angels drew the curtains closed, sat down and made themselves comfortable. And they began to sing a song:

> *The meadow is grown with hemp,*
> *In the meadow we see a maiden fair,*
> *The meadow has a stump and a log,*
> *And old Marya is sitting there.*

GULLA KHIRACHEV

Salam, Dalgat!

Translated by Nicholas Allen

Dalgat felt bad as soon as he entered the crush of the bazaar but found some respite in the shelter of the separate stalls. Even then he was still overwhelmed by washing powders and household soaps, then dazzled by the sunny gleam of shampoos, wire dish brushes, hair ties and bands, cellophane packets of henna, basma and laurel bunches.

Then in another rush of colour he found himself hemmed in by brassieres with enormous cups, heaps of cheap, gaudy lingerie, and twice he got wedged between two heavyset women as they rummaged for items in the aisle.

"Buy these young man, you won't regret it," screeched a gold-toothed shop assistant of about forty, shaking with laughter as she flapped a pair of red panties under his nose, triggering a wave of female mirth around her.

After he had extricated himself from the narrow paths between the stalls, Dalgat found himself in the bright sunshine again, only narrowly escaping being knocked down by a filthy iron trolley that flew round the corner with a clatter, pushed by a shabbily dressed man.

"Gang way, mind your backs!" came a low coarse shout swallowed by a local pop star's voice coming from the loudspeakers. "Come on, get your bargains here ladies, get them here, over you come!" The reverberating clamour swelled on all sides. The noisy traders stood and sat everywhere, sheltering from the sky with pieces of cardboard, blackened by the sun and haggard from their toil in the burning glare.

A few men could be seen sheltering in the shade of their Kamaz trucks, the backs of which spewed out heaps of ripe, heavy watermelons. Among piles of raspberries that towered towards him, Dalgat's drunken eyes made out a sign scribbled in pidgin Russian advertising "Sweat apricots". Green hazelnuts lay alongside like torn paper wrappings. Apples, pears, oranges, persimmons and tomatoes rose in neat, soldierly formations, flanked by peas, cherries, large, small and oblong bunches of green, violet and red grapes. And among this rich abundance there prowled a moustachioed tax collector who for some reason carried a long whip.

Against the masses of food leant pieces of paper with the biro-scrawled names of the villages they had come from, Gergebil, Botlikh, Akhty, while half-blind, flea-ridden kittens crawled under the stalls between crushed pomegranates and peaches. All around people thronged relentlessly, sweaty and exhausted, with dark agitated eyes, cautious old ladies with neat ponytails, weary girls in sparkling evening dresses and heels who lugged buckets of cucumbers, women in veils and young men in track suits.

"Get your greens here sonny, come on!" they urged Dalgat. "Parsley, coriander, dill, all fresh... Check out these potatoes, the very best, no worms, weigh some for you?... Come, have a bit of this apricot ... Try these sweet apples, not at all tart!"

Ahead of him a young woman in a straw hat swayed on her feet, blocking his way.

"Nice hat miss, let me try it on," shouted a woman selling carrots while immediately snatching and placing it on her unkempt head and doing a turn as her neighbours came up to help her tie the ribbons. The owner of the hat tried to reach for it in confusion, prompting a male trader with a kindly smile to spit out the straw he was chewing and call out from across the aisle: "Take your hat back yourself, lady, she's got dirty hands, she'll make it all grimy!"

Dalgat walked on and turned into the small meat hall stinking of blood, but dark and cool. Long sides of veal, mutton and other meats hung from the ceiling while the men worked quickly and deftly on carcasses with axes.

"Here you go young man, the finest mutton just for you!"

"Chickens, get your chickens!"

In the fish section the latest catch flipped around on the floor, sucking last gasps of air through bulbous lips. A man in a dirty blue apron thumped the head of one large fish on the counter, while women in the row were busy gutting and filleting, surrounded by gleaming scales.

Dalgat remembered the religious programmes they used to show on television every evening, hosted by an uneducated, incoherent *alim* with some spiritual rank or other. By comparison, the young *mufti* on the show was smart and educated, but he then got murdered. In these programmes they would talk about genies and *suras*, prescribing what you can and can't do. People would ring into the studio, like the guy who asked if it was allowed to sleep with your back to the Koran. One girl even inquired what colour you should paint your nails according to Shariah law.

"Hello Dalgat, what's up?" came the voice of an old classmate who stood before him, his broad smile accentuating the old rip in his ear.

"Ah, Maga, how you doing?"

"Great – got your phone on you?"

"Yes," Dalgat answered, reaching into his pocket.

"I haven't got any money right now and I have to call the boys, one of the junkies has started to mess us around. I was talking to him and he started playing up, so I suddenly gave him a smack, that shook him, but then wham-bam, suddenly he was on me. I threw him off and gave him a good beating, messed him up real good. Now he's gone to get his boys, so I have to gather our lot."

As he talked to Dalgat, Maga took his phone, said something about the model and its power and suddenly yelled into the handset.

"Hey, Murad, it's Maga, what's up! How are your dad and mum, brother and sister? I'm calling about that son of a bitch Isashka's brother. He wants to take us on! Where are you now? Get over to Street 26, let's roll the lot of them, show him who's boss. Give your brother a call, and Shapiska too, get them over. Okay, thanks buddy, talk to you later."

Maga ended the call and started to fiddle about on the buttons.

"You got any girls on here?" he asked Dalgat.

"No, it's a new phone," he replied.

Maga looked at Dalgat closely, exposing rows of healthy teeth in a big grin.

"What's the matter with you, you getting weedy? Don't you work out no more?" he teased, playfully prodding Dalgat in the shoulder and back. "Come for a spin with me, the boss gave me his car for a while, let's zip round and see the lads and then take a ride along Lenin Street and back."

"I've got to get to a place around here, drop me off?" Dalgat asked as he followed Maga to a new foreign car.

"No problem."

As they got in they were suddenly surrounded by a bunch of Uzbek dervish beggars who had been sitting on the pavement eating chunks of watermelon.

"Sadahah! Spare some change," whined some swarthy urchins, shoving their filthy hands in through the windows of the car.

"Yo!" Maga yelled to an Uzbek woman standing back from the kids, "Get them away!"

"Sadahah! Spare some change, in the name of Allah," the woman bleated back as she looked up from her watermelon.

"You're richer than me anyway!" Maga shouted back, and turning to Dalgat told him: "These beggars make a killing here, she won't even look at bread, all she wants is money!"

As if she had heard him, the Uzbek got up and held out her hand: "Give me bread, we'll eat it, Allah punishes thieves, but we are not thieves."

Maga was deaf to them as he stepped on the accelerator, whipping the car forward through the unruly flow of vehicles, oblivious to the traffic lights ahead. He quickly reached the turn, screeched off to the left and veered into the opposite lane, ignoring the whistle of a traffic cop standing by the road.

"That whistle was for us," ventured Dalgat, gripping his seat.

"So what, the boss will have the lot of them," Maga shot back, maintaining his speed while rifling through a pile of CD's with one hand and then filling the street with the sound of a female Avar singer.

"Ah, Lazat," Maga exclaimed appreciatively, beaming at Dalgat. Suddenly the car stopped with a squeal of tires and, winding down the window, Maga shouted over the music.

"Give you a lift somewhere girls?"

A group of attractive girls in glitzy clothes and shiny shoes and with neat hairdos made their way slowly along the roadside, not stopping.

"Hey, are you deaf or something, hold up!" Maga yelled.

"You're not going our way," one girl replied, haughtily adjusting her hair but laughing.

"Let's go Maga," said Dalgat, remembering his task.

"See you later girls," Maga promised and gunned the engine again. "Once I was driving with Nurik and there were these two chicks walking along by the Anzhi bazaar," he said to Dalgat, turning the singer down a little as he spoke. "We crawled along behind them for a while, then one said to the other, these guys are okay, let's get a ride with them."

"Then what?" asked Dalgat.

"We drove them to Manas, where there's a nice sandy beach, and invited them to take a swim. Then they started to make trouble, Nurik grabbed one and she started to create. He shouts at her 'you speak properly to me' and the like, and she screams back that she'll get her brother, it was dead funny!"

"So what happened?"

"Well, we got down to it in the end. Nurik's was a right little cow, but mine was a bit of all right. At first she wasn't up for it, but then she lightened up. I recognized one of them from Idris's yard — now the lads there don't leave her alone," laughed Maga. "Shall we get you something to smoke?"

"No thanks — you can stop here," Dalgat replied, and then they both got out of the car at the mouth of a cul de sac.

"Okay pal, mind how you go," Maga called after him, frowning as Dalgat went to go.

Sensing he had not done right, Dalgat paused and extended his hand. Maga shook it and half joking, half seriously, dropped Dalgat onto his back in the road.

"Got no strength these days have you, eh? You know the form, Dagestan boys are strong!" he said, brightening again.

"He who isn't with us is under our feet," Dalgat replied with a grin as he got to his feet and shook himself off. "Thanks for the ride, take care!"

"OK, I'm off, stay in touch," Maga shouted before the car shot off, hitting every pothole as it sped out of sight, leaving Dalgat alone with his ears still ringing from the blare of the stereo.

Now Maga had gone he tried to remember which of the tight rows of houses belonged to Khalilbek. Small clay-built dwellings adjoined larger, well-to-do properties, most of which were still under construction. The pavement was dotted with piles of sand, ballast and garbage, and children in ragged shorts and wearing triangular leather amulets around their necks ran around on the dirty street.

The area was populated by the Akhvakh (one of Dagestan's numerous ethnic groups) and one gate even bore the proud sign "Akhvakh = strength". By the gate stood a cluster of women in cheap headscarves and housecoats who looked Dalgat up and down and called out: "Who are you looking for?"

"Khalilbek's house."

"You see that corner? Go straight through there and you'll find a red-brick house, that's them, they're in now."

He strode a few steps to the corner and saw a gang of five or six rough-looking youths squatting by the roadside, all aimlessly spitting on the ground at their feet. Noticing the skinny stranger approaching them the group perked up.

"Hey, no *salam* for us then?" a ginger-haired youth in black shorts called out to Dalgat.

"Assalam aleikum," Dalgat said, approaching and holding out his hand as nonchalantly as he could.

"How about giving me a go at your phone?" Ginger asked, slapping Dalgat's palm in greeting but not getting up.

"No phone I'm afraid, it's being repaired."

"I bet you anything he's got one," said another of the pack, pulling a fistful of sunflower seeds from his pocket and squinting lazily at the sky.

"Hey, what do you think you're up to monkey boy, I said give me your phone!" the first added, hackles rising.

"No way," Dalgat said firmly, resolving to brazen this out. "Want me to call my buddy over here, do you?"

"I'll take care of your buddy too," hissed Ginger, losing his composure. "What's your problem, eh?"

"No problem," Dalgat managed.

"Hey, Ibrashka, tell him," Ginger said to one of the others, now evidently close to boiling point.

"Don't start anything here if you're smart," said Ibrashka, standing up menacingly and swinging a rubber shoe on his bare foot. "What's your game, pal?" he added, suddenly grabbing Dalgat's wrists.

"You going to take him Ibrashka or what?" another asked.

"I'm going to kick his face in, that's what I'm going to do," spat Ibrashka, throwing Dalgat from left to right by his wrists.

No one had struck him yet but they pressed in from all sides, hampering each other in the process. Ginger was the most determined to get in close to him.

"What are you showing off for then, eh?" he hissed, jabbing him in the forehead with a big paw.

Behind them they heard a boyish shout of "fight!" and Dalgat saw a crowd of kids run out of the adjoining streets to watch. Someone rushed forward to separate him and Ginger, and when Dalgat dropped the leather folder he was carrying another kid stamped on it with a trainer. A little guy in a tracksuit with a self-important expression tried once again to separate them until Ginger elbowed him in the nose, only to receive an unexpected blow to the ribs in retaliation. Then amid the noisy melee someone shouted "Cool it boys, that's the White Khadzhik's cousin!"

Dalgat felt the crush slacken slightly and then saw Khalilbek's son Khadzhik and two of his friends, one of whom was making a show of talking into an expensive mobile phone. Khadzhik himself was muscle-bound and fashionably dressed, his fair hair falling down the nape of his neck and with a pair of pointy shoes decorated with a chain shining on his feet.

"What do you think you're doing hassling my cousin, eh, are you stupid or what?" he barked at the crowd.

"It was Ginger who started on him," someone shouted angrily in a high-pitched voice.

"What do you mean me," Ginger protested, hitching up his shorts. "I didn't say anything out of order to him. I just asked to use his phone and he starts to get het up and then scared. Act normally and nothing will happen to you, got it?" he said to Dalgat, throwing his thick arm around him as if to show they were now friends.

Dalgat broke away from the embrace and picked up his dusty folder with its fresh covering of footprints.

"What are you getting all offended for now, moron?" Ginger snapped.

"What did you say?" scowled Khadzhik, feeling for something tucked in his pocket.

"Me, nothing..." Ginger mumbled.

"Any more lip from you and I'll open you up good and proper," growled Khadzhik, drawing his hand back from his pocket and leading Dalgat to some black gates behind which a red-brick house was visible.

"So did that little punk get the better of you?" Khadzhik asked. "Don't have anything to do with him, that Ginger is a shithead."

"Are you leaving now?" Dalgat asked.

"I'm off for a ride with the boys in town, you come in though, Arip is home. Give me a call if you need me, and I'll drop you off wherever you want later."

"Thanks," said Dalgat, shaking Khadzhik's hand as he left.

"Any problems, let me know," said Khadzhik as he went to join his friends, issuing a word of warning to the gang on the road as the boys scattered. He got into a foreign car and raced off round the corner in a pall of dust that lingered behind them.

Dalgat quickly went through the gates and found himself

in a small inner yard with a fire-cock jutting from the ground and a moderately sized two-storied house. The second floor was unfinished and the yard stank of lime.

Aunt Naida came out of the house and hugged him.

"Wow, Dalgat! Where have you been? How come you're so disheveled? How's your Mum? Come in, we're going to have hinkalis."

On the wall of the room, under the stucco ceiling, hung a rug with a woven portrait of the imam Shamil in a *papakha* sheepskin hat. Under it, on a sofa covered with decorative cushions, sat Khadzhik's older brother Arip, a dark blue gold-embroidered skull-cap perched above his thick eyebrows.

"How did your T-shirt get all stretched like that?" he asked as he greeted Dalgat.

"Em, here, I had a bit of trouble by your house, Khadzhik gave me a hand."

"Where has he gone off to this time?"

"For a ride in town he said."

"He'll ride straight to hell," Arip snorted. "No matter how much I tell him not to go driving with these jackals he still goes and gets himself in a fix somewhere. Have you started praying yet, Dalgat?"

Dalgat sighed heavily.

"I told you before..." he started to say.

"You listen to me, I've been telling you all along to go and start praying on your own, haven't you been paying attention?" Arip said condescendingly.

"I..."

"You saw those little junkies by the gate? Khadzhik, as Allah willed it, doesn't touch weed, because I'd batter him if he did. But those little punks take whatever they can get their hands on or just sit around, scrapping or running after girls half naked and bothering them. What is this world of unbelievers coming to? They've set up clubs here, discos, and just look at the state of the women on the streets! What's going on? If we had Shariah law there would be none of this contamination here, agreed?"

"There's no point in discussing this with you, Arip," Dalgat said, sighing once again.

"It's my duty to instruct you. 'He who brings to fulfillment will be rewarded, he who abandons will be punished'. We know from the *Hadith* that a person will plummet 70 years to the bottom of Hell for but one wrong word, so who's to say what punishment a wrong deed will incur?"

"I don't believe in the tales of the Prophet," replied Dalgat.

"Do you know the story about that guy who was a Communist but then became a believer? He began to pray diligently, then everyone used to get him to sing *mawlids* on Mohammad's birthday, which he was pretty good at. Then one day someone tells him their relative died and he should come to Buinaksk to sing *mawlid* prayers for them. But some other people in Derbent told him their son had been circumcised and that he should go there to sing for them. And you know what? He appeared both in Buinaksk and Derbent at the same time."

"How do they know that?"

"How do they know that? They phoned each other: Salam – Salam. One person says Nadyr is reading the *zikr* for us here in Buinaksk, while the other says 'no he's here with us in Derbent' – it's all true I swear," said Arip. "And do you know about Allah and the tomatoes?"

"No."

Arip got out his mobile and, clicking some buttons, showed Dalgat a close-up of a tomato without a skin, the white veins on its flesh twisted and bent like Arabic script.

"See, it says 'Allah'," Arip crowed. "This tomato was grown by godly people."

"Photoshop," Dalgat countered.

"What Photoshop," Arip snapped in sudden exasperation. "I'm telling you, these are real tomatoes! And do you know about the man who heard the prayer?"

Dalgat batted his hand in dismissal.

"No, listen, we all know that every living thing from animals to plants, gives praise every day to the Almighty, and this person, a guy from my village, began to hear how the animals and plants say 'One God'. He couldn't sleep or eat and went to seek advice in Chirkei from Sheikh Said Apandi, who told him that his was a great gift. But the man had real trouble living with this gift and he asked Apandi to free him of it. There is so much proof you know. Take that American astronaut who was in space, he heard the call to prayer there. Everyone knows that!"

"Arip, fools tell you stuff and you believe them..."

"Do you know Kamil from Izberg?" Arip interrupted.

"Yeah, what of it?"

"Now that guy truly is a fool. It's because of people like him that others hate Islam. He speaks of jihad but he's got it all wrong. He even used ICQ to send me the mufti's fetwa, imagine! So I say to him, what are you playing at, Kamil, someone has been messing with your head, you must adopt the true path — think of your poor mother! But he didn't listen to anyone and joined the rebels in the woods. All the worldly sins, he says, saunas with girls, bribes, this and that, came from Russia. There must be Shariah law and infidels must be put to the sword."

"Do you think that too?" Dalgat asked.

"They're right about Shariah, but we still have to be with Russia. All this *haram* emanates from our own leadership here. We have to change them — one ethnic group grabs power and starts fleecing the others. If we beheaded people for taking bribes, no one would do it."

"How about you teach those hardcore believers some morals first," said Dalgat. "Are they supposed to be better than me because they pray five times a day and then buy lots of goods to bring back with them when they go on the Hajj?"

"Don't judge everyone by their example! If some hypocrites pray five times a day and then go filling their pockets and robbing, it doesn't mean that you shouldn't pray five times a day. Go and see the Sheikh, he'll explain everything to you."

"Did you send Kamil to see the Sheikh?"

"Kamil's gone, no saving him now. He didn't read anything about Islam, and knew nothing about it, just called everyone infidels. His whole family was penniless, they went round the neighbourhood to collect money for a bribe to get his sister to college. And so he started to fall in with the Wahabites, and they aren't true holy warriors, their Islam is wrong. You don't get into Paradise by killing innocent people, but they lead lads like Kamil to their deaths. It's America that gives them money to kill our boys and wage war against Russia. They reject the sheikhs, our teachers, the holy places, and *mawlid* celebrations, everything. All they want is to use other people to mete out death."

"As long as they don't send troops here too...," said Dalgat.

"You don't say. And it'll only get worse!" Arip exclaimed. "Mark my words, there will be a total mess here, God only knows how bad it will get. Once I got a call from Osman, asked me to go to the bazaar at Batirai. I couldn't make it because of the traffic so I asked him what was going on. Osman said there was a security operation, they didn't take anyone alive, just carried out the bodies in front of everyone, and there's a big jam of cars and people everywhere, sheer chaos. The bodies of the rebels were just lying on the street. One Wahabite was still alive so the Black Berets finished him off with a rifle, just like the others got it inside. Then they started to break up the crowd, roughing people up, beating on the cars, Osman still has a big dent in his bonnet. What sort of lawlessness is this, eh? They might have left one of the Wahabites alive, I mean, don't they need information? And couldn't they have kept people away earlier? We are finished if we give these Black Berets free rein, I'm telling you!"

"Our police aren't any better," Dalgat started to say.

"Take our neighbour, Djamaludin, 90 years old, had that operation in hospital. His grandson Musa is a well- brought-up boy, always carried our mum's bag at the bazaar. Then one day he gets a visit from people wearing masks, they search his house and when he asks what for they tell him nothing, and no warrant either. Then they left, taking Musa with them. The family's passports all vanished in the raid, money went missing, including the old man's, and they wouldn't release Musa from custody. His dad went to the police station where the district commander swore by God his men wouldn't harm his son and that he should leave. He was lying, they beat Musa for several nights in a row, asphyxiated and electrocuted him, pulled his teeth out, forced him to sign a confession that he was a Wahabite. They didn't let a lawyer see him, then three guys from the special forces came for him, took him out to the highway and they too beat and abused him so badly his own father couldn't recognize him. For two weeks these animals kept him lying injured in a cell. Tell me, Dalgat, how can we let them get away with something like that?

Dalgat sat in despondent silence.

Aunt Naida carried in a dish of plump Avar dumplings, pieces of dried meat, cream cheese with garlic, flax seed butter and spicy *adjika* sauce. She then plumped down in an armchair covered with a coloured drape and fished out the TV handset from under her.

"Can I switch on the television, Arip?" she asked.

"Of course, no need to ask," he answered, before reciting

the *bismillah* grace. Dalgat realised how hungry he was and set about dipping his dumplings in the sauce, while Aunt Naida fiddled with the worn buttons on the remote. Eventually she found a Dagestani music video in which a rising star of the local pop scene swayed her hips and sang about her beloved walking through Makhachkala's beautiful streets.

"Change it," said Arip, gnawing on a piece of meat.

The singer disappeared and was replaced by the mayor and the pinched faces of some local officials as one of them received a dressing-down for the latest breakdowns in the power and water supply. The officials practically cowered before the mayor as another of their number was taken to task over the garbage cans that burned around the city.

"Has your house got water at the moment, Dalgat?" Aunt Naida asked.

"I don't know, I haven't been home for a while."

"We went without for a whole month, and then only the hot came on — Sokhrab would bring us canisters of cold water from his place."

"Will Uncle Khalilbek be long?" Dalgat asked. "I need to give him this folder."

"You'd better give it to him yourself," she answered. "He should be in the Republican Library now, I gather they are launching some book there."

Loud music suddenly blared out in the yard and Aunt Naida exclaimed "Khadzhik!"

"Coming," came Khadzhik's voice through the doorway. "Come and eat!"

Khadzhik entered the room cheerfully and shadow boxed for a moment.

"What are you all down in the dumps about then?" he said, still hopping about.

"Come on, I want a quick word with you," said Arip, wiping his stubbly chin and leaving the room with his brother.

"Have a quick bite to eat, Khadzhik, then you can give Dalgat a lift," Aunt Naida called after him, and then turned and asked Dalgat with a smile: "Did you see the video of Magomed's son's wedding?"

"No," Dalgat replied sleepily.

"I'll show you a bit now before you go," said Naida, pushing a cassette into the player.

Some familiar figures of adults and children appeared dancing on the screen. Aunt Naida pressed pause and turned to Dalgat.

"Who's that," he asked.

"It's Madina, the daughter of your Uncle Abdullah, she's studying medicine. Do you think she's pretty?"

Standing motionless on the screen, her arms raised in air and her hair neatly styled, was a girl in a strapless evening dress.

"Forget it, Aunt Naida," Dalgat said irritably. "I don't like her."

"Why not? Look what a beauty she is, and she's good around the house too."

Dalgat got up from the sofa and made for the door.

"Think about it," she said as he left. "They've nearly finished building their house and they've got a plot in the mountains..."

In the hall Khadzhik was putting on his shiny shoes.

"I dropped my phone, during the scuffle I guess," Dalgat said.

"Don't panic, I'll have a word with them later and shake it out of them."

"Take care, Dalgat," Aunt Naida called after him. "It's Zalbeg's wedding today, maybe we'll see you there."

Arip gave him a firm handshake as he left and said, "Don't sit around son, think about the Almighty, and take this." He handed him a slim book on how to offer prayer.

Dalgat promised to read it, slipped it inside the folder and followed Khadzhik out of the house.

It was windy outside. As they drove, Dalgat gazed at the boxes and wrappers that flew around the dirty town, and at women who were dressed like tarts and battled to hold down their skirts and hair in the swell on the streets. Khadzhik looked at them too and laughed.

"Get a load of that!"

Khadzhik got out of the car a few times on the way to greet people he knew crowded on the pavement or cutting capers with their cars as on horseback.

"Nice little runner, isn't it? Ten minutes in her and I'll catch up with anyone you like. At night it's sheer fun, me and the boys just cruise around all over, at any speed on any street."

"Are the traffic lights broken then?" Dalgat asked.

"Forget the lights, there aren't any cops on the streets now anyway."

"Where are they then?"

"Sitting at home, afraid of snipers. You can do what you want. Then again, there's not much petty crime here."

"Are you working anywhere these days?" Dalgat asked, watching a small Arab prayer charm bounce about beneath the rear-view mirror.

"There's nothing about now, the boss promised to get me a job in the prosecutor's office, he's got a friend there. Know how much it costs to get into the traffic police now as a beat officer?" Khadzhik asked unexpectedly.

"No."

"250,000 roubles, even though the cops tend to get killed a lot now."

Khadzhik did a kind of feint manoeuvre and then mounted the pavement and stopped, almost hitting a minivan whose driver swore back at him. A car full of young men zipped past them at full speed, the occupants laughing and leaning out of the windows holding the roof as they drove, including the guy at the wheel.

"See you later boys!" Khadzhik yelled after them.

Dalgat tried to stay in the shade as he walked, but there was hardly any shade to be had. Some dolled-up women were gathered in the road, blocking his way. Skirting round them he ducked round the corner where there was a crowd of middle-aged men and a large, ample woman in a silk shawl, hands on hips during the customary conspiratorial haggling over price. One of the men grinned in embarrassment at some girls who gaped at the spectacle as they passed, and urged, "Keep moving girls, there's nothing for you here." Dalgat's heart skipped a beat when he saw the crowd and the place where he once stood and haggled before spending two hours with a shameless wench with high cheekbones.

On a long fence, behind which the construction of a sports complex had dragged on for years, someone had scrawled in charcoal "Sister fear Allah – wear hidjab". Further on, between the bright posters advertising concerts and beauty salons, more graffiti exhorted: "Dagestan, defend the religion of Allah in word and deed!", and finally, "Death to the enemies of Islam! God is great!"

He was then almost deafened by the roar of traffic at a large crossroads where idle policemen usually loafed around with rifles, chewing on sunflower seeds and hassling local beauties as they passed. From the jeep, which shook to a cacophony of Dagestani pop, a pair of bare feet and fingers clicking to the music protruded. Along the roadsides old ladies dozed with sacks of seeds at their feet, while voices floated overhead from adjacent yards where a sea of bed sheets dried on lines.

The houses encroached on the road, threatening to

consume the pavement with its heaps of garbage. The fences of some properties actually ran along the footpath, another had swallowed a tree and an electricity transformer block from public land. One owner had even used a tiny square of land to build a five-storey house that jutted overhead. As if forgetting they were built on level ground rather than in mountains, the houses huddled together, while the surrounding apartment blocks had sprouted huge extensions and glassed-in balconies, and the private sun-baked smallholdings high walls made of fashionable yellow brick.

Dalgat turned towards the little side streets and Jewish quarters clustered around the port and the Anzhi-Akra Hill with its small beacon on the crest. He could already hear the sound of the *lesghinka* dance and saw the 'Halal' sign above the banquet hall and its open garret with figures moving busily about inside. In its yard a mass of children played beside 20 or 30 parked cars festooned with garlands of flowers. The bride had evidently just arrived because as Dalgat went up the stairs he saw a sweaty *zurna* piper and drummer being plied with mineral water after their greeting performance. The hall was set for 3,000 guests and was already packed with people, most of whom he knew or had seen somewhere. A happy, portly relative ran up to Dalgat and threw his arms round him.

"Salam aleikum, Dalgat! Look, Israpil, this is Akhmed's son, don't you remember him? You're so like your father. Wah!" he exclaimed, introducing Dalgat to the men around them. Most recognized him and clapped his palm to shake it in greeting.

As he made his way through the throng, Dalgat found himself trapped between some women in aprons with oily hands. They asked him about his mother, who he said was now away in Kizlyar, and led him to some old women in long, light-coloured shawls seated in a row at the laden tables. The kisses and hugs began. Dalgat let them kiss his hand; his answers were irrelevant because no one could hear any questions or answers anyway over the thundering music.

After he managed to get away he remembered he had to make his contribution to the wedding; two women sat with a calculator at a table by the entrance and jotted down who had given how much. Dalgat went up to them and made his hello audible before turning over most the money he had in his pockets.

"Salam, Dalgat, what are you standing around here for, get a move on!" shouted a young male relative who appeared at his side and then led him past countless tables into the heart of the event.

There was a tumult of wild dancing in front of the newlyweds' table, behind which hung a red rug with the names "Kamal and Amina" shaped with cotton wool. In the middle of a tight circle the bride moved slowly and clumsily in a flared skirt, her heavily made-up face drooped in embarrassment over her plunging neckline. Ritually edging the groom away from her, his friends pranced around like goats for her attention, one leaping into the air and throwing his shoulders out proudly before another muscled in to cavort before her. Then a third man seized from his hands a white stick clad in chiffon frills, thundered with his heels and twirled his arms around the bride, locking them momentarily around her waist and then trailing them over her head while showering her with scrunched up banknotes. The infectious music almost got Dalgat dancing too, but instead he plunged into the thick of the crowd and stood clapping.

The bride continued to lazily cross-step her feet in time to the music, fanning herself and holding down her crinoline skirt while the young men tirelessly competed with dancing leaps and cartwheels, to the accompanying cries of *'assa!'* The young women looking on were all smartly dressed and coiffed, glistening with various decorations and gems. As the chiffon-covered stick flashed from one set of manly hands to the next, a skinny woman stepped up to collect the bills that fell on the bride's head, landed in the folds of her dress or tumbled to her feet.

After a few more minutes the bride finally tired of her laboured dance and set off just as slowly back to her seat together with her girlfriends, who straightened her outfit as she went. As he watched the tall, smiling groom follow her, Dalgat remembered how as a child he had attended a wedding in his old village. All of the neighbours sat up on the flat roofs of the houses and down in the street someone placed a brightly decorated goat's head on the happy couple's table. The guests were served heavy trays of hinkali dumplings and boiled meat; a mummer poured wine for seven days straight as the guests celebrated to the sound of the zurna and drums.

As Dalgat mused, the circle broke up into separate pairs of dancers. A girl touched his elbow and offered him a twisted serviette as an invitation. Dalgat recoiled and was about to decline, but not wishing to embarrass the girl took the serviette and raised his fists in the air in acceptance.

After managing three circuits with the nimble girl he felt awkward about his amateurish movements and stopped, bowed his head and applauded his partner to signal the end of the dance. The girl gave him a surprised look and walked away, while Dalgat quickly crumpled the serviette and stuffed it into his pocket, lest anyone else want to dance with him.

"Salam, have you seen Khalilbek?" he asked a deadpan guy in a felt hat who passed him.

The man looked at Dalgat with interest and asked "Whose son are you?"

"Son of Akhmed the son of Musa," Dalgat replied.

The man suddenly looked animated and led Dalgat to his table.

"Come and sit with us," he shouted over the roar of the

lezghinka. They sat down at the table laden with *golubtsy* stuffed cabbage leaves, and hot meat dishes heaped with Dagestani *chudu* cream cheese and potato-filled pastries, greens and other morsels. A circle of guests drinking vodka poured a measure for Dalgat.

"So, tell us, how long will this carry on?" a burly, gloomy-looking man at the table asked, motioning at the heaving mass around them.

"What was that?" shouted Dalgat, leaning towards him to hear better.

"This nonsense!"

The music broke off for a moment and in the ensuing silence the man's words rang sharply. Dalgat said nothing in reply and silently served himself some *chudu* and aubergines. There was a murmur from the huge loudspeakers by the wall and then an accented, unsure sounding voice spoke up hoarsely.

"And now, dear friends, relatives and guests, I give the floor to a very fine and respected man who... er... has achieved so much in his life, knows no bounds when caring for family and helps them in everything they do. And today, as the hearts of our dear Kamal and Amina are united, he will say some... er... parting words to them. Listen closely Kamal, you'll get a chance to speak later, after dear Aidemir advises you how to proceed in your future family life. So Aidemir, what do you want to tell us...?"

"You're at a loss for words yourself, aren't you?" the burly man said to Dalgat, ignoring the faltering utterances of the *tamada* master of ceremonies.

"No I'm not," said Dalgat, impaling a greasy *chudu* on his fork.

"This is a mess, just a mess," the man said, shaking his head as the voice of Aidemir issued from the loudspeakers.

"Today we see united the hearts of representatives of two

peoples, two great peoples of Dagestan, the Avars and the Lakhs," said the voice, laden with a mix of inspiration and pathos. "We are overjoyed that our Kamal, who I remember when he was knee-high, has grown into such a horseman, an eagle of a man, and that he has wed this most beautiful girl Amina from the village of Tsovkra, so celebrated for its tightrope walkers. I wish Kamal that his life with her will be much easier than treading a tightrope, so let's drink to this new family! May Kamal and Amina have ten children and that all are a joy to their parents!"

Aidemir had evidently raised his glass as all the men now stood up. Dalgat also sipped at his vodka for appearance's sake, and once they were seated the burly man again turned to him.

"Those Lakhs are good folk, but the Dargins are devils, two a penny they are," he pronounced.

"Why's that?" Dalgat asked.

"What do you mean why's that? Everyone knows it's true, they're nothing but a bunch of shopkeepers," his neighbour said passionately. "Let's drink."

"Hey, you lay off the Dargins, Saipudin," said the guy in the felt hat. "Our people do their share of business too, Akhmed's son will agree with me on that."

But Saipudin merely downed his vodka in silence and turned again to Dalgat.

"My whole life I worked with my hands," he lamented. "And everything gets spent somehow, this much goes to so and so, I have to give the teacher something at school, cough up for the college exams. I've got a house that I can't finish, I've been building it for twenty years but now I'm supposed to find the money to fix my son up with a job. I even told the wife that she must sell her gold necklace. He'll want to marry then, but how are we supposed to pay for a wedding? I'll have to steal."

"Steal what?" asked Dalgat.

"A bride for him!" Saipudin exclaimed. "Then there's no need to throw a banquet, just do the marriage ceremony and that's all."

"No, it's bad to steal a bride, that's what the Chechens do, not us," interrupted a grey-haired man sitting opposite them who despite the heat wore a tall Astrakhan fur hat.

"Wah, Dalgat, why are you sitting here, we're going dancing?" said a second cousin of his who suddenly leant over his shoulder, all wise-eyed and white toothed.

"Hello, Malik, I'm coming," Dalgat said in relief, springing from his chair.

"Wait, I knew your father," Saipudin said, rising unsteadily to his feet and swaying for a moment before he threw himself at Dalgat in an embrace, and thumped his puny back.

"Here, take this," he said, producing a crumpled note from his pocket. "Allah didn't give me much money, but still I give to everyone."

Dalgat carefully distanced himself from Saipudin and the banknote.

"I have money, thanks, give it to your son instead," he said, looking round at Malik.

"Don't you dare offend me!" Saipudin exclaimed and, egged on by the presence of his friends, stuffed the note in the pocket of Dalgat's jeans. Startled, Dalgat tried to return the money, but Malik grabbed him by the shoulders and led him away.

"Forget these people, we're going to kidnap the groom now," he said gleefully as they moved into the melee.

From behind the long table some girls watched them with curiosity.

"Who's that, Dalgat grandson of Musa?" Zalina drawled to her friends.

"That's Dalgat," Asya replied, laughing.

"Heavens, he's so thin!" Zalina added.

Asya laughed again.

"They haven't fed him for five years, honestly!"

They were joined by a large girl in a tight golden skirt with a heavily made-up face and a tinted fringe.

"I'm so thirsty in this heat, I'm going to drown myself in mineral water now," she puffed, filling her glass.

"Patya, where did you get your skirt?" Zalina asked, inspecting her friend from top to bottom.

"From a boutique in Moscow. It's Gucci," Patya replied self-importantly, gulping her water and blowing air up at her fringe.

"It's lovely — is it really Gucci from Moscow?" Zalina added, emphasizing the last words.

A middle-aged man appeared behind Patya and offered her a sprig of flower buds. The girl heaved a sigh, then slowly straightened her skirt and hair, rose rather inelegantly from the table and followed him.

"Just look at her," Zalina said to Asya. "Did you see how she went after him?"

"You don't say... And her skirt is daft. She bought it at the Eastern Bazaar, I'm telling you, so she can cut the Gucci nonsense," said Asya, watching in amusement as Patya circled the man's galloping dance steps, lazily twirling her hands around him. "Did you know her fiancé called off the engagement?"

"Get away, Datsi called it off?!" said Zalina, lighting up with interest. "They'd already booked a bridal room at the Marakesh and Patya even had a tattoo done and what not!"

"Datsi saw her at the Pyramid discotheque and told her it was all off. She had to return all the presents, including all the dowry stuff his parents gave her in the suitcase."

"It was probably a poor haul anyway, all from the village," Zalina scoffed.

"You're joking, there was a fur coat, clothes, boots and a fancy mobile phone — in fact there wasn't a whole lot she didn't get. And now look what a spectacle she's making of herself, why did she even bother to come here at all?"

"Zalina, look at Zainab!" Asya whispered loudly, pointing a claret-coloured fingernail at the next table where a girl sat in a pretty *hijab* headscarf.

"She's covered up," said Zalina, looking sideways at Zainab's Islamic garb.

"I knew she'd cover up after what happened."

"Why, what happened?"

"Well, her family left her on her own with a girlfriend in the village one night and to cut a long story short, she went off into the mountains with some guys. Her cousin happened to come by and knocked at the house, then raised the alarm. She came back the next morning and they took her to a doctor immediately to have him check her for signs of intercourse."

"And...?"

"I don't know. She wanted to get married but now she pretends she's too pure for it."

"I also want to cover up," Zalina said earnestly.

"Is your brother forcing you?"

"No, it's my choice, because what I do at the moment isn't enough, even though I observe the *sawm* fast, say my *namaz* prayers, although maybe not always. But I don't wear a headscarf. Have you heard what they're saying in town?"

"What's that?"

"That during Ramadan the rebels will kill every girl they see without a headscarf. They already killed two."

"Stop making things up!" Asya retorted. "They even said on TV that people are deliberately sowing panic among the population. So it's not true!"

"I'm still scared," Zelina replied.

Suddenly Khadzhik emerged from the crush with a happy smile on his face and asked Zalina to dance. She beamed and got up, her long strapless dress sparkling. Asya looked first at Zalina and Khadzhik and then at Patya, who was already dancing at full pelt with the groom's brother, then at an old woman who was twirling her hands in an ancient dance, and then the guest singer, a woman who was quite well known in the city. A young man got her up to dance and holding the microphone, she daintily wiggled her bottom in Persian style.

Malik and his friends managed to discretely kidnap the groom while the bride affected a playful look of dismay during this wedding ritual. But Dalgat continued to look for Khalilbek. The song finished and the *tamada* and some of the esteemed guests were already cosying up to the laughing singer and pawing her. Among them were Aidemir, Khalilbek and the groom's father Zalbeg, and some important guest officials or other. Uncle Magomed clapped Dalgat on the shoulder.

"Invite Abdullah's daughter Madina for a dance, there she is sitting down, see, next to my mother," said Magomed, pointing at the neatly-coiffed girl Dalgat had seen frozen in mid-motion on the videotape. "Go on, when the music starts."

Dalgat shied away.

"I need to talk to Khalilbek," he told Magomed.

"You have your talk later, don't muck me about, go and ask her when the music begins."

The tamada took the microphone and resumed his faltering spiel: "Hello, anyone out there, right, so basically our groom has been stolen. Why is the bride sitting alone, eh? A group of us have already gone to look for him, and we will... er... sort out those friends of his who did this, that's right, even you Khalilbek! I now give the floor to our esteemed Khalilbek, who found the time to attend the wedding of his close relative Zalbeg, who is marrying his son to pretty Amina from Tsovkra. And, without more ado, Khalilbek will say a few words, and share some of his wisdom..."

"Salam, Dalgat!" came a voice behind him and Dalgat

turned to see his cousin Murad, unshaven and tired-looking. "Let's go outside for a talk."

"What happened?" Dalgat asked.

"I need your help."

Dalgat looked reluctantly at the tamada and Khalilbek as he prepared to give a speech and then trailed behind Murad, who led him to the edge of the open garret. Below them the children were still running around the parked cars, men stood smoking and women in baggy garments carried wedding cakes across the yard.

"I've got a package rolled up inside a carpet, you can keep it a few days at your place while your mum's away," Murad told him.

"What package?" asked Dalgat, impatiently looking back towards the hall and its echoes of Khalilbek's voice.

"It's nothing but I can't keep it at home," said Murad, wiping his red eyes.

"Is it heavy, because I'm not going home right away, I have to talk to Khalilbek?"

"No, not now, I'll bring it round to you in the evening, you just hide it at yours for a couple of days. Your mum's in Kizlyar, isn't she?"

"OK, fine," Dalgat agreed, keen to end the conversation.

Suddenly Khalilbek's voice was interrupted by women's screams and the singer's music cut in momentarily. People standing on the street ran upstairs to investigate and Dalgat also raced up into the hall where he saw a sea of shocked faces, especially that of the shaken tamada as he held back Zalbeg from a crowd of men crouching over something on the floor. Someone shouted for an ambulance.

"What happened?" Dalgat asked the nearest guests, but they just clutched their heads.

"Wahi, wahi!" the old women shrieked, covering their mouths with scarves and looking fearfully at the melee.

"Someone shot Aidemir," said a shaggy-haired young man, his eyes bulging. "I swear someone shot him, I saw it with my own eyes. He was standing there and suddenly from out of nowhere got a bullet in the head!"

"The side of this hall is open, you could shoot from anywhere," said another voice. Someone led the bride in her billowing skirt from her table without letting her look round, while Saipudin blundered past Dalgat, spluttering as he went.

"God have mercy on us," simpered the girls as they poured out of the hall in an ornately dressed crowd.

"Let's get out of here," said Murad, suddenly appearing at Dalgat's side and dragging him out.

"Khalilbek..." Dalgat started to say.

"Khalilbek has gone to meet the police, he hasn't got time for you now."

"Was it an assassination?" the women on the stairs asked each other. "Aidemir works at the prosecutor's office."

"If he's hit in the head they'll not be able to save him," someone else added, while the old women just whispered "Wahi, wahi!" and fumbled with their beads.

"Now the police are here they'll search everybody," said Murad, "They'll say that because it was a wedding that someone just got carried away with their celebrating and fired at the ceiling and hit Aidemir by mistake. Everyone's got guns here, they always do, we'd better get out of here."

They were already walking along a dirty, stuffy alleyway when they heard a police siren wailing in the direction of the "Halal" banqueting hall.

"What happened, I don't get it?" Dalgat said. "I wanted to go closer and look at Aidemir."

"What do you want to look at that dog for," replied Murad, quite unbothered.

They walked onto the city beach. Taking off their sandals the pair walked down the well-trodden sand to where noisy, happy clusters of people lay basking on sheets. Dalgat looked at the duck-shaped silhouette of a derelict factory on the island bobbing in the distance on the choppy grey waters of the Caspian Sea. In the foreground, bathers splashed in the mucky shallows. A group of old and young women waded into the sea in long clinging nightdresses, teenagers squealed as they scooped water at each other and two girls in bikinis squealed as someone grabbed their ankles. Children laughed and ran around shouting in unfathomable mountain dialects, chomping on corn on the cob handed to them by domineering mothers.

"Hot pies!" shouted a woman as she picked her way through the wet bodies around her. Dalgat saw a group of girls, one of whom wore a Muslim tunic and hijab, while her friend sported a cheap red bandana and long, semi-transparent skirt with slits down the side. Others wore fashionable knickerbockers. They were followed by a posse of boys who joked and, gathering handfuls of little shells, tossed them playfully at the girls' backs or bottoms. Murad hung his head in silence, hitching up his trousers as he went.

Some Chechens in wet, sand-covered slacks kicked a ball about noisily and, as usual, a group of heavily-built men and youths congregated around a metal chinning bar dug deep in the sand. Further on behind heaps of rocks they could see the cranes of the deep-sea port in the distance. Murad and Dalgat climbed up the rocks, past some Russian fishermen standing with aluminum buckets for their catch, and at last sat down right at the water's edge. Dalgat sighed.

"It's not good to refer to someone you don't know as a dog," he said.

Murad chuckled and dangled his hairy legs into the spray of the waves.

"Who doesn't know him? He's a thief. Do you see those big houses over there?" Murad asked, pointing. "He owned three of those."

"Why are you speaking about him in the past tense, he's still alive?" Dalgat mumbled.

"He's a filthy turncoat, abandoned our faith and went and became like all the rest of the infidels and traitors with their ignorant ways," Murad replied, spitting into a wave that rose beneath him. "It's all down to *kufr*."

"What's that?" asked Dalgat.

Murad turned to Dalgat and scratched a stubbly cheek as he looked at him.

"Don't you know what kufr is? It's everywhere, everywhere! It's a lack of morals, a refusal to believe in the miracles of Allah. Just now at the wedding Mala and Rashid were boasting about how they pray even more than five times a day, morons!"

"So what?"

"They say their prayers and then drink beer, it's sacrilegious, it is. That Aidemir built two mosques but his son raped a dozen of our sisters, students and suchlike. He was also filming them with his mobile phone and emailed them around to his friends for fun."

Murad pulled a green tubeteika scull cap out of his pocket and put it on his head.

"I'm coming over to yours this evening, don't forget. There's a lot that needs explaining to you. You live on your own with your mum, no one has much use for you, and no one will set you up with normal work because of all the infidel employment practices. You have to fight for things," he instructed Dalgat. "You know how the Sufis have taken over almost everywhere? They account for the imams in almost all the mosques and sit on the Muslim councils, and they suck up to the Russian infidels and submit to them entirely. It's wrong, the family of Muslims, the *umma*, shouldn't be divided like this, otherwise there will be a *fitnah*, an uprising and split in Islam, understand? We Salafites, Wahabites if you like, believe that we must return to the true Islam they had in the time of the Prophet, peace be unto him, and that the Muslim Imamate should be independent."

"Who's been putting all this talk in your mouth?" Dalgat asked.

"None of your lip," Murad snapped, rising to his feet and straightening his trousers. "I know you're one of us at heart. By the way, I won't be alone when I come to your place later. You might be a bit of an oddball, but I know you want justice. Have you got a girlfriend?"

"No."

"Good lad, not a fornicator then," Murad said, smiling as he stood above Dalgat. "Our sisters are another story. Expect me around midnight, and make sure you're at home."

Murad nearly slipped on the wet rocks as he went off without shaking hands and vanished from view.

Dalgat got up to go and, passing the fishermen again, he jumped from the rocks onto the sand and back into the hubbub of the beach. There was no sign of Murad.

"Hey kid, want some?" a short man with a moustache in an unbuttoned shirt shouted at him as he rinsed a watermelon.

"No thanks," Dalgat smiled back.

"My treat," the man shouted, but Dalgat had ambled on, staring idly at a motor launch taking people on board until he reached the men heaving themselves up and down at the chinning-bar.

"How many pull-ups can you do then sonny?" someone asked, slapping Dalgat on the shoulder.

"Not today," he replied. "I pulled a muscle so I can't."

This drew a burst of laughter from a couple of girls who had stepped out from the crowd to watch. Angered, Dalgat strode quickly to the taps and washed off his feet, put on his sandals and went into the archway over which goods trains periodically rumbled. Beneath it a young couple was enjoying a furtive embrace, while at the mouth on the other side a cross-legged beggar rocked from side to side, yowling a tortured melody.

There was still a throng of people around the banquet hall.

"Khalilbek is at the police station on Soviet Street," an agitated teenager with long eyelashes told him. It was close by and sure enough Khalilbek's white car stood outside when Dalgat got there.

"This is the place," he thought and then decided to wait outside and watch the crowd.

Trendy Muslim girls in lace stockings and velvet dresses tripped along the broken pavement on high-heels while older women fanned their busts as they walked along. Minivan drivers jumped out of their vehicles to greet each other loudly and shake hands on the busy street, bristling with the signboards of beauty salons and dental surgeries.

"Hi Dalgat!" came the voice of Mesedu, one of his classmates.

"Have you had your hair cut?" Dalgat asked as he turned to her.

"Yes, don't you think a square cut suits me best?" she asked coquettishly. "Let's go into a café and sit down for a while, I haven't seen you for ages."

"I'm waiting for someone, he should be here any minute."

"You're not getting away that easily, give him a call," she said.

"My phone got stolen."

"So use mine," Mesedu replied, leading Dalgat to a fashionable glass-door café called Maryasha. By the door hung a framed sign: "No sportswear or weapons".

It was cool in the café and little fountains gurgled beneath large screens showing music videos.

"Let's sit in a booth," Mesedu commanded.

Once they were settled she took some cigarettes from her bag.

"Well just look at you smoking now," Dalgat said.

"Don't make me laugh, Dalgat," she trilled back, clicking her lighter. "Almost all of us smoke in secret while pretending to be nuns. Haven't you noticed how the girls shut themselves into the booths?"

A waitress with penciled eyebrows and rosy cheeks came up.

"Lamb kebab and a litre of apricot juice," Mesedu told her. "And what will you have, Dalgat?"

"Nothing for me, I have to go soon."

"What, are you fasting?" she joked.

"The fast is long over. So what are you up to now?"

"I'm moving to St. Pete to work in a translation bureau. My Dad is against the idea, of course, but what is there for me to do here?"

"Find a husband," he suggested.

"No way, husband — are you crazy?" said Mesedu, arranging her hair and flicking her ash. "There's no one to get married to here, unless you think I might go for you," she said with a peal of boyish laughter. "I've heard there are lots of skinheads in St. Pete," she continued, suddenly serious. "But I don't think I'll have any trouble, I look like a Russian."

"You do in that outfit," Dalgat answered, studying her linen jacket which was spangled with buttons.

"Do you like it? The girls here stare at me like I'm crazy. Hey, I saw Dima."

"And?"

"He just finished his army service, he volunteered, wanted to see a bit of the world. With his university degree he only had to do a year.

"Everybody does only a year now."

"This it happened before they changed the rules," Mesedu frowned back. "But generally they dislike the one-year guys more than anyone in the army. Anyway, he got sent to the Smolensk region and though they try not to send too many Dagestanis or any Caucasians to one unit, there were five others there."

"But Dima's Russian himself?"

"That's what he says, 'I'm a Russian but still they take me for a darkie'," Mesedu said with a laugh. "Anyway, our boys sorted everyone out there, had the sergeants washing their feet and the officers tiptoeing around them. And our Dima was one of them. They didn't have to clean toilets or sweep floors. Our boys saw one Lezghin with a broom and they stuck his head down the toilet!"

"I don't understand why he would go into that wretched army of his own accord?"

"Well actually Dima says our boys want to go and even bribe their way in, because afterwards you can get a job in the police or somewhere like that. Anyway, he got summoned to the political officer who asks him 'You're a Russian, so why you're behaving like a black-ass from the Caucasus?'"

"So what does Dima say?"

"Well, he's happy to keep his nose clean but then his Dagi mates will give him a beating. So he tells the officer he has no problem observing regulations if his personal security is guaranteed. But that's nothing they *can* guarantee. They stuck him in the glasshouse for a while with a guy from our Tsumadin village. Neither of them ate in there so they wouldn't need to go to the toilet, they just peed in a bottle and passed it through the bars. On the third day Dima got in a fight with this guy and the officers watched them through the bars and bet on whether 'black or white' would win. Eventually Dima got sent to a disciplinary battalion or whatever they call it in the army. Everyone's a wimp there, always afraid of someone else, one guy even tried to cut his wrists. Dima was surprised by the pathetic state of them all."

"Stay here Mesedu, what do you need to go to St. Pete for? They all think we're thugs and savages."

"And here everyone thinks Russian men are all drunks and weaklings and the women are whores, so what's the difference — at the end of the day everyone hates everyone else."

"I was just talking to this guy, kind of a resistance fighter," Dalgat confessed.

"You're kidding?"

"He wants to come and see me at home, or invite me to his, I'm not sure."

The rosy-cheeked waitress came in and went out again, leaving a plate of steaming kebabs and a jug of cooled juice on the table.

"Don't go, Dalgat!" Mesedu implored him, filling her glass. "Do you know what happened to my cousin Gimbat? He got to know some guys and went with them to a flat. And that was that, they started to talk about religion and how the republic is riddled with corruption and has gone to the dogs. Of course he agreed with them, said sure, things are indeed in a bad state, that something has to be done..."

"And what then?"

"Well it turned out that these Wahabites had connections in law enforcement and it was all being recorded on camera in order to blackmail him. They came to him later and said here's a tape showing you in the company of extremists, so now choose, either we turn you in or you join us in the resistance."

"Why do they need to go to such lengths?"

"That's how they recruit. It's to their advantage that things are in such turmoil here. Gimbat was lucky that our dad also worked in law enforcement. When he heard his son was being sucked in he went white as a sheet, spoke to whoever he needed to ensure it all worked out okay in the end. Gimbat was lucky, but what about all the rest? So don't even think about hanging about with these people."

"Maybe you misunderstood," said Dalgat. "It doesn't seem very believable."

Mesedu laughed again.

"You're so funny, Dalgat."

"I have to go now, in case I miss this guy. It was good to see you. Enjoy your meal."

"Hang on a moment, take a bit with you," said Mesedu, separating some of the meat for him.

"No thanks, and pay with this," Dalgat said, leaving Saipudin's banknote. "Bye."

It was dusk when he came out onto the street. He could see that Khalilbek's car was no longer parked outside the police station. At that moment an officer with a big nose and a rifle over his shoulder poked his head out of the door and then disappeared from sight.

Dalgat was upset to see the car gone.

"No money for the bus either," he sighed to himself and then sloped off down the street, occasionally reacting to the wild honking of the drivers, loud laughter and the nearby sounds of the *lezghinka*. It was now completely dark. A few idlers sat crouched along the kerbsides, lit up in the gloom by the blue light of their mobile phone displays. Not a single streetlamp worked and the only real illumination came from the little shops which resounded to cheery voices inside. Some girls strolled towards him, clasping each other's arms, high heels clicking on the pavement and drawing soft wolf whistles behind them.

Dalgat walked slowly, trying not to step in the pits in the road and on the various construction materials that spilled out before him. Turning into the city's main drag he went straight to the central square of Makhachkala. It was unlit and deserted there too, and the great daisy-chained inscription on a wall that boasted "Best city in Russia" was lost in the dark. Dalgat went and sat on the marble steps to Lenin's monument, his back to the blue shadows of the pine trees beside City Hall, opened the folder and groped around for the message for Khalilbek. Then he threw his head back and gawped up at the stars as they vanished in the fog that swept in from Tarkitau. Suddenly he heard steps behind him and someone quietly called his name.

Dalgat turned and could make out the figure of a man under one of the pines.

"Who's that?" he asked, thrusting the folder under his arm and standing up.

"Salam, Dalgat!" said the man, striding up to him confidently. At that moment he could hear drum music erupt on the next street and cries of 'Assa!' as someone danced.

Dalgat watched the approaching man, knowing that he had come for him.

POLINA KLYUKINA

Translated by Anne O. Fisher

FREE

The Simferopol train and dusty wool blankets. The train conductor with her tangled black locks and her sheepish "shh" in the phrase "Hush now, girls, hush now;" the clinking of the metal tea-glass holders. The rail-thin female convicts, puffy with drink, are crawling back home to Novosibirsk. The road consists of short stories about other people's long lives and the smiling phrase "Now don't you go being afraid of us," there between the loudspeakers and the inner ear membranes. The embarrassed passengers cover children's ears at the words "little bitch" and listen curiously to stories about murderers as cellmates.

The car is silent: Sveta is talking about Lyokha, the cannibal from Block Three, and sweet human meat. Calmly, she describes the uncle she killed, as if it were the rude saleslady. "He used to treat my grandma real bad, he'd smother her with the plastic bag from a loaf of bread and rap two fingers on the table whenever he asked for money." Sveta taps her plastic nails on her knee. Alyona agrees with her, adding, "People like that need to never even get born at all, much less live their lives; I would've also... except I've got kids, they'd never forgive a mother who was a murderer." They've left behind them tons of innocent people, guilty only of rapping on their knees the same way. They don't throw their cigarette butts on the floor for fear of being put in the hole for ten days, and they don't buy things on the cheap from their cellmates so they won't get their parole deferred. Parole is a term that gets heard a lot but is rarely explained. It's like the long-awaited pa-royal treatment, or pa-roll in the hay: all it means is getting out before your sentence is up. But lots of the ones looking through bars (ones like, for example, Alyona) decode this term differently: pa-rope to hang their husbands with, or else their relatives, whoever locked them up for a couple years. You can always put the rap on your fellow inmates, you'll get out earlier, but you won't get any respect. "My whole life, it's like my whole life is gone…"

As they approach Novgorod, they start seeing abandoned little shacks, with long, straight rows of potato plants sticking up out of the ground. They are right next to enormous white brick dachas protected by barbed wire, with little holes in the walls for cats. "I can't f…. believe we're back!" "I'm gonna get the kids back out of the orphanage! My little girl is starting school this year."

An elderly woman catches up to Alyona and Sveta on the platform: "Hey, Alyona! Alyona! Here, take some money, you're going to see your kids, after all. What were you in for, anyway?" Alyona pushes the woman back. "I stole three million…" The woman shoves the money in her pocket and trudges heavily past the train cars. "Just don't go and get back at 'em, girls, don't get back at your relatives; you've done real good, you got out, now just don't go and get back at 'em!"

Months go by. Other Alyonas and Svetas fill the prison cells and the Novgorod walls add on more layers.

It's been six months now since Sveta returned to her grandmother's widowed house, its unswept floor covered in spruce needles. She put away the glasses that were on the table, moved the stools out of the middle of the room, and freed the icons from their black drapes. As she went out to the courtyard, she knocked over an overflowing enamel bucket and bumped into Tamara. This old lady always seemed like she was part of the worn window divided into two unequal triangles by a meandering crack. No one in the village knew who this woman was waiting for, except maybe her husband, who replaced her from time to time. They nodded habitually to passersby without ever smiling and didn't shoo away the dirty urchins playing in the mud with a tractor gear.

"'Lo, Aunt Tamara!" Aunt Tamara gave her usual nod, muttered an aside, and turned away, and to her silhouette was added a silhouette in a cap. Sveta glanced at the clock and remembered that it was suppertime. In prison camp, this was when they used to take the lids off cauldrons of porridge, belching their burnt smell.

Alyona arrived at Uprising Street, made it to the fifteenth building on the auto-pilot she still hadn't lost even after camp, and went into apartment thirty-nine. She went in by herself. She sat down on a stool by herself and by herself she turned on the gas. She hadn't ended up getting her kids back since her husband filed a denunciatory scrawl with the district court that, like an ink blot, marred her already far from spotless motherhood. In the kitchen, the radio peeped out nine o'clock, started singing about dreams in a male voice, and imperceptibly went quiet, leaving behind a familiar, unobtrusive "shhhh," which gradually faded into the "sss" of the gas. An hour later the neighbors from apartment forty, who'd started coughing uncontrollably, opened the windows in apartment thirty-nine and called an ambulance to pick up the dead woman.

The stray dogs were barking furiously, upset at their interrupted sleep; the little boys were getting their heavy toothed disc stuck in the muddy road, growling and making sound effects with every move. "Wait, boys, let me just get by:" Sveta was headed for her relatives, and was stepping in every stirred-up puddle. She'd put on a bead necklace, bought some wine, and said a prayer for mercy and forgiveness for all. When she arrived, she knocked on the kitchen window, but when no one came, she went into the outer hallway. It smelled like the frost was drunk. Her brother was sleeping on a mattress, surrounded by colorful cigarette butts. He didn't notice either the tired barking, or the children's laughter at the gear stuck in the mud, or Sveta's appearance in the room. "Pasha, Pasha, I got out, Pasha, I'm back!"

The courtyards turned morose. Sveta was going back home and was mad at the prayer that hadn't done her any good. In her hand she carried a thread with the remainder of her beads on it and all the way back to her house she kept repeating "I hate 'em all!" — familiar words to the cell. She took off her boots, walked in, and started shuffling over to the stove, but feeling a sudden pain, she looked around at the porch. It was the leftovers from the funeral: once the spruce needles had turned into sewing needles, they'd waited that whole time for someone's feet. Sveta poured iodine over the pinpricks and limped over to bed on her tip-toes.

"Sveta! Sveta! Something's wrong with my old man! Sveta, we've got to get an ambulance! Wake up, dummy!" Tamara, wrapped in a calico-print housecoat and holding her shawl in her hand, stood in the doorway. "He can't talk at all, he's just moaning something, Sveta, go for help, go right now, or else he's gonna die!" Forty minutes later the ambulance ambled, rather than raced, up to help Tamara. "Now what are you all panicked about? Old age is just like that..."

Neither Tamara nor Sveta could sleep that night. It took Sveta three pots of mint tea to recount several years of incarceration and a couple of days of freedom. "They took everything from me, the bitches," combining her brother and the prison camp in the same word, taking a deep drag and, apologizing each time, spitting on the floor. She sobbed, wiping the tears into her crude cheekbones and embracing "dear Aunt Tamara, my favorite, my best grandma."

She came back home at noon. She took the clock off the wall, turned on the radio, and caught the song about dreams, then got to work on the needles on the porch. It wasn't until evening, when the grey stream of warmth from the oven had swallowed the peeling walls, that Sveta wrote her letter:

"Hey, Alyona! Hello, little sister! It's hard for you, right? It is for me too. My house isn't mine anymore. Now I fall asleep on my grandmother's bed looking at that same floor, where he was lying, rapping his fingers on the table, remember? It's really cold here. Almost as cold as in the cell. I stoke up the stove and choke nights from the smoke. Turns out that's what freedom smells like: carbon monoxide.

Alyona, so how are you? I can just imagine how happy you are now! You probably go and get the kids in the evening, and you all go for a walk around town. Then you come home and make supper together, and you put them to bed as you sing one of your dumb little songs, like "dreams come true..."

Alyona, everything's really hard for me these days, but summer will come, there won't be any smoke, it won't be cold, and I'll probably even find another place to live. And I was here thinking, maybe I could just go on and move in with you in town? Alyona, we can do it. I promise you. We did it in prison camp, we did it with dignity, but here... Alyona, we're free here..."

DIMWIT

The map of Russia looks like a two-ton Crocodile-Dinosaur that feeds exclusively on the Kamchatka-Fish. It's a country lit from below by refugees' lighthouses. Every day it selects nice little gilt hooks and bait, but there's no need for them: the mouths of the fish-states swimming by are shut tight.

Not many people are able to catch forty winks behind the conveyer belt. Little female machine operators have come here from all four corners of the land to get the destitute Moscow suburb back on its feet. They get to work by eight and they always remember not to leave their dry meals — composed of six slices of bread with some topping, three packets of tea, and a consolation apple — in the communal hallway. They labor until their mustached boss comes in and says, "Thanks everyone! See you tonight," which means eight in the morning. The whole night through they pick at the conveyer belt, changing rolls of plastic film and carting boxes with a wonderful French title in and out.

In Lenin's Tomb, it's the same conveyer belt and the same flowing stream, but here it's the curious gazes of Swedish people that are moving past, not swollen magazines. A waxy person who practically makes you throw up keeps impeccable count of yet another group of foreigners; he isn't afraid of working too hard, since any pallor will be hidden behind a plastic rind of paint.

"All cameras must be turned in at the entrance to the Tomb!"

"I don't have a camera."

"Go ahead."

Sonya was forty-nine when she visited Lenin's Tomb for the first time. She put on a little brown dress that went lovingly with her grey-tinged hair and covered her eyelashes with clumps of black mascara. She smiled as she strode across the cobbled square and was windblown, succulently, from her upthrust chin to her scaly knees, which is why she didn't notice the main street's oppressive heat. She hurried to enter the sepulcher of dark-red granite. When she was five steps away from the crystal dome over the treasured sleeping comrade, she stumbled.

"Keep moving, don't hold things up, there's quite a line behind you!"

Sonya pulled the hem of her skirt back down and chastely dragged herself into the porphyry burial vault. As she went down the stairs, she became aware of the cool, mortuary air and the light odor of formaldehyde that was being exuded either by the figure reposing in the hall, or by the people who were keeping watch over that pantheon. But maybe it was her own odor, strongly manifesting itself precisely here, in the abundantly ventilated room. The stench got stronger with each step, thus Sonya's walk grew thin, provoking an indignant Swedish "*Dumbom.*"

Even though she had no interest in a translation, she guessed it anyway: "They had to've called me a dummy." She was so upset that her cheeks instantly caught fire and she threw up, without being able to make it outside first. *"Lakarvard! Lakarvard!"* panicked the little Swedish ladies, upon which they quickly evacuated the timid Russian woman to the square. They sat her down in the park where she wouldn't get in the way of the tourists on their tours, handed her a can of Coke, and left her with a pitying "*Kraftlös!*" which meant "Sickly!" in Russian.

This had never happened to her before. She had been upset before, of course, and she'd been sick before, but one had never been a result of the other.

Once, when Sonya was living in Chelyabinsk and teaching chemistry, the mother of a Vietnamese schoolboy had come in to school. She'd come gravely into the office, freed her neck from the shawl's knots, and offered Sonya a crimson box with a cake inside. Both of them immediately broke into a sweat and then stood, completely frozen, for three minutes, until they calmed down a little and began their conversation:

"Why did you bring me a cake?"

"People told me to, they said that's what you do."

"Quite the opposite, now you've put me in an awkward position. What do you want from me?"

"My son, a ninth-grader, Pham Vin Chong, isn't making it in your class."

"He isn't, but I don't think the problem is with me."

"We used to live in Hanoi, it was different there, they..."

"I know what was different there: he had his native language, and kids his age..."

"Pham wants to go back to his homeland later, but for that he has to finish his studies, you see? In Vietnam, for him to get this kind of education..."

"What, is it hard?"

"Yes, but you don't have to be so angry."

"Now why do all you people think we're such wolves? There's no point in us getting angry at you, it's just that everybody's got his own homeland, so why do you need to escape to anyplace else?"

"My son has made a place for himself in Chelyabinsk, he's capable, but his homeland... his homeland is like a religion, it's deep down inside him... otherwise he wouldn't be going back to Hanoi."

After the Vietnamese woman left, Sonya got out the gradebook for the ninth grade "E" class and found the last name Chong in the class list. The homeroom teacher had written "Pham" down as "Foma," and all the little squares for IQ indicators were regularly filled out with his scores. It was evident that this child was attending school eagerly and trying zealously to figure out the spelling rule for when to use one "n" and when two, that he was able to find the discriminant, and that he had watched a paramecium hunting lactic acid bacteria.

Finals began at the end of May. Foma approached them conscientiously, as usual, and only chemistry, with its "eitch enn oh three," was capable of corroding away his future diploma. The vice-principals and a few teachers had gathered in the teachers' lounge. A Korean petty trader was pulling speckled poplin tops with pearlescent buttons out of his checkered bag and hanging up festive white blouses smeared with the occasional lipstick mark. These traces were left over from when the teachers at neighboring schools tried them on, and there the trader had also answered "Fi hunnet fitti" when asked "How much?" That same Vietnamese woman, Pham Vin Chong's mother, peeked into the office, stood around for about three minutes, and then gathered up her courage to ask for Sonya. Sonya went out into the corridor without taking off her finery and led the Vietnamese woman into a classroom.

"I know why you've come to see me."

"Yes. But you've got to understand, please, my husband sends me to see you every time Pham gets a D. I... he... he ..."

"What, he beats you?"

"Yes."

"Maybe you should go to the police..."

"What are you saying! What for? You don't know him. He's just like a child, I promise you. He came over here and it's like he's gone crazy. He was smart before... he was generous, and how understanding he was! Just you don't know. I can't go to the police."

The Vietnamese woman plucked at her shawl and minced tirelessly back and forth from the blackboard to the teacher's desk. Grey curls were bursting out of her shiny gold kerchief. They were coming down over her lined forehead and disturbing her train of thought. The thing to do was shout, but the Vietnamese woman couldn't remember the Russian words, the ones she had heard people say more than once as she walked past. She could only stick up for her husband with the usual "No!"

"But if he beats you...!"

"What are you saying... and even if he does, you don't know anything about it... He's unhappy, he's sick... He wants justice, he believes that it exists, justice, he is just, he is!"

"What's going to happen to you?"

"I don't know, but we're together, we're the same. He's desperate, we're being kicked out of our apartment and nobody else will rent to us... because we're not Russian. So all our hope is on our son only, maybe they will treat at least Pham as a human being here. My husband worries a lot, that's why he's losing his mind. He's counting on you. He believes that another life could begin. And in those moments he kisses me even. And he buys our son everything he needs for school. Have you seen his pencil case? It's full of all kinds of pencils and pens... it's gotten empty lately, that's true, but that's just because we don't have any money right now. It hurts me to look at him..."

"Well, of course, with a life like that, a pencil case is the only thing he can give."

"But don't you feel sorry for him? I was cruel to him so many times, I remember I asked him for money..."

Sonya fell in step with the Vietnamese woman's pacing, and this conversation started sounding like a conspiracy.

"It has to be stopped!"

"But what can we do? What can we really do?"

"What can you do? You and your son need to get free of him. I'll do what I can for you, I'll try to help Foma."

"Thank you. For the love of God, forgive me."

Sonya went back into the teacher's lounge. She stood there for a little while, then walked over to the shelves with the class gradebooks, found the spine of nine-E, and was just about to return to the chemistry room's alkaline-breathing walls when she was abruptly stopped by the "Lilliputian," as everyone, including the teachers, secretly called the head teacher. The small, stick-thin woman with an enormous birthmark on her cheek stood up on tiptoe and whispered nasally in Sonya's ear, "We know what that chink wants, looks like her son's getting himself a nice little D in chemistry, hm? Now look, don't you dare! Otherwise the entire faculty'll find out about it. No point in helping them, let them go back home and get A's there."

The day of his final, Pham dragged in an armful of globeflowers. The teachers, a carnivorous yellow glint in their eyes, met the little boy with a smile, but the minute they got closer, they swerved to avoid him. The reason was the killer ticks sitting in the forest flowers' intimate areas, or else it was the wall newspaper (ticks kids are everywhere) the school nurse had put up yesterday, a green poster without any punctuation. As a result the flowers adorned the director's desk, since he was seldom there, while Pham, having unloaded his dangerous cargo, went off to the chemistry final. That day five teachers had decided to be on the final exam committee, including Sonya, who was pensively wandering the room picking cribs up off the floor. She pulled up the schoolboys' white shirtsleeves in order to reveal secret formulas. Several times, whenever she walked past Pham, she tried to pause and slip him the answers she'd prepared the night before, but suddenly the Lilliputian appeared. Stretching her birthmark out in a smile, she grabbed Sonya under the shoulderblade and led her off to the blackboard, and then raised one eyebrow, which made her birthmark triangular, and began nodding significantly.

Three hours later the cleaning lady was rocking from side to side just like a Weeble, pulling out the "accordions" and "bombs" left by the nervous students. These bits of paper had turned out to be worthless: the committee, including the Lilliputian, mercilessly exposed the sly scribblers. Then they compared versions of correct answers equally mercilessly, and wrote in C's and D's on all the pages that didn't correspond with them. All the papers were divided into four piles and laid out in descending order on three tables. The last pile was granted one more assessment, a more humanitarian one, where an extra point could be scraped together. Pham's three half-empty pages headed that pile. The evaluation was entrusted to Sonya, the teacher most knowledgeable about acids.

Pham didn't come to either the end-of-year dance or the "Last Bell" end-of-year ceremony. For him, the test slip had been good for a one-way ticket to Hanoi. The boy had no choice after this examination: the day after the test results were announced, the mother turned up in the emergency room, and a trial was pending for the father, the kind of trial that happens every single day of the week.

Matryoshka dolls gradually filled Red Square. All the doors flew open with the words "Velcome, comrade tourists!" and the evening gloom disappeared, consumed by illumination. Sonya was still sitting on the bench. She watched people drift past, their index fingers extended, and dozed occasionally. Sonya hadn't slept for a long time, she'd forgotten how long it had been. These moments of sleep on the bench seemed like a reward for the humiliation she'd endured: "You threw up right in the mausoleum! What a disgrace! It's like seeing Paris and not dying of happiness!" The chimes rang out eleven times. For Sonya that meant that in an hour she'd have to be back at the clanking, belching conveyer belt, just like yesterday, and the day before yesterday, and a week ago, and that she'd already missed the eight o'clock shift. It'd been four days since a new batch of glossy magazines awaiting their inserts and tear-out cards had been delivered to the shop, and now she was in for several nights in a row of gratifying them.

Sonya tossed the empty can aside with a clatter and immediately felt a passing policeman's eyes on her. She pulled the hem of her skirt down, gave a guilty smile, and marched off to work.

In any city, whether it be Moscow, Chelyabinsk, or even

Sweden, they always turn off the hot water earlier in the outlying suburbs, and the heat disappears much earlier there too than downtown – strictly according to schedule, regardless of whether it's warm or cold outside. And it gets dark earlier in the suburbs, too. The streets begin getting snarled as early as nine, and by midnight they're just a tangled, shaggy knot of yarn. The neighborhood where Sonya's workshop was set up was four stations past the Garden Ring, so the road there felt like the road out to the suburbs. The streets were joined by heavy-set buildings, all different kinds of factories: some baked vanilla buns, whose morning aroma invited everyone to go back home and have breakfast, while others were print shops whose odor chased passersby to work. At night the odors stopped: the industrial bakeries would turn off their ovens and mix their dough, while the industrial print shops, in contrast, would work twice as hard, but by then no one cared about the smell of printing ink. At night, Moscow would break down into a great number of smaller towns according to income level: you could see who had rich fiancés by their Garden Ring, while you could tell the slightly poorer ones by their incessant, nervous smoke. Sonya's workshop happened to be in one of the suburbs that didn't have an authoritative ring, and that smoked at night, isolated and silent.

Somehow managing to make it through several stations, Sonya came out of the Metro onto a deserted square. She only saw one person at the bus stop, a nice young lady completely wrapped in a red muffler, hoping against hope to catch the after-hours trolleybus. She sat on the bench tapping her miniature velvet slippers in time to the children's song "My grandma had a little grey goat" and jumping up every so often like a woman possessed in reaction to the sound of somebody's engine. Sonya had gone about five meters when she suddenly heard the girl's voice: "Don't touch me! Please, don't touch me!" Now the muffler was off to one side, and the possessed girl, sobbing and waving her hands around, was slowly sliding down to the ground.

"What is it? What happened?"

"They took my purse."

"Get up."

"I'm... I'm not from Moscow, and everything's in it..."

"Just get up, dear..."

They walked two blocks silently, they went past Sonya's shop, caught wind of the earnestly-striving print shop, and walked up to the train station.

"Let's spend the night here, it's too late to go to the Metro now, but where do you live?"

"I... I'm renting a room from a friend of my grandmother's."

"What in the world were you doing at the trolleybus stop at night?"

"I was going home from work, we usually don't finish this late, it's just that today..."

"So what are you going to do now?"

"Now I have to replace my papers, I get paid in two weeks, I'll have to get by somehow until then..."

"Where are you from?"

"I'm from Chelyabinsk."

"Really?!"

"Well, sure."

"And you say you'll get by somehow?"

"Yeah. I'm not going home, there's no reason to."

"Me neither. I'm not from Moscow either. I do have a husband back home... He lives with a young tramp, about your age. The neighbor girl. I used to feed him..."

"You did?"

"Yes, me, who else would, not that idiot of his. She doesn't work, and he's handicapped, category two... So I moved to Moscow..."

"What for?"

"I went to Lenin's Tomb for the first time today... I got sick there all of a sudden, and I sat down on a bench, I sat there and watched the people: here's Lenin with his beard coming off, selling matryoshka dolls. He's standing there yawning. He takes the matryoshkas apart, sets them up, pulls the little baby ones out of the big fat ones. I was watching as he dropped one, a really tiny one, and he didn't even notice. Everyone was walking right past him, and they all saw it, but not a single person said anything..."

"That's funny, Lenin with his little beard coming unglued! If only he'd known, the leader of the world proletariat..."

"There you go! 'Any cruel actions are morally justifiable, as long as they are intended to free the proletariat from exploitation and as long as they contribute to the victory of the proletarian revolution...' "

"Wow! You've got it memorized! That old lady, the one whose apartment I'm staying at, also quotes him a lot: 'There is no such thing as a common human morality, only a class-based morality...' So who was walking past him, foreigners?"

Sonya glanced at all the occupied seats around them, pulled the hem of her skirt down, and rose resolutely. "Listen, wait here, I'll be back in fifteen minutes."

Sonya's feet marked time for a few hundred quick steps on the marble floor, and ten minutes later she was sitting next to the "possessed" girl again, listening to her gradual pacification. In one hand she held the red muffler that had slipped off her shoulder, while in the other, she held a train ticket for a six-hour trip and a little tiny matryoshka. She knew that she was getting a new life for free, and that she wouldn't have to pay a lot for it, she wouldn't have to pay with some grand future feat...

APPLES

There was something special about it. There had been since morning. How many days had it been since the long-gone sun had come back out... but that morning, it came out. The early reveille was quite a surprise for many connoisseurs of thirteen hours of sleep a night. The languishing scent of the freshness being baked up in industrial bakeries and candy factories, a scent that stepped over the train tracks, went up to the bridge, and walked along its edges for three blocks — everything set this morning apart.

Church was also different that day. Sunbeams fell on praying people's heads, and icons' shadows fell on praying people's heads, and all of it was accompanied by the singing of a choir and children's voices. A picture like that just looked ideal. It's rare for separate parts to come together into a whole, with no need for chemical bonding, or even for screws and angular bolt-heads to be machined; only the mentally ill can look at chaos and see a still life.

Vic the Steering Wheel "wheeled" circles around the parishioners, smiling at each one and offering to give each one a ride. The ones who were a little younger, with headscarves that were a little brighter, sat down in the back seat and ran after the driver, chortling, and then tactfully hopped out without catching a foot on the illusory doorframe and walked to Sunday service. Elderly judgmental eyes hid under kerchiefs, then led the under-age damsels behind the fence to nag them about their careless treatment of poor feeble-minded creatures. Vic didn't consider himself one; he woke up in a feather bed like many other people, and he performed his ablutions with the same soap as everyone else, and every morning he ate scrambled eggs and headed out to "wheel around," same as the businessmen in ties. He lived with his father, which is why he was always clean and fed, why he "drove an expensive car," and why he was like family for both children and adults, convincing the former to play games and the latter of their capacity for compassion.

No one knew whether Vic had been that way since he was little, or whether something had happened to him that made him find a heavy metal steering wheel covered in a peeling layer of plastic in the Gaiva dump and start "driving around," imitating the sound of an engine, but everyone just saw him as he was at the time: the strange local boy. He was around thirty when he and his father moved into this outlying district of Perm, when they passed the two cemeteries and the bridge over the Kama (the bridge off which, according to local lore, a pregnant girl jumped because of her poverty and hopelessness) and settled into a tiny house with an aluminum tub on the porch and a freshly-whitewashed stove. The story about the pregnant girl could have become the biggest one from the Gaiva Forest to the Gaiva grocery store, and made everyone who was driving past look sorrowfully at the railing, but the endless flow of the water, accompanied by the violent belching of foam, took people's minds off mourning.

The older he got, the more people found out about him. Stories about Vic from Gaiva, who never let the steering wheel out of his hands, and whose smile was a familiar sight at all the local bus stops, gradually spread throughout the city, and now it wasn't at all unusual for residents of one end of the city to be telling residents of the other end about the boy with the steering wheel, and then for them to start waving their index finger around, exclaiming delightedly, "He was over in our neighborhood too, that sick boy, he's gotten all over town by now!"

The parishioners moved in single file through the church, gradually filling the altars with tiny flickerings and then, after crossing themselves and sighing heavily, heading for the exit. The ones who were a little older could never quite make up their minds how many candles to light for their health, but they always knew exactly how many to light for the peace of departed souls. Every so often someone would confidently buy several candles, recite something in a murmur just as confidently, and then walk away, still with that same confidence. The majority of the flock spent the first ten minutes at the Mother of God, tortured, trying to decide whether to pray for this one or that one, or whether it was time to let their dear ones go on by themselves. They spent the second ten minutes choosing the right interjections and verbs, formulating their request to the Lord to take good care of them — or to be good and rid of them — then hurried to appeal right away for a meeting with them. But the children were so confident, racing right up and sticking a candle anywhere they felt like. It was a native scene, looking more like an old postcard done in inks that were still fairly reserved, but real: a little five-year-old missy in an intentionally modest blue piqué dress lighting a thin candle, with absolute harmony between her energetic little heart and her endlessly curling thoughts, who smiles once she's stepped back a bit and assessed what she's done. She whispers something, turns suddenly away, and, without finishing her sentence, takes her thoughts away with her, continuing her whispering on the fly. As if she can really see, or really *is* seeing, that gentleman upstairs, and likes chatting with him, and doesn't have a clue that one could ask him for something, while everyone else wanders vainly through the church, pleading. They scrutinize the icons and then turn their curious, submissive gazes on each other.

When the door opened with an exhausted sigh for the new arrivals, the drone of Vic's car whooshed into the church along with the air. His engine went silent every time some sad new person appeared at the front entrance and put three fingers together in a way Vic didn't understand, but that had always and forever been that way, ever since he could remember.

Behind the church, staircases led one after the other down to a drainage ditch. Uncle Victor, the watchman, was checking the church inventory, lugging spades and rakes from place to place. "There's a lot of 'em these days, a lot of leaves. That means there'll be a lot of snow, too."

Sanka, a six-year-old ragamuffin in his grandpa's sweater, was putting scraps of cellophane and colored paper into a washtub full of trash. They mixed in with the smooth, charred apple leaves and the brown fruits, faded from being burnt, and turned into a colorful, living mass.

"Look! Look!"

Sanka the ragamuffin poured a remaining family of juicy sour apples out of the aluminum tub onto the ground and jumped on top of them, making the apples hawk up the remnants of their juice and grow emaciated with a crunch.

"Sonny, you can't do that to food, you don't act that way with bread now, do you?"

"But there's not much of it."

"And if there was a lot of it? What does the dear Lord give us food for?"

"What's the dear Lord got to do with it, we give it to ourselves."

"Well, that's just what you think, is that we do it ourselves, but it's all from him."

"And he gives it to Vic too?"

"Yes, and even more than he does to you and me."

Vic, busy and concentrated on the clattering of his motor, stepped on the apples and tore over to the old man.

"Hey, Uncle, does Sanka feel like going for a ride with me?"

Sanka appraised Vic with a practiced adult eye, and, without waiting for his grandpa's reply, he stepped over the scrofulous fruits, leaking the last trickles of juice, and opened the invisible door with a stern gesture. His awareness of his own maturity and understanding caused a little furrow, a juvenile one, but one that still expressed all the seriousness of a six-year-old boy, to divide his brow.

"Step on it."

"Just for a little while. A few laps and be right back."

Victor swept the fruits into a heap and found among them piebald birds' feathers drawn in all colors of the rainbow on graph paper. He bowed to pick them up, then stacked them together and put them in his pocket.

"Must be Yashka's feathers."

Eight years ago his son Styopa used to copy sketches of ostriches out of popular magazines about animals. He caught the parrot Yakov's pirouettes, a parrot he'd once renamed Yashka when the latter was dying in his cage. Yakov was dying because he'd soiled his seed-tray and decided to declare a four-day hunger strike just to spite Styopa, but, since he was a small creature, he grew weak in those four days, and then the only thing left to do for the bird was bury it. Styopa mourned for about two weeks, watching over the bird that'd starved to death, and kept wishing he could turn into Victor Frankenstein, so he could resurrect the dead Yakov and turn him into Yashenka, never mind if he was slow, never mind if he wasn't such a capricious fellow, at least he'd be alive, at least he'd be airborne, sending Styopa's sketches flying with gusts of air from his wings.

Styopa's childhood had been remarkable for a special attachment to certain living things. Until he was fifteen, he'd had no doubt that his father's love for him was eternal. It was an immutable part of life, like trips to Grandma's, like the scenes at Sunday breakfast caused by Styopa's blunders, which, between the open windows and the smell of bread, were almost effaced. He used to remember his family's New Year's Eve "tours" in Velikie Luki with trepidation, when eleven obsessed adults and seven carefree children, all succumbing to the general sense of expectation for the magician from underground, would gather in one house. With him in the lead, the children would sit down on the floor and set up little tables on stools by laying down immense, boundless sheets of wood that looked like the boards of easels and that were heaped with snowdrifts of flour, and a chipped yellow enamel pot full of ground pork would be set at knee level. When Auntie let him, Victor would take a hunk of the sourdough bread his Nana had baked and spread with a thin layer of meat, a layer so thin you could count every unchopped piece of onion and every bloody knotted vein. Styopa got the most exciting part of the holiday *pelmeni*-making* process: he stuffed them with surprises. After dinner everyone would agree that the *pelmeni* were a huge success: not the ones with pig veins in them, or even the ones with gristle, but the ones with a filling that his hungry carnivorous relatives weren't expecting. In the end, over half the wooden sheet ended up filled with his dough, and thus one of the rounds that got served would lose the name *pelmeni* and turn into something else, such as "grade-A dough." In this way he was trying to give happiness to his numerous family members, as he in his childlike sincerity forced everyone to choke down their New Year's dinner. Back then he still didn't know that good things come in small quantities, and if they didn't, they would invariably be followed by some calamity, such as indigestion.

Whatever happened, he always knew that he had his dad, and his habit of falling into a deep, deep sleep in his arms whenever he felt sad, and his habit of locking himself with Dad in his room with the Lilliputian window. All of Styopa's memories went back to when he was nine years old and they all centered on three things: the clinic, grocery store № 7, and the

---

* Pelmeni are small pockets of dough that are filled with ground meat, pinched shut, and then boiled, much like ravioli.

massive green slide projector with a broken wheel. He'd made his first acquaintance with it when he was five. Since Styopa didn't have a mommy, Victor had to take on all his childhood problems, whether it was allergies or skinned knees, and only later, when he started the third grade, did he let his father get back to the combustible world of beginners and bosses and start going to the doctor by himself. It was a particularly ceremonial ritual: he would wake up at eight o'clock in the morning and complain that his throat was swollen, and his dad would open the yellowed plastic box reeking of bandages and Tiger Balm and take out Styopa's accomplice, the thermometer. They'd reach 37.4°* together and then the best part would start. Having waited until Victor finished his stinky coffee and listened to the shapeless, mediocre melody of the weather forecast, he would begin, slowly, to get dressed. He did everything just like his father taught him: he washed his ears scrupulously, combed his hair back with a wet comb, and folded his white shirt collar down over his jacket, so that he would look like the neatly-dressed son of a parent respected in the community. Styopa never understood what all these formalities were for, since after all, any lady doctor puts on motley slippers stained with milk and rips the covers off her offspring, yelling "Time to get up!" just like he does, just like all parents do. And she even curses under her breath the same way when she looks at the clock hands as they race around their circle without checking with her first.

On the way home from the clinic, having endured the hour of screaming and whimpering from kids who were no match for him — kids who weren't grown-up yet, like him — he headed for grocery store № 7. His father, as a rule, used to leave him a tasty bill he was obliged to use to buy bread and milk, and the change from which he was far from obliged to

---

* Normal body temperature is 36.6° Celsius.

use to buy sweets. He would do everything according to his instructions, with just one difference: he would forget to buy bread, which always provoked a fit of anger from his dad in the evening. But the cake he chose was three-layered, the kind that could fit the whipped cream, and the chocolate shavings, and the tiny marshmallow rose on top. And then there would be no way he could walk home, so he flew, never looking at the winter sledding-hill of the sidewalk, keeping all his thoughts on the baker's intricate creation, and anticipating the vanilla flavor of the precarious sugary miracle. Styopa thought it was a crime to put the cake on a plate and eat it sitting at the kitchen table, and so he discovered a pastime that complemented the dessert better than anything else: watching slide-shows. "The Matryoshka's Fun" and "Rag and Cloud" were the first slide-shows he watched. That time, Victor woke him up in the middle of the night and pointed the slide projector at the ceiling. They got comfortable on the bed in the bedroom and clicked the little wheel of colored frames. There was text too, but because it fell right on the sheer curtain and the hilly, wavy drapes, his dad became a writer and chose words that made sense only to his son. The cake would be eaten and "Sinbad the Sailor" would be shown for the hundredth time with text by his father, the narrator. The only film Victor didn't bother to adapt for a child's perception was "Where Children Come From," and in the middle of the showing, somewhere around the eleventh click, Styopa started to groan, he said that it wasn't interesting, and for the rest of his childhood that filmstrip didn't appear anymore, it was sent up to his mom's brooches and buttons in the storage space under the ceiling to await its hour. Their film clubs went on until Styopa turned sixteen, until the time all the light bulbs in the slide projector burned out at once. Back then, because of the shortage, it was impossible for even the resourceful Victor to find new ones, and Styopa had to take his pencils in hand and discover his own artistic talent. No less than a hundred slide-shows remained intact in his memory, both sad ones like "White Fang" and funny ones like "Where Children Come From," ones that he did end up liking, but not until he was a teenager.

After that Victor didn't understand what was in his son's pictures anymore, he just believed very much that Styopa missed his father's voice, the smell of the heated film coming from the slide projector, and the ceiling, stained with colored images. He'd been missing his son for years now and every night as he filled his shot glass, he brought back the bready smell of a family get-together and the intelligible dubbing of the meaningless daily frames.

A person consists of his memory. He moves at a speed that's right for him alone, and encounters events that are right for him alone. Then he falls down and realizes that it's better not to walk on shaky ground; he gets up, rubs his knees, and keeps going. And everything is more or less like it was before, but now his walk looks like he's moonwalking in place. Around him everything is changing, and that doesn't mean that things are catching up to him... it might just be that everyone else around him is also moonwalking... everything's just changing. But as for him, he's just started consisting a little bit more of his memory.

Sanka came back forty minutes later, when all the emaciated apples had been piled in the aluminum basin and looked like grandma's forgotten preserves. Victor was collecting rakes and greeting the parishioners coming out of church, shaking hands with some, and answering others with a modest nod, then quickly turning away. His greetings differed because his memories of those people differed. For example, he remembered Dasha as the cook who lugged cream of wheat to his house for Styopa and borsht for him for four months, and Nikita as someone who secretly hated him and called him a leper, but Lyudochka was just Lyudochka to him. And, strange as it might seem, he rushed to shake hands more than necessary with none other than Nikita, showing him how good he felt and how his forehead had healed up. But Dasha and Lyudochka had to be content with just a five-letter "'lothr," which meant "Hello there."

Victor took the drawings out of his pocket and laid them out on the ground. He straightened the crumpled corners and called Sanka over.

"Look, sonny, this is what I was telling you."

"Yasha?"

"Looks that way."

"But how'd they get here?"

"God only knows."

"Again. It's always him, him, him!"

"Have a nice run?"

"We went around the church a few times, then we went down to the swamp, we chased each other like silly idiots, and he's not strange at all..."

"He's not strange, he's just mentally ill."

"That's right, and there you were saying he gets more than us, but who is it that's making him ill, then?"

Victor rolled up the drawings and sat on the ground.

"Have you ever seen a car accident on TV? Of course you have. One car slams right into another, there's an explosion, the brakes squeal..."

"I've *seen* that!"

"But why do things like that happen, do you know that?"

"Nope."

"Because in real life everything's full of potholes. And once I ran into a pothole. I ran into it, but here I am, still going. My forehead healed up, the car is in the dump... But then Styopa... Well, fine, I met you, fine, your mama left you and ran... so you'll face a lot of potholes too, and I'm raising you different than I did Styopa. Now you, sonny, always keep the most important thing in mind, you know, the thing that I'm always telling you..."

"Be a passerby?"*

"That's it. The only ones who can do that are children and the mentally ill. Old people see that when they come up against death: there's nothing at all, there's only memories of kids and grandkids. So you, do you think a lot about which way is better?"

"I don't know how yet."

"And why should you. Now look here, sonny, take a person with a rucksack and a person who wakes up every morning to go to work. Which one of them do you think is more satisfied?"

"Let's go home already."

"We're going, we're going right now."

"One doesn't know where he'll wake up tomorrow, but the other one does. He *thinks* he knows, but *really*..."

Victor bent over the basin with grandma's forgotten preserves, where flies had already started collecting, gathering for the tasting with clumsy little flights, and spat into the very middle. His saliva trickled onto one of the crumbled apples and immediately soaked into it, while the rest of it slid softly down an unbroken apple and settled on the basin's aluminum bottom.

"We're going, call Styopa."

The barefoot boy raced off to the parish.

About seven minutes passed before Sanka's voice rang out, calling Vic the Steering Wheel, and why he was Vic, why he'd been carrying his father's name for several years now, was clear only to the three of them. Gaiva was falling asleep so as to wake up the next day. Victor was lying motionless.

ALEXANDER GRITSENKO

from the *"Dreams"* cycle

Translated by Lisa Hayden Espenschade

IN THE TUNNEL

It happens often: a morning Metro train somewhere in the middle of a black tunnel between stations suddenly stops for no reason. The car falls abruptly silent. You can hear music playing through some student's headphones at the other end. Then someone gets irritated. "Good Lord!" the person says. "People are going to be late for work..." But their dissatisfaction sounds meek, modest, hushed.

The train will sit for a couple of minutes and then move along.

Why did it stop in the middle of the tunnel? What was it waiting for?

To let children by. Children were crossing the tracks.

The underground children generally walk around at night. A little in the morning, very rarely in the evening, and never in the afternoon.

They don't know themselves where they're going. They look like a group of kindergarten or elementary school children crossing a street. Except that it's not a kindergarten or Phys. Ed. teacher leading them but a fuzzy teddy bear with a torn-off paw.

Only the Metro drivers see all this. But the children's shadows on the tunnel walls are sometimes visible if you ride at the front of the first Metro car. Take a look if you want. When I found out about this, I started to take a closer look and saw them a few times.

That's why all the Metro drivers drink. After a shift, it's a full glass right away. It helps you loosen up, you sit for a bit, have a smoke, knock back another hundred grams...

And the children walk around. At night, generally, but sometimes in the morning. Where are they going? It's as if the children are asleep: they have blissful smiles on their faces. Not idiotic but, well, only a baby can smile like that.

Sometimes they stop on the tracks and look at the train. The driver looks back and can't avert his gaze. They look at each other: The children smile, the driver cries. Then the teddy bear turns, frowns at the driver, and makes a sign to the children. Let's move along, he says, there's no need to stand here. The bear seems to know, what he's doing, why and where he's leading the children.

When an overcrowded Metro train suddenly stops in the middle of a dark tunnel during morning rush hour, don't be scared, don't swear, and don't think about being late for work. Cry a little. Not for the children: they're happy. Not for the teddy bear: he's leading happy children. Not for the driver: he cries for himself.

Cry for yourself. Feel sorry for yourself.

THE BOY WITH THE BANGED-UP KNEES

There's a secret room in every middle school. Usually it's found near the coat room, and if you listen hard, you'll be able to hear a rustling and the scrape of a goose feather on paper through the wall. These noises come from the Outcasts. They're banished temporarily, till they reach initiation age, and it is these children who will eventually become presidents, government ministers, oligarchs or, at the very least, governors. They were chosen to run the world, though they have their own selection process, too, and not all will take high posts – they can't withstand the competition.

There are Outcasts in every school. Their peers despise them and tease them during breaks between classes. But that's not so terrible – that's how it should be. They should experience suffering to learn to be cruel. They should learn about life and science.

Only lucky chosen children become Outcasts. They are already singled out in elementary school by teachers who inspire horror, unattractive women with an apathetic gaze and men with mechanical, lifeless movements. They give the students the choice to either become what is expected of them or to die from a terrible illness. By the way, not all agree. They're hindered by a primal fear that could only be compared with the fear of the first sexual intimacy. But that's stronger.

It's not just the teacher who evokes horror. It's also his office, cold, soulless, and empty, like the moon.

No matter what a student's answer might be, the teacher will force a semblance of a smile, then go over and pat the student on the head, causing an absolute vacuum to penetrate his insides, which causes his innards to compress and even his heart to jump and stop, and his mouth go dry. Only if the child is observant will he understand the reason: the teacher's body doesn't smell of anything, there's no scent, and you can feel its absence in the room, too, where it's quiet and empty, where every object causes severe unease.

And then there is either death or long lessons in a secret room without windows, where people speak only in whispers. Candles stand on the walls and floor. The children copy books with quill pens and ink and every day they must tell the educators what they copied. There's no punishment here for lack of progress: after the third error, the student simply disappears without a trace...

A strange portrait of a boy with banged-up knees hangs on the wall of every Outcast room. The educators teach children to treat the image with awe, as if it were God. Clearly, the solution to the mystery is in the portrait.

Rumors circulate among the Outcasts that it's not an actual boy but the image of the soul of a dead child, the collective image of all the children who died too soon, all in one picture, where each brushstroke expresses despondency and suffering. The child misses family and the ordinary life that everyone has.

Some students think it was Lenin who founded the Outcast Society; others claim it was Lomonosov in the eighteenth century. But then what does a boy with banged-up knees have to do with anything? Another version of the story seems more plausible to me: the artist who painted this frightening picture founded the society.

The Outcasts have to lead double lives. They hardly ever turn up at home but their parents don't notice. Once they become adults, former Outcasts think a lot about why their parents never suspected anything. Most of them think that the boy in the portrait came to the parents, in their likeness: the dead child took as payment parental warmth, something he received little of during his short life.

Maybe that's how it is, maybe not... In any case, there's no solution to all this and, at the end of their education, the Outcasts understand that the mystery they're part of is more ancient than a person can imagine and that the mystery involves Lomonosov and Lenin and the artist...

But time to think only comes later. Until then, the students copy books during evenings and nights, and come to the classroom during the day. Ordinary children hate and beat them because they can sense that they're different, incomprehensible. They sense that the Outcasts are more important and that they, ordinary children, are only decorations for their future play, so the ordinary children take vengeance for that while it's possible. They beat the Outcasts and humiliate them in all sorts of ways. Some of the Outcasts manage to gather their peers around them at school and become leaders. The teachers don't hinder them.

After graduating from school, the Outcast will enroll at a university or take on something else, but the boy from the portrait will always be a presence, like a guardian angel that prevents misfortune and brings success. And one day the chosen person will occupy a high place in society, earned and ransomed from the strange spirit.

That boy will be a guardian angel until the end of the chosen person's days. And yet, despite all the success, money, and power, the person will become more depressed and miserable each year. And there won't be a remedy for that melancholy. All because the dead boy cannot bring joy to a living person. Only grief and sorrow.

METAPHYSICAL WORMS

It happens like this: you're a full one hundred percent sure of something, then suddenly someone tells you that white is black. Of course you argue and stand up for what you're sure of. But you realize that somehow you've started to doubt.

The more time goes by, the less confidence you have in yourself. The day will come when black will start to seem like white to you and vice versa.

This is because metaphysical worms have penetrated your brain.

These worms are quite dangerous, and they're passed from person to person through the ears. The processes that they cause are irreversible for the soul. An infected person spits out these worms in conversation, and some fall onto his opponent and crawl into his ears.

When we say "Don't try to pull the wool over my eyes!" we don't suspect that this ancient expression is a spell against metaphysical worms. In the past, everybody knew about their existence and tried to protect themselves by saying these words.

After penetrating thorugh the ear canal into the body, the worms devour energy from the brain and soul. People infected with the illness will soon begin to doubt themselves and believe in things they used to deny. This is the first stage of the illness.

Some individuals have lifelong immunity to the illness because their souls and brains are too much for the worms, but they are few and far between. The illness develops slowly in most people, and they manage to die from old age before the worms drain the brain of blood and fully destroy the soul.

Those who are less fortunate lead a half-conscious existence until their bodies die. Their view of the world is distorted and gets more so each day. In the end they stop distinguishing colors and shades — everything narrows down to black and white. In their understanding, the world is simple to the point of meaninglessness. All attempts to tell them about the colors of the rainbow provoke aggression. That's how the second and third stages of the illness progress.

In the fourth and final stage, the infected person mistakes black for white and vice versa.

The loss of one's self and the loss of an understanding of the world lead to the loss of the soul's immortality: it dies, eaten away by the worms. Individuals infected with the disease feel their own metaphysical decline, which makes them irritable and aggressive. Fear of the Abyss forces them to do the most inept things. A lot try to infect as many people as possible in their last days.

One may be infected by this metaphysical plague in direct conversation as well as by the Internet, television, radio, newspapers, and letters. Be careful. If you have stopped seeing the colors of the rainbow and it is suddenly clear that this is the end, then my advice is to shoot yourself. That way you cut off one of the chains of infection and save yourself from suffering. But more importantly, you save the souls of those around you from disintegration!

DESPERATION

Patches of sky flashed through naked branches. The driver accelerated. No snow had fallen yet this winter, but the cold snap was terrible: twenty-five below. This was the second day of freezing-cold temperatures; winter was just beginning. Oleg imagined how chilly it must be in the woods.

The Tatar driver, withered, lanky, and resembling an evil jinn, turned his head from time to time and said with self-satisfaction, "We'll get there in time" or "I can make two hundred kilometers in two hours" or "It's only three in the morning." Nobody paid him any attention. Oleg and the fleshy, well-dressed woman sitting next to him in the back seat were thinking their own thoughts. "How old is she, I wonder? Probably fifty," thought Oleg.

A double chin and very thin lips coated with violet lipstick... She wore huge glasses covering half her face, the lenses magnified her eyes. It could have been worse.

Oleg glanced at the woman, trying to be inconspicuous. She answered with a serious stare... The car smelled of stale cigarettes.

A woman like this doesn't let anything go. Oleg had only worked at the newspaper for three months, but he'd heard quite a lot about her from colleagues. The woman had come to the newspaper as a rank-and-file manager, but soon she had enlisted the support of the general director and editor-in-chief, removed the advertising director, and taken his place. Ruthless!

She had no children. She had long ago turned her husband into a pathetic creature who didn't make a move without her. He often came into the newspaper office. Pale, always frightened and submissive.

Oleg looked at the plastic, long-legged doll with prominent breasts hanging from the rear view mirror and swinging like a pendulum. Right, left. Right, left.

The woman felt sorry for Oleg for some reason. They had met the day he first came to the paper. And the woman began to protect him from that first day. She said only complimentary things about Oleg to the editor. If an advertising article was in the works, she would inevitably assign Oleg to write it: "Nobody else here writes as splendidly as Oleg." Occasionally one of his articles wouldn't work out, and the advertiser was dissatisfied, but she always covered for Oleg.

It was great fortune for a provincial journalist who hadn't even graduated from the university to work in a well-known paper's news bureau. Oleg received Moscow-standard fees for his articles, so he was able to live large in Kazan... He loved to be generous, adored expensive alcohol, restaurants, clubs, adored women, to smoke in bed with them, to spend money on them.

Oleg had been living it up lately. In addition to money, he had a sort of recognition. His classmates, for example, considered him a talent, a future star, and respected him very much. There was envy, of course, but nobody did any harm.

The plastic girl swung, and there was a smell of stale

cigarettes. The woman placed Oleg's hand on her hip. He stroked it, thinking, "She planned this whole business trip just for two."

He remembered that the woman was his mother's age.

His mother lived in a village near Kazan, only three kilometers from the city, but they hadn't seen each other in two years.

The woman directed his hand. He felt repulsion but overcame it, unfastened, got underneath, stroked.

She lowered her pants and pulled his head down. Oleg tensed his neck, resisting, but then gave in. Before leaning over, for some reason he looked at the girl, swinging under the mirror. "Like a gallows..." thought Oleg. He caught the Tatar's glance in the mirror.

The woman's legs were plump and lumpy, and dark blue veins snaked along the skin. Oleg felt nauseous and it seemed that the car spun, tilted, and then fell...

He opened the car door. The water was icy. He gripped the ice with his fingers. It kept breaking.

Oleg felt that he was sinking. He tried to grope for the ice. His hands were numb.

He crawled along the ice. It seemed that the ice was about to crack. The shore. Oleg lay still, and he shivered. He coughed and lay a bit longer. He raised himself up a little and looked at the river.

The car had fallen into the river. The driver had lost control on the bend just before the bridge. "The river is quite small." He saw the other side of the river distinctly: a sandy slope, dry grass at the top. Silence...

He went to the roadway. Snowflakes melted on his wet clothes. It was cold. The damp soles of his shoes slipped on the slope. To keep from falling, he grabbed onto the sparse dry grass.

The road was completely empty. He didn't know where he was. There were trees on both sides of the road. He couldn't remember how many times during the trip he'd seen oncoming headlights. It was the forest.

Should he set out without knowing where he was going?

Headlights appeared in the distance. Oleg stuck his arm out. The headlights lighted his pitiful, hunched figure and unbending arm. The car drove past. Oleg couldn't believe his eyes. He breathed out a thick cloud of steam and began to cry. It seemed that even his eyeballs had frozen.

He walked to meet an oncoming car and tried to aim carefully between the headlights. The driver noticed his silhouette from afar and braked, then carefully drove around Oleg.

...He saw more headlights. Snowflakes, snowflakes, snowflakes. He took off running. The car stopped. Oleg tried to open the door, but couldn't. The driver grinned. The car began moving. The man drove slowly; he was smiling. Oleg beat on the glass with his fist. Snowflakes, snowflakes, snowflakes...

He wanted to press his face against that woman's legs...

It was getting light. A child and an old man were walking along the snow-covered roadway. The shafts of a wooden sledge carrying brushwood pressed into their shoulders, and the sledge's runners caught on hummocks. The snow was falling in large awkward flakes.

"Where does snow come from, Grandfather?" asked the girl in Tatar.

"From the sky," said her grandfather.

"But who throws it?"

"Allah."

"Does Allah throw it with his hands or with buckets?"

The old man didn't answer. He had noticed a frozen body in the road. Snow had almost covered him. The old man touched the stiffened body with the toe of his boot.

"Allah alone knows how he throws the snow," said the grandfather.

He lifted the corpse with difficulty and set it on top of the wood. The girl watched with wide eyes.

The wayfarers set out again. The wind tossed around flakes of snow, and the trees nodded joyously at the man and his granddaughter.

THE FLIES
a novella

Another Fury: And how beautiful!

First Fury: Yes, we are favored. Only too often criminals are old and ugly. Too seldom do we have the joy, the exquisite delight, of ruining what's beautiful.

The Furies: Heiah! Heiahah!

Third Fury: Orestes is almost a child. I shall mother him, oh so tenderly, with my hatred; I shall take his pale head on my knees and stroke his hair.

First Fury: And then?

Third Fury: Then, when he least expects it, I shall dig these two fingers into his eyes.

[All laugh.]

First Fury: See, they're stretching, sighing, on the brink of waking. And now, my sisters, flies my sisters, let's sing the sinners from their sleep.

Jean-Paul Sartre, *The Flies*

CHARACTERS:

MOTHER, *aged 70*
ANNA, *aged 45*
VERA, *aged 42*
her three daughters:
LYUBA, *aged 25*
ANDREI, *Anna's son, aged 23*

Scene 1

A Russian *izba* — a rustic wooden house. It is dark. Light comes only from a small lamp hanging by an icon. A woman kneels; she is praying. Her face is radiantly serene. She is dressed in black, with a black scarf on her head. The flame from the icon lamp reflects in her eyes, casting dappled light on her face. The woman's name is VERA.

VERA. Our Father, Who art in heaven, Hallowed be Thy name. Thy Kingdom come. Thy will be done on earth, as it is in heaven. Give us this day our daily bread. And forgive us our debts, as we forgive our debtors. And lead us not into temptation, but deliver us from the evil one. Now and ever, unto the ages of ages. Amen.

She has barely said "Amen" when the door opens wide and MOTHER waddles in. She carries her bulky body with difficulty, and breathes heavily. A thin woman with a wrinkled face slips into the room behind her. This is ANNA. Both are wearing black dresses. The mother has on a black scarf; Anna's head is uncovered.

MOTHER. There's been a misfortune, Vera, dear!

Vera's face instantly loses its piety and placidity. Now we see that she is older than she seemed at first.

VERA. What happened, Mama?
ANNA *(in tears)*. Our sister has lost her mind! She's definitely not right in the head!
MOTHER. Maybe the Kuznetsovs were right when they said that as soon as a person starts to earn a lot of money, things don't turn out well. And we thought they were envious.

Vera gets up off her knees, sits down in a chair, and silently looks at the women.

ANNA *(crying)*. And how is it they killed Anton, left Andrei legless, and this woman is mixed up with them...

Vera slowly crosses herself. Mother settles her bulky body into a chair.

VERA. Did she get mixed up with a darkie then?
ANNA. Not just any darkie. With a Chechen. *(Anna pronounces the word as if she's choking. She crosses herself.)* Oh, Lord!
MOTHER: My poor, unfortunate daughters. Anya, Vera, both of you... Andrei must not find out!

There is a thick curtain covering the window that makes it dark in the house.

Scene 2
But outside, it's daylight. Autumn. Leaves are falling from the trees. Many leaves. Spring is a beautiful season but late autumn is wiser, when living nature has already recognized its end but plans a last celebration anyway.

Scene 3
In the yard. Trees with huge piles of leaves underneath. Chickens and ducks are pecking around outside a shed, and there is a dog kennel with a huge dog on a chain. He seems threatening. An unexpected gust of wind blows a heap of yellow-red leaves around the yard.

Scene 4
Wispy clouds in the sky. Wild birds take up half the sky — they are migrating. Their cry is audible.

Scene 5

A bathhouse stands at the end of the yard. Inside, ANDREI, wrapped in a sweater, is sleeping on a bench. Nightmares torment him in his sleep. He groans, breathes heavily, as if he's trying to run away from someone. He doesn't have legs. His prostheses stand beside the bench. They are imported prostheses of the best quality.

Scene 6

MOTHER. Well, if he finds out, he'll kill him!

ANNA. And let him kill! She gave me money to buy his prostheses! Probably the Chechen gave it to her! Oh, he'll find out and kill me too!

VERA. Bless us, O Lord.

MOTHER. That's why I invited her here. *(Takes a mobile phone out of her pocket.)* This was her gift, too. *(Puts the phone on the table.)*

Vera looks askance at the phone and crosses herself, "Bless, o Lord!"

VERA. Bless us, O Lord! *(Looks askance at the phone and crosses herself).* The devil's creation!

ANNA. She's not my sister anymore! I'll borrow money, but I'll repay. And she... May she never set foot here again!

MOTHER. She's still my daughter.

ANNA. Have you thought about Vera's and my children? SHE'S NOT MY SISTER!

Scene 7

Through the bathhouse window we see Andrei, asleep. His teeth are clenched, and he's all stretched out. He begins to wave something aside, as if there is something flying around him. After a short time, he sighs hard and turns to the wall.

Scene 8

A car is driving along a village road, drawing closer. Through the windshield we see that a young woman with light-blonde hair is behind the wheel. Her face is nicely made-up, and she has a serious expression.

Scene 9

MOTHER. Maybe she's using drugs there in the city and that did something to her head?

ANNA. I wouldn't be surprised! She's probably shooting up. It was that Chechen who put her on drugs.

VERA. We shouldn't have let her go live in the city. We're the ones to blame.

MOTHER. I thought maybe she'd at least live like a human being.

They hear a car pull up outside. The dog starts barking.

VERA. It's her! *(She crosses herself.)*

MOTHER. Sit here. I'll open the door myself. *(Gets up, goes to the door, swaying and lamenting.)* Andrei must not find out.

Scene 10

In the yard. LYUBA walks toward the house. She is dressed in a short skirt and top. She has a pretty face, a lithe, shapely figure, and nice legs. The huge dog barks welcomingly, not threateningly.

MOTHER goes into the yard and stops after a couple steps. When LYUBA walks up to her, MOTHER hugs her, crying, and kisses her on both cheeks.

MOTHER. My dear daughter...

She hugs and kisses her again.

Scene 11

Anna and Vera are inside the house.

VERA. How can I look at her?
ANNA. There's no reason to look at her, the hussy!

MOTHER and LYUBA walk into the house.

ANNA. Here she is! Like a painted whore, almost naked! For shame!
LYUBA. What's going on? Why are you speaking to me like that?
ANNA. Do you have to ask? I'll pull out all your styled-up hair right now and you'll know!
MOTHER *(heavily catching her breath)*. Now don't yell, girls. Sit down. We need to talk.

LYUBA sits straight down. Then ANNA. They are silent for a long time. Then suddenly:

MOTHER. Is it true you're dating a Chechen?

Lyuba looks at the floor and doesn't answer. Pause.

MOTHER. Are you planning to get married or you're just loving each other?
LYUBA. He proposed to me.
VERA. O Lord!
ANNA. You're going to be a nanny to little Chechens, grandma!
MOTHER. My daughter... Lyuba... How can you do this to us?
ANNA. They tore off Andrei's legs and killed Anton, but you!
MOTHER. That's how the war touched us... How could you?

(Pause) I had you late in life... The doctor told me the baby could be born handicapped.

LYUBA. You're handicapped yourselves! *(Cries.)*

VERA. Lyuba, dear, you know you're not just a sister to me, you were like a daughter. You grew up with our children, with mine and Anna's. Don't you remember Anton? How they brought him in a coffin?

LYUBA sobs.

MOTHER. They killed Vera's son — your nephew — and your other nephew, Anna's son, was left crippled. And you're all mixed up with them!

LYUBA. I'm not mixed up with anyone! He didn't even fight in the war!

ANNA. So? They're beasts! Barely human!

LYUBA. Do you want me to live like all of you, without a husband? For my whole life to be out of kilter? I want a husband to love! I want to have his children!

Her face, stained with mascara, is frightening. She looks like a woman possessed, like a Fury. The light of the icon lamp reflects in her eyes, and her eyes seem to burn with an unworldly, devilish fire.

ANNA: How is it you're planning to have his children? If you start carrying a child, I'll squeeze that wolf cub out of you myself!

LYUBA jumps up, grabs the first thing at hand, the mobile phone, and throws it at ANNA. She misses. The telephone smashes. ANNA stands up. As if she wants to hit LYUBA.

MOTHER: I'll talk with her myself. Get Andrei something to eat.

VERA rises obediently. She pulls something out of the sideboard, takes something off the table. ANNA resumes her seat. Her face is stony. Everyone is quiet.

VERA. I'll go to our darling.

Exits.

Scene 12
VERA walks across the yard. The wind spits leaves at her. Her gait is angular, hurried. She is thinking about something serious. The dog begins barking and stops quickly, as if something had closed its mouth.

Scene 13
VERA knocks on the bathhouse door. A voice calls out, "Come on in!"

Scene 14
In the bathhouse.

VERA. God bless you!
ANDREI. And you, Aunt Vera.
VERA. I brought you something to eat.
ANDREI. Oooh! Great! I'm hungry as a hog! *(Laughs.)* Why're you sad?
VERA. Maybe you'll come back into the house? Why are you here like ... O Lord, forgive me ... like a dog?
ANDREI. Nah, Aunt Vera, I'll live here a while longer. It's not very cold. I can't be with you... It's depressing enough. And then there's all of you.
VERA. Well, God be with you. You know best.
ANDREI. Don't look, Aunt Vera.

Vera turns away. Andrei puts on his prostheses.

ANDREI. All done, Aunt Vera. You can turn around.

He gets up, makes a few uncertain steps, then walks deftly, as if on his own legs, not prostheses, and goes over to the window.

ANDREI. Oh! Lyuba's here! My sister! Why didn't you tell me?
VERA. She's your aunt, dummy.
ANDREI. She's a sister to me.
VERA. Do you love her?
ANDREI. Who could be closer to me, Aunt Vera?
VERA. Well, yes, you were raised together.

VERA sighs deeply. ANDREI goes out.

VERA. At least have something to eat!
ANDREI. Later! Let me go see my sister!
VERA *(in a whisper)*. God bless you.

The door of the bathhouse slams behind ANDREI with a bang that makes one's blood freeze.

Scene 15
MOTHER, ANNA, and LYUBA are in the house. Andrei bursts in. It's not noticeable that he is wearing prostheses.

ANDREI. Lyuba, dear, hi!
LYUBA. Hi, Andrei.

ANNA gets up, her face stony. She wants to say something.

MOTHER. Be quiet, you mad woman!

LYUBA runs out of the house in tears.

ANDREI. So! What's happened here?! I'd bite off the head of anyone in the village over Lyuba... And here's what I want to say. Why are you always making digs at her? Your husbands left you. All of you! I can't live in the house, I stayed in the bathhouse all summer. Now I don't know where to go for the winter. Why do you nag her? You don't like anything! Let her live as she sees fit!
ANNA. Well, you just don't know.
MOTHER *(to ANNA)*: Be quiet!
ANDREI. I don't want to know!

Leaves the house.

Scene 16
LYUBA runs across the field, over dried grass and clumps of leaves. She runs aimlessly, but as fast as she can.

Scene 17
ANDREI walks very quickly across the same field.

Scene 18
LYUBA falls on the grass, on the leaves. She is in hysterics.

Scene 19
ANDREI walks across the field.

Scene 20
MOTHER, ANNA, and VERA walk across the field. The daughters support their mother.

Scene 21
ANDREI reaches LYUBA. He hugs her shoulders, says something to her.

Scene 22

MOTHER, ANNA, and VERA reach ANDREI and LYUBA.
MOTHER pushes ANNA and VERA away and sits down on
the ground.

ANDREI. Why are you following me?
ANNA. Andrei, you just don't know anything!
MOTHER *(to Anna).* Be quiet!
VERA. Bless us, O Lord!
ANDREI. Granny, take these Furies away! I beg you in the
name of Christ!
MOTHER. They won't leave.
ANNA. She's living with a Chechen! And you're defending
her!

The wind blows the leaves. Everyone is quiet. LYUBA's hands
shake, and her lips tremble. Her eyes are wide open.

ANDREI. Lyuba, is that true?
LYUBA *(crying and shouting).* He never fought in the war! He
was born in Russia! I love him! Kill me for that!

ANNA begins to cry.

ANDREI *(calmly).* Don't be a fool.
ANNA. He killed Anton!
ANDREI. He? Are you out of your mind? Another one killed
Anton. And they killed that "Chech," too. Almost right away.
VERA. Bless Anton, O Lord!
ANNA. They killed my Anton, left you legless, and your auntie
is mixed up with them... They're scum!
ANDREI. They killed my cousin, crippled me... But another
"Chech" carried me out. A Gantimirov fighter carried me three
kilometers, I was bleeding and without legs. And he carried me

through a minefield. I get letters from him now and I write back. I don't think there's any dearer, closer person for me. Never was or will be. So kill me, too, since you want to kill Lyuba!
MOTHER. You never talked...
ANDREI *(yelling)*. Well, fuck, why talk about it!

ANDREI sits on the grass and beats the ground.

ANDREI. Don't touch her. She loves someone, good! She loves, that's so much in this world! Don't touch her!

ANDREI cries and hugs his MOTHER and LYUBA. They all cry together.

Scene 23
The whole family walks back across the field.

VERA *(quietly, to her MOTHER)*. Maybe it's not so bad that he's a Chechen. Let them live together. It turns out they saved our Andrei.
MOTHER. Let them be, forget it.

Scene 24
In the house again. It's already night and dark. Light comes only from the small lamp hanging by the icon. VERA again kneels and prays. The flame from the icon lamp reflects in her eyes...

VERA: Our Father, Who art in heaven, Hallowed be Thy name. Thy Kingdom come. Thy will be done on earth, as it is in heaven. Give us this day our daily bread. And forgive us our debts, as we forgive our debtors; and lead us not into temptation, but deliver us from the evil one. Now and ever, unto the ages of ages. Amen.

VERA stands, yawns and goes over to her bed. MOTHER and
ANNA are sitting at the table. LYUBA is asleep.

VERA. It's impossible to just leave everything like this. They
carried out Andrei, but killed my... And she'll have a baby and
what faith will it have? No, that's impossible.
ANNA *(rigidly)*. We'll talk her out of it.
MOTHER. I'll talk to her tomorrow. Go to sleep.

A sudden breeze blows in the room. MOTHER, ANNA, and
VERA look unnerved. The wind has blown out the icon lamp.
It's dark.

Scene 25
A bed in semi-darkness. LYUBA is asleep, wrapped in an old
blanket. She smiles in her sleep. There is an angelic look on
her beautiful face.

Scene 26
The bathhouse. ANDREI is asleep. He groans in his sleep. He
is having a bad dream. He waves it away with his hands.

ARSLAN KHASAVOV

Translated by Ben Hooson

BRAGUNY STORY

If you go onto Google Maps and enter "Braguny" in the search box, you will see a satellite photo of our village. Near the bottom, on the right, if you look hard, you will see a telephone tower next to the village council and shaped like three sides of a square. It is not actually the tower you see, but its crown and its shadow on the ground — a long spire, close by the cemetery.

It was a warm summer night. A faint wind, coming from the Sunzhi or the Terek, ruffled our hair and stroked our hands. The quiet of the village was only occasionally broken by the muffled howling of dogs or growl of an engine as some speed demon raced through the empty streets of Braguny.

Sated with monotonous village leisure, we started to climb the tower. Height is good for thoughtful gazing into the distance and frank conversations. Climbing up, trying to get closer to the sky, you leave your everyday life on the ground, behind your body as it clambers up the metal platforms of the telephone station. There weren't many of us — only myself and Arthur.

We climbed higher and higher, up the metal ladders, flight after flight, starting to feel afraid. The higher you go, the more you feel the vibrations of this metal framework, its slight but perceptible swaying from side-to-side.

Finally, just short of the top, we stopped. I sat down on a

crosspiece with my legs dangling over the side, while Arthur stood, holding onto the reinforced concrete.

What surprised me was the difference between a village and a town at night. A town, and particularly a big city, is enlivened towards night, it enters a second life illuminated by thousands of lamps. But a village is still, like the body of someone who has died. There are a few signs of life, here and there — a weak glow from under a tent over a courtyard, somebody's shadow moving along a street in search of adventure, but mainly silence. The light soon disappears, the person is swallowed up by the night, leaving no trace, and you understand that... No, I don't know what you understand.

"I don't know what to choose," Arthur said without looking at me. "I want to change the world, become someone important, fight, destroy, smash, but at the same time, I want to create, support my mother, respect my father, study..."

"It's a crucial choice. Choose what's closer to your heart. You can't do both. It's either, or — there's no in-between, there can't be... if it's a genuine choice you're talking about, from the heart."

"I'm afraid," then after a pause, "afraid of making a mistake."

We said nothing...

Before me was the silent village, behind me were eloquent graves. I turned my head towards eternity — from on high the gravestones looked mysterious in the dark. Life and death. Someone has lived, walked these streets, maybe just recently, and today he is no longer among the living. People will not see his smile again, or hear his voice, feel the warmth of his look — never. Only his family will revive his image in their memories, recalling various incidents from his life.

I was overcome by melancholy and I remembered Rustam. Though "remembered" isn't quite the word — I always thought about him and kept a part of him in my soul.

It had been in the middle of Braguny, by the village club, that Rustam and I had really got to know each another. We played billiards at his friend's place, and then went out under the starry sky. We came up to a group of local boys where two streets met. Rustam talked to them, he knew them all well because he'd been living for a few years in Gudermes, occasionally coming over to Braguny to visit his grandmother. He had drunk a can of beer over billiards, and now he was smoking cigarettes one after another. The conversation was leisurely, with much laughter. I didn't understand a lot of it and lost the thread.

Car headlights lit up the darkness of the road. At first they were small and far away, then bigger, and then they enveloped us all in their light. The boys moved aside to let the car past, but Rustam stayed in the middle of the road, serenely inhaling the tobacco smoke.

The car revved its motor a couple of times in warning, but naturally did not dare run him over.

A heavy silence hung in the air. There was only the hum of the engine, and the wordless figure with the smouldering cigarette in his mouth. Finally, the car's front bumper nudged Rustam's knees, bringing the tension to a head.

Rustam broke the tension, throwing his cigarette-end onto the car bonnet.

"What the...?" A short man with red bristles jumped out of the car and came right up to Rustam, frowning at him threateningly. "Where d'you think you are chucking your cigarette-end?" He spiced this innocent question with a couple of strong words.

Rustam found it funny. He smiled and put his arms round the man.

"Arsen, are you serious?" They knew each other.

Arsen brushed off Rustam's hand with a nervous jerk and went on glaring at him like an angry bull:

"I sure am!"

Rustam's expression changed instantly. There was a fight.

I loved him and respected him. For his daring, for always keeping his word. I've never anyone, even since Rustam's early death at the age of the Prophet Jesus, who could accuse him of any dishonesty.

I stood up for Rustam in that fight and did the best I could — I was still a young lad then — and took quite a beating. But Rustam was pleased, it was a test for me, which I fortunately passed.

"Good boy!" He said, admiringly. "Never be afraid! Even when you see that the opponent is stronger, strike first. Good boy!" And he put his warm hand on my shoulder.

He trusted me after that. He had trusted me before, but our relationship of trust was on a much higher level now. He told me about his personal life, his thoughts, about things he maybe hadn't told anyone else. And he would apologise for not having talked to me before. Really talked to me, I mean openly.

"Never mind that I drink and smoke," he said to me once out of the blue, "and I don't say my prayers. So what? I know that I have faith here," he pointed to his chest. "I am good and decent. I have much more faith than a lot of people who obey all the rites. I know people who pray at home, even go to the mosque, but tell lies to people, betray them. I am not like that..."

And indeed he wasn't like that. He was real, genuine, and, even when he departed into the unknown he left a question mark behind him. Who was he? Why was he struck down by illness so young?

They tried to console his mother — my aunt — at the funeral:

"Allah takes good people when they are young."

Someone said:

"Four Hadji who've been to Mecca are standing at the corners of his grave, so he is sure to enter Heaven."

A third added:

"He died in the month of Ramadan, and everyone who dies then automatically goes to Heaven."

But his mother still cried inconsolably, mourning her grievous loss.

"Shall we go down to the cemetery?" I suggested.

"Why?" Arthur asked, surprised.

"No reason..."

And we started down. When we reached the gates, we found that they were locked from the inside. We had to leap over the fence.

"Bismillahir Rahmanir Raheem," I heard Arthur whisper, and repeated after him.

Silent tablets engraved with Arabic script looked at us from all sides as we went further into the cemetery. We stopped by some graves and Arthur said, pointing at the overgrown heaps of earth:

"That is my grandmother and that is my uncle. He was a good man. He was killed in a car accident.

I decided to start with grandmother, and began to pull at the deep-rooted grasses.

"What are you doing?"

"Let's weed the graves."

He helped me.

It wasn't easy. As if grandmother was holding on to those weeds, digging her heels into the earth from the other side. I had a vivid picture of her tense, wrinkled face and knew it was a sin.

But what could I do, I sinned the moment I was born into the world with these thoughts in my head.

The ground around the graves was marked with holes — snake tracks.

"May I be punished if I am doing wrong!" I declared aloud. "May I be bitten by a snake and die."

But we had already finished weeding grandfather's grave and the snakes did not bite.

We suddenly had a sense of dread and ran off. Just before the gates, I looked back — among the bushes and gravestones, under the light of the pale moon a figure in a hat stood watching me. I jumped quickly over the fence, and didn't tell Arthur what I had seen.

We were in no hurry to get home and decided to make for the Sunzha. The moonlight was reflected on its turbulent surface, and the tired forest stared at us from the other side. We stripped to our trunks and decided to dive in.

Arthur went first — he was more resolute than me, and as a village boy it wasn't the first time he had done it. But I hesitated.

He was already swimming back towards me when I saw his appraising look.

"He won't jump! He won't dare!" his eyes seemed to be saying.

"May I be punished if I've done any wrong in this life!" I said to myself, took a running jump and pushed off from the bank.

After less than a second of flight I was in the water. It literally swallowed me, flooding into my nose, filling my mouth, pouring down my throat, and painfully burning my eyes. I came to the surface with difficulty, trying to cry out, but I could only make gurgling noises, which were instantly swallowed up by the river current. On the other bank, between the trees I saw the silhouette of the man in the hat. And the water swallowed me again.

ANOTHER CHANCE AT FAME

A small but heavy beast has crept into my stomach. It is placid and doesn't give me any trouble, except for being heavy. My stomach is gradually becoming detached from my body, starting to live its own life and I thought it was worth giving it one paragraph in this story.

Time passes painfully slowly when you are waiting for a girlfriend. Time seems to disappear completely. You sit and sit and the clock still says 15.45. You start walking up and down, to have something to do, you look at the clock, and the hand finally moves lazily to 15.46.

I was killing time like that in one of the halls of my university. For want of any other occupation, I went up to a board with wall newspapers. The main paper was richly illustrated and gave an account of an Arab evening, which had been "magical", at least that is what the text under the photographs said. I bent forward slightly with my hands behind my back, studied the faces of the evening's participants and read about their merits.

Students who were unremarkable on ordinary days turned out to be actors who "coped outstandingly with the difficult roles assigned to them", singers who "left the audience spellbound", and dancers who "brought a storm of applause". As always in this institution, the newspaper was full of false admiration. This endless sucking-up to such events was a debased toadying to the teachers. "Special mention should be made of the invaluable contribution made by the Faculty of Arabic Philology, and particularly by..." This wasn't exalted praise, it was debased, when fear takes the place of respect and one's own opinion gives way to the need to please.

These thoughts were teeming inside me, mixed with glances at the clock, when the head of the department came over to the stand. A short Jewish man of about sixty with a characteristic homosexual walk and unhealthily dry skin answered my greeting.

"So then, where are you here?" he said, studying the photographs from the Arab evening, "You're an Arabist, aren't you?!"

"I'm not there," I said, though it would have been in my interests to have been the hero of the evening. Despite my honest answer, he pointed at a boy dressed in a white Bedouin costume and asked:

"Isn't that you?"

"No. I was the... what do you call it?!" The word had slipped my mind. "I was the scriptwriter, that's it."

"Scriptwriter?!" he glanced at me skeptically.

"Um-hmm, the scriptwriter,." I went on lying brazenly and, for good measure, promised, "Next year I'll be the star of the evening. My photograph will be right here." I pointed at the very centre of the wall newspaper.

"Hee, hee," he laughed approvingly.

According to the rules of the genre, our conversation should have ended at that point, but the department head was feeling sociable and stayed, wanting to talk more. I thought this would be a good time to boast a little:

"Did you know, Serafim Mikhailovich, that some of my stories have been published in *Yunost* magazine. You may have heard of it?!"

"Of course I've heard of it. Critical stories, I should imagine?"

"Not about you," I joked subtly, and was rewarded by the laugh we all knew.

Then he said:

"Even if they were about me, so what?" Again he laughed. Still in a playful mood, he asked when my Arabic exam was.

"On the fourth," I answered.

"Are you ready?!"

"Yes. I mean to get a good pass!" I teased him.

"A good pass?! Hee, hee, hee. I would never say that about myself! Hee, hee, hee."

"If you don't believe in yourself, how can anyone else believe in you?" I countered.

Serafim Mikhailovich stepped back, still laughing, then turned around and strode off.

Now time, which had edged forward a little during our conversation, again stopped. I sat down and stared at a recommended text book.

I held the book in my hands and my eyes ran down the lines, but my head was thinking about time. I was unable to catch the meaning of the words so after a short struggle I slammed the book shut with irritation and left it for a better occasion.

Now, I think, we need a little action to liven up the narrative!

I slung my black bag over my shoulder, cast a last glance at the wall newspaper and made for the exit.

Outside, the month of May greeted me. A clean sky and clean air with a slight touch of dust from some reconstruction work on our faculty building, the most important red-brick wall in Russia after that of the Alexander Gardens by the Kremlin. Everything around me and I myself in the midst of it all was so insignificant and at the same time so significant. After looking around and finding no friends, because I have none, so it was senseless to look, I thrust my hands in my pockets and made for Okhotny Ryad.

The surroundings there had not changed at all since my last visit, but I decided to have a look around, to kill some time in idleness. Shops, shops, shops, cafes, shops, shops, cafes...

Walking around the air-conditioned shopping mall, I came little by little through the sensation of time, which was forced to retreat by the impenetrable armour of my resolve to wait it out. Backing away, as Serafim Mikhailovich had done a little earlier, time gradually moved forward, casting its minutes treacherously into the furnace of history.

Finally, she made contact.

"Hello, my love! I'm done!" She told me in a happy voice on the mobile. "Where are you?"

"I'm already at Okhotny! Come straight here!"

Our coordinates met at the entrance on the second floor, which leads straight into the underpass on one side and to the quartet of portly horses, splashing in the sounds of water, on the other side. Dasha pushed the red handle of the glass door and made for me with an airy smile on her face. We hugged each other tight, kissed and strolled slowly, hand in hand, through the inside of one of the ravines of civilised society.

"How are things, my love?" This question was the start to any conversation between us, and she nearly always exercised her right to ask it, getting another relaxed chat underway.

"Everything's OK! What about you?" I played along.

"Same..." I might have guessed.

We walked, each in our own thoughts, protected by each other, by our feelings for each other. I'd just had a first publication in a literary magazine, and I was thinking for the hundredth, maybe thousandth time about my chances of becoming a more or less decent writer. My plan consisted of several stages within two or maximum three years. But I fully realized how approximate, even unstable, the plan was: if just one stage didn't turn out as I fantasised it, then everything that followed from that stage would collapse like a house of cards.

We exchanged phrases as we passed shops with eye-catching window displays. I remember many smiles. It was one of those days when our faces were never without a smile, though I look fairly idiotic when I smile. It was one of those days when time stands still, so long as she is by my side.

She is quite small, with dark hair — catch up with me somewhere after lunch and I'm more than likely to be with her, if nothing changes in our way of life.

"Look at that dress! What awful fake gems!" Dasha points at a golden dress spangled with shiny stones.

"Uh-huh."

Suddenly I feel a pressure on my shoulder:

"Hey dude, what's up?" I look at her, and she smiles impishly, pretending that nothing unusual is happening.

She pushes me towards her favourite shop. I think she would go past it a hundred times a day if she could, and look inside a hundred times a day. But what might be surprising to some is that she rarely looks at anything for herself — only when I insist. As a rule she starts running around the men's department, with all the passion that a girl is capable of, usually choosing a new shirt for me.

"Oh no, dude," I laugh at her habit.

Unexpectedly her face turns serious:

"Why don't you want to put me in a good mood?! Don't you love your little Dasha anymore?!" She turns out her lower lip in a specific fashion.

"Of course I do," I say to her today, kissing her. But when I'm in a bad mood, I say, "Yes that's right, if you think it depends on whether I want to go shopping or not".

I'm in a good mood today, so we go into the English shop, Topshop, which opened not so long ago. Dasha immediately pulls away from me and starts to navigate alone. She runs up to one hanger, then another, feeling the various fabrics, studying the different colours and labels. Her face expresses the utmost concentration of which the human mind is capable.

I can barely keep up with her. My companion seizes one thing after another. She prefers bright but gentle colours: pink, turquoise, yellow. She occasionally makes comments, such as:

"Wow! Look at that!

By the time I have grasped which shirt she means and looked at it to form an opinion, she is already gone, and I see her in another part of the shop, looking at another shirt or tee-shirt or trousers and calling me urgently to take a look at it.

Finally her enthusiasm and the light in her eyes wane. Her pace slows, she calls me less often to look at the wares and I, also tired out by now, take her quietly by the hand, pretend to look at things, but move closer and closer to the exit, and finally pull her out behind me into the spacious halls of Okhotny Ryad.

We are at a loose end for a while, parked against the rail of one of the many balconies, with people walking across a marble floor beneath.

"My darling!" A swell of love hurls my girl against me, fastening her arms around my neck and compelling her to declare, "I love you so much."

We stand there for a while and then decide to walk up Tverskaya, to a Sberbank branch, to see whether her monthly stipend has shown up on her card.

I stopped getting any money from the state long ago. If you get a C on an exam, you lose your stipend. I lost mine because of Arab ethnography. Dasha is a far better student and gets her thousand and a bit regularly.

It was a sunny spring day. Leaf buds, green grass, all the things that inspire people, were in abundance. Not on Tverskaya, of course, but in the air. The air smelt of spring and encouraged a mood to match.

"What was his name, Cho Seung-Hui, was it?! You know, the one who massacred people in a university..." I began, thinking out loud.

"Yes, yes... that loony."

"No, he's no loony. I was thinking, what if I did the same?!"

Dasha spluttered, but I went on with my fantasy.

"Suppose they gave me a D for Arabic, I'd say to them, 'I haven't had anything from you but a bad face,' and the next day I'd come and shoot the lot of them."

"Ha-ha..."

"I'll start with the security men, then go upstairs, look into all the offices and shoot, shoot, shoot. I'll polish off the old bursar woman, then Serafim Mikhailovich, I'll shoot his secretary and then him. I'll say, 'Eat lead, you old queer! That's for corruption in the country's main university!'"

Well-bred Dasha frowns automatically at the word "queer". Bad words offend her ear, so I only use them in front of her when absolutely necessary.

"I'll pop in for a cup of tea with Chernogortsev! Then on to the faculty! 'Gulchara, you old hag, Adelia, you irresponsible cow, Mrolov, you bearded ape...' All of them, one after another. Their eyes will fill with horror, they'll beg for mercy, and I'll say something impressive like, 'The Fascist Jihad International Terrorist Group, of which I am the leader, has condemned you to death!' And I'll read a guilty verdict to each of them, if there's time, and if not I'll shove a note in their mouths."

"What are you on about?!" She laughs, knowing that I'm joking.

But I'm carried away and rush on like a hurricane, as if nothing can stop me:

"Why not, they all deserve to die! Well, OK, let's think what we'd get out of it..."

"That's where we should have started," says Dasha. "You'll be the talk of the town."

"That's what we need! I'll be top of the world news, just think?! Everyone will hate me, and a few, who knows, might understand. Cho killed himself, but I won't. I'll reap the rewards of my fame. I'll get life in prison, unless they make an exception and give me the death."

"People will read your stories!"

"Ah, yes! My stories, poems... I can imagine how people will study them, re-read them a hundred times and think about the motives..." I fall silent, thinking out the rest for myself.

There was money on Dasha's card. She instantly decided to spend it on a new shirt for me.

"No, no, no..." the world's biggest newsmaker played up, "I already have a pile of stuff to wear. I don't need clothes right now, enough!"

"So you really don't love me?!"

We kiss and go to the Metro. After a long good-bye, we part.

On the way home I decide that I'll have to kill her too, for the sake of completeness.

OLEG ZOBERN

Silent Jericho

Translated by Leo Shtutin

The Young Pioneer camp Red Pine near Moscow was slumbering in the predawn mist when, quietly, so as not to disturb the other kids in the dorm, the bugler from the third unit slipped on his T-shirt and shorts, put on his sandals, and deftly made his bed, plumping the pillow into a pyramid. He washed and smoothed down his mop of fair hair, stuck out his tongue at his reflection in the mirror, and went to the special room where important things were stored, such as banners, balls, pioneer ties, and a long bronze bugle, the pride of the camp — a quality trumpet used for signalling. The Young Pioneers all knew that its clear reveille would put you in a good mood for the rest of the day and drive away any bad dreams you might've had. Even the camp leaders believed this, and enlightened fresh intakes about the bugle.

The bugler unlocked the room with his own key on a string around his neck. The black velvet case was sitting in a special plywood recess next to the banner. The boy took out the instrument, carefully wiped it with a soft rag and hurried off to the mound in the middle of the camp from where the reveille would be clearly heard by all.

The sky beyond the far-off forest changed colour. Early birds were chirping. His sandals slapping the damp asphalt path, he sidestepped frogs and puddles with pink worms at the bottom — it had rained during the night. At the canteen he turned right, towards the second block, and brushed his suntanned knee against a wet nettle overhanging the balustrade. He had to stop and scratch the stung knee, now dotted with white blisters.

He walked past the sports ground, climbed up the mound, and sounded the call. In a few minutes the pioneers would come running out for morning exercises, looking respectfully at the bugler, and Vera from the fourth unit would give him a smile...

The bugler had had his eye on Vera for some time, only he didn't have the guts to speak to her, scared she might laugh at him. And tell her friends all about it.

Everyone agreed that Vera was the fittest girl this season. Olive-skinned, green-eyed, fiery-tempered, she'd won many a lad's heart, and even one camp leader's, but the bugler had one advantage over the rest: sounding reveille, lunch and tattoo was a mark of distinction. Some envied him — oh, he's a one, they'd say, a proper hero... Though it only seems easy, does bugling. No: you have to do it with feeling, especially the reveille. You've got to focus mentally, imagine the trumpet call resounding across the Land of the Soviets, echoed by other buglers in every Young Pioneer camp, soaring over fields and forests, over our beloved expanses, awakening everything and everyone, from the tiniest little critter to the General Secretary of the Communist Party.

As he made his way to the mound, the bugler realised it was time to declare his love for Vera. He'd take her aside in the canteen, go all red in the face and tell her that he —

"Can't keep tormenting myself like this," he thought. "'Course, I *am* a bugler, a pioneer leader. Doesn't mean I'm made of iron, though, does it. Even Party leaders've been in love, they say. So I'll go up to her and —" He didn't know what words he should use, he only felt he had to keep his fear in check and make a decisive move, even in the face of potential humiliation.

He clambered up onto the mound, fixed his tie, gulped in as much morning air as his lungs could hold, and sounded the call. The birds went quiet, and the sky was suddenly shrouded in black clouds that floated in from God knows where. The bugler was taken aback, but carried on. The sun, it seemed, had changed its mind about rising and hung beyond the forest, its murky crimsons bleeding into the grey sky.

No Young Pioneers came out for morning exercises, while the camp's living quarters disintegrated before his eyes. Glass shattered, plasterwork peeled away, asphalt paths cracked open. The plaster Party leader flaked and tilted over in front of the boarded-up entrance to the canteen, the parade ground became overgrown with grass, and the heroic granite memorial among the bushy firs was vandalized by summer cottagers.

The bugler finished sounding reveille and listened. Not a sound. He inspected his bugle which for some reason had lost its sheen. He'd polished it to a mirror-like shine only recently, but now the bugle was suddenly become lustreless and speckled with greenish rust, as if it hadn't been used for years.

The mound also seemed to have shrivelled under his feet. The bugler came down onto the path, approached the flung-open door to the fourth unit where Vera should have been, and peered cautiously inside. In places the floor was rotten through, rusty beds lay overturned, some rags were scattered about, the white paint on the ceiling had flaked and cracked; all that remained of the lavatory pans was pink ceramic stumps sticking out of the floor.

"Vera, Ve-era," the bugler called quietly, holding back tears. "Anyone in here?"

A draught rustled the torn and yellowing pages of a Politizdat brochure on the floor.

Figuring out what to do proved hard and painful: five minutes ago the guys, the camp leaders, Vera, they were all here... Where'd they all get to? Who'd take him home? His parents had no idea what'd happened here.

Still hoping someone was there to hear him, he yelled even louder into the building's damp emptiness:

"Guys! He-e-y, guys!!!"

No answer.

He squatted down, leaning against the rough wall, and put the bugle down.

He felt cold.

He wrapped his arms round his knees.

It started spitting, raindrops pitter-pattering evenly on the tin window ledge.

A crow cawed revoltingly...

For a moment the bugler was on the verge of legging it out of the camp, but then he thought Vera might still be around. "Though if there's no one here," he reasoned, "Vera must've gone too."

He began to cry, feeling his tears drip down on to his frozen knees. He sat like that for a good long time. Then it occurred to him that Vera would be taken aback. A bugler was supposed to be a brave Young Pioneer, and there he was, crying.

He got to his feet and picked up the bugle.

And decided to get away from the ruins.

From the road he glanced back at the blue metal gates of Red Pine, wiped his nose and set off.

He remembered that after exiting the motorway they had driven through a forest, then past a big state farm, after which the road meandered through the forest again, right up to the camp. He was having fun then, in the bus with the other kids, and had hardly looked out of the window. These details just randomly stuck in his mind, the forest and the state farm — was it Sunrise? There'd been a brick road-sign with radiating scarlet rays made out of painted steel above the name of the state farm.

He decided to keep walking till he met someone he could ask how to get home.

Soon he was soaked. Dirty stains sprawled on his white knee-highs, his damp shorts and T-shirt provided no warmth. The trees lining the road rustled, the rain came in dribs and drabs. The bugle under his arm felt cold. Shame to throw it away, though, it wasn't just any old trumpet after all. True, it was heavy, it slowed him down, and yet without his bugle he wasn't a bugler, but God knows who.

When he was completely frozen he stopped to sound a call. Maybe this would perk him up? The trumpet made no sound. He plodded on, sandals squelching.

When the rain stopped, walking became a bit easier, and he seemed to have more strength. He felt thirsty. He chose the clearest puddle he could find by the roadside, with pebbles and dark leaves on the bottom, bent down, and lapped up some water. He saw his reflection and suddenly realised that he had grown up.

He didn't want to grow up, but his boyish face had coarsened, the fluff on his chin had grown into stubble, and his shorts, too tight for his muscled thighs, ripped as he was getting up. He kicked off his tight sandals, pulled off his dirty knee-highs. Going barefoot was easier. The bronze bugle now felt lighter and smaller.

"I'm growing," he thought, ready to set off again, "but where should I head now? I've not even got to the state farm yet. Really need to bump into someone before it gets dark, find out about the way... And I'm hungry."

The bugler's thoughts were more grown-up now, he was aware of getting smarter, his head felt heavier. He looked around: what else do I need to know? He counted the young spruces at the roadside to the left:: eighteen.

The grey asphalt ribbon of the forest-flanked road turned

and stretched on towards the horizon. There was a noise in the bushes, it sounded like someone crashing through the branches.

The bugler stopped, grabbing the bugle by one end so he could wallop any nasty piece of work. Might be robbers. He remembered the ten-rouble note he had in his back pocket. His parents had given it to him before sending him off to the camp. He took out the twice-folded red tenner with the portrait of a squint-eyed Lenin and clutched it in his fist.

There was a hubbub behind the trees, then, pushing through the wet bushes, a lanky lad in a track suit with a big green box on a strap emerged onto the road.

The bugler had seen him somewhere before...

The lad approached and held out a hand:

"Hi, bugler, so our paths have crossed. I remember how you used to sound the call back when we was kids – top man..." He put his box down on the road. "What you traipsin' all barefoot for, though?"

"Oh, you know, I've grown out of my sandals," the bugler said, then remembered: this was Lyokha from the same unit at the summer camp, the buddy with whom he had gone for secret evening swims in the river and smoked cigarettes; they had both been in love with Vera.

"Lyokha, I didn't recognize you. You're proper tall now, got a whole head on me. So many years..."

"...'ve gone by," agreed Lyokha, looking around. "I've lost my way a bit. Headed for the marshlands first, but nothing doing, all staked off there." He shook off some leaves stuck to his jacket. "I was busy here in the pine grove, then... never mind. Time for me to start a new life, get back onto the straight an' narrow. Now we can go together. How d'*you* get here?"

"I sounded reveille, and everything just started falling apart."

"It happens," sighed Lyokha. "I see you've got your bugle with you. Heraldin' your pioneer's joy just like before, are you?"

"Nah, I'm just carrying it. Shame to chuck it."

The bugler was happy to meet a friend: he'd got sick of walking on his own. It'd be easier together. Looking at Lyokha, he remembered his childhood, the camp, Vera. He felt relieved and noticed that everything didn't look all that gloomy any more. Nature, forest air. Wouldn't hurt to get hold of some shoes, though.

"How's Vera doing, d'you know?" he asked.

Lyokha smiled wryly and scratched the back of his head:

"She's workin' in the Diversion Service. Hob-nobbin' with darkies*, the bint. I did warn 'er. She was after the glamorous life, but there ain't no glamour there."

The bugler looked absentmindedly into the distance, where it had brightened up a bit with a sliver of blue sky.

Lyokha picked up his box, and they set off.

Soon the forest thinned out and was gone. Endless fields stretched on either side of the road and in the dry grass they could make out the circles of fresh tree stumps.

"Look at that," Lyokha nodded at a pile of sawdust. "Forest around here was top class, now it's a wasteland. Nothin' growing."

The bugler was surprised: "Where's all the trees?"

"Went into Finnish paper. You know, all nice and smooth, like. And what's more, we're basically giving it away. In return for spirits and exotic bric-a-brac. Let's stop for a bit, need to send a signal."

"You what?"

"I'll explain," said Lyokha, putting the box down on the

---

* Approximation of "cherniye" (literally "blacks"), a highly derogatory term for Caucasians and Central Asians.

ground. "We're travellin' together, right, so we need to send communications to the Future Controller."

The bugler remembered that he'd already heard from someone about the Future Controller. Or maybe he'd not heard about him, but figured things out for himself.

"We need to send regular communications so as the Future Controller doesn't get upset," Lyokha took out a canvas bag from the green box, which turned out to be a big military two-way radio. "Give 'im detailed reports. 'Bout everything."

He switched on the contraption, picked up the receiver and adjusted a shiny dial. The radio started to hiss, the instrument pointers trembled.

Suddenly Lyokha yelled so loudly that the bugler jumped.

"Can you 'ear me all right?! Yeah?! I've run into the bugler! Yep, bugle's on him! On his way! Ain't got no shoes, though, gaddin' about barefoot. Should give some out to 'im! ... What d'you mean, ain't none left?! That's no go, autumn's around the corner!"

The bugler felt uneasy that the Controller disapproved of his bare feet, and gestured to say: No need, I'll do without shoes.

Lyokha paid no attention and carried on yelling:

"Yeah! Yeah! Can't do without shoes, can he! There will?! When? A stiff?! Perfect! No, hold on, forest's all gone 'ere... Yep, all of it!"

As he was putting the radio back in the bag after the communication session, Lyokha happily announced:

"We'll get some off a stiff. Officer's leather boots. What you starin' at me like that for? Controller said there'll be a stiff lyin' further on somewhere. No good to him now, his boots! And you need some pants and a jacket too. Don't worry, we'll get you dressed. Man up, mate."

"Who is this Controller?" the bugler asked.

"The bulwark of the workers. Capable commander, unanimously elected to control."

"Maybe we shouldn't be taking boots off a corpse?" the bugler said doubtfully. "I've got money, we can buy some. Look here."

Lyokha smirked. "Think *that's* money? You're a bit late, can't buy nothin' with that. They've changed it, d'you understand? So chuck away your tenner, you won't be needin' it."

The bugler crumpled up his tenner and threw it into the grass.

He remembered his parents and felt homesick.

"You know, Lyokha, I kind of want to go home... my folks're prob'ly worried about me..." he said.

"You ain't got no parents," Lyokha replied flatly. "You ain't got no one. You're alone. I don't count. No home neither. So there. We'll keep going, you and me, we'll keep sending our signals to the Bulwark-Controller and with a bit of luck things'll sort 'emselves out."

The bugler's face darkened. "How's that then — completely alone? What about my parents... Surely, people are born, which means others have to... I'm a grown-up now," he thought. "Still, something's not quite right. Maybe I just don't have enough knowledge?"

"Am I smart, Lyokha? What d'you reckon?"

"Everybody's smart, in their own way. You can play. Right, do the call for lunch, it's time."

The bugler did so, and Lyokha fished a paper bag with some cheese sandwiches out of his inside pocket.

They ate.

Then set off again. While the bugler counted cumulus clouds and the stumps in the field, Lyokha told him about his peregrination, his failed early marriage, and also about the election of the workers' Bulwark. How the masses finally grew exhausted, spontaneously self-organised in the hope of an easy life, and nominated the Bulwark as Controller. It turned out that Lyokha was hand in glove with the Bulwark, he'd met him during his forest tribulations, hence his familiarity during communication sessions.

The bugler even cheered up a bit: things wouldn't go astray with Lyokha around — well, at least not straight away.

He didn't long to go home any more. What'd be the point if there was nobody there?

Meanwhile, up ahead of them, in the field, some huts had materialised. They were scattered anyhow, almost at random.

They drew near.

The huts were empty, boarded up; next to one a grey nanny goat with intelligent eyes was grazing. When they came closer it stopped munching grass, raised its head and looked up: who's coming?

They decided to knock on the door, find out if the owner was in, then report to the Bulwark-Controller. "He has to know everything," said Lyokha, "for our own good. We're workers too, in our own way."

The bugler stepped up onto the decrepit porch and knocked.

No answer. He pushed the door open and got a fright. In the hall, feet facing the threshold, lay a body dressed in a German army uniform from the Second World War. Big leather boots caught the bugler's eye.

"Lyokha, the stiff's in here!" he shouted.

Lyokha came in, gave the body the once over.

Black uniform with embroidered silver eagles and lightning bolts. Severe face, arrogant expression. Massive jaw, big pale eyes open. A note on the chest. Lyokha took the note and read aloud:

"Take that, you Fascist bastard, it'll teach you to gorge

yourself on McDonald's, take that, you scum, this is what you get for scaring us. The Ryazan Scouts."

"Who?" the bugler asked, confused.

"The Scouts are kind of like Young Pioneers, modern kids. See what they get up to. Thing is, the krauts' manner ain't to their taste, specially their marchin' style. Right, get his boots off." Lyokha grabbed the body under the armpits so it wouldn't drag on the floor.

The bugler pulled the leather boots off the corpse's feet and put them on. The dead man's service coat went over his T-shirt. All he needed now was to change out of his ripped blue shorts into some pants. But they left the fascist's trousers alone.

"It was with their rebukes that they finished him off — can you see, there ain't no wounds on the body," said Lyokha. "We've got to report this to the Bulwark-Controller."

They brought the radio into the hut.

Tuned in.

Gave their report: the hut's empty. Only an old pedal-operated Singer sewing machine in the otherwise vacant icon corner. It's unclear who lived here. Maybe the Fascist (they're not fussy), maybe someone else.

"Let's go," said Lyokha, "we've got loads of stuff ahead of us, no use stickin' round here with the stiff."

They got twenty yards or so away from the hut.

"He-ey, he-ey," someone called out behind them.

They looked round.

It was the goat bleating.

Lyokha went back, untied the animal, gave it a green apple (he had *everything* squirreled away), and the goat bolted down this offering right off his hand.

The further they went, the livelier their surroundings became. In the field they came across cooperative kiosks and whole villages with live workers. Their road intersected with other roads, passersby appeared — normal ones, like anywhere else.

The bugler started counting and memorising everyone he saw, just in case, for the report, but Lyokha said there was no need to give such detailed accounts.

People gazed at the travellers in surprise, even pointed at them: Look at the fascist, now that's a sight and a half (in his service coat the bugler was taken for a kraut)! Where'd he blow in from?

It started to get dark.

They had reached some big buildings, citizens scurrying about, car horns blaring.

It became hard to breathe, as if there wasn't enough air.

They sat down on the pavement, next to a shop window with a lingerie display. From out of nowhere, security appeared, telling them to beat it.

They trudged on and came upon a small park. They wandered among the benches, peered in bins. Collected bottles. Lyokha said they could turn them in, get some money for grub and vodka.

When they'd filled two cloth bags (Lyokha had bags on him too), some local hobos showed up in the park. Sling yer hook, they said, this is our site, so get yer dirty mitts off what ain't yours.

They wanted to take the bags with the bottles, but Lyokha said he'd report this abuse to the Controller, and the hobos admitted defeat.

They went to the nearest drop-off point to turn in the bottles. Didn't make it in time. Now they'd have to wait till tomorrow. Lyokha thought for a bit and suggested they head to the nearest church, beg from workers. Not too late to go there.

They picked up the radio, the bugle, the jangling bags, took a backstreet route to the church. They sat down on the porch next to two little old women in black, who began mumbling grumpily.

"Take it easy, grannies," Lyokha soothed them, "there'll be enough alms to go round."

The bugler hid the bugle inside his jacket.

He had the impression that he'd got a little older still, and he'd grown a beard (he ran his fingers through it.) Lyokha had too. He was gazing devoutly at passersby and bleating like that goat he'd treated to an apple:

"Go-o-od people, spa-a-are a little cha-a-ange..." And coppers started dropping into his palm, till there was enough for some bread and vodka.

A car pulled up to the church.

From the passenger door emerged a priest in a blue cassock, and solemnly made his way to the clergy house.

The bugler looked and saw a beautiful sad Angel hovering over him. The Angel bowed its head to the priest and said:

"Sell your new car, father, and deal the money out to the poor..."

Awed by this unearthly beauty, the bugler got out his bugle and played a salute to the Angel.

"Stop it," said Lyokha, cutting him short.

They hung about on the church porch a bit longer, then went to the shop. They bought some rye bread, a packet of mayo, and some vodka.

They reported what they'd seen to the Controller. The Controller was pleased.

They went to sleep in the basement of a multi-storey building.

The bugler sounded tattoo.

Crickets chirped in the basement throughout the night.

In the morning they turned in the bottles and aged about ten years more. They also felt more feeble.

And so began a procession of tattered days, each one like

all the others. Autumn arrived, then the first snow flurries. The German uniform got worn out, so the bugler picked out some warm pants for himself at a dump, also a decent padded jacket.

They kept tramping about, ridden with lice, but unfailingly got into contact with the Bulwark-Controller, reporting on how things were going and what successes had been achieved and by whom, until one day the Controller disappeared. Lyokha called him again and again, shouted out call signs, but all to no avail.

The bugler sounded tattoo, and they chucked away the unwieldy radio set, seeing as there was no use for it now, though it did pain them to do so. After all, it's hard to get used to the thought that no one's there to control you any more, and that your whole life's of no interest to anyone.

A year after the Controller's disappearance some Ryazan Scouts appeared in town. They prowled the streets in studded leather, chains, and knuckledusters. They hounded good people and left the bad ones alone. So the bugler and Lyokha holed up in an empty well.

One spring day they sat on a bench in the park. The bugler played, Lyokha listened. Some underage gopniks* walked past. There was no one around, so the gopniks set about duffing them up. Decked 'em, kicked 'em, took the bugle off the bugler.

"Prob'ly found it in the dump, the dick'ead," said one gopnik.

"Let's flog it to a scrap dealer, innit," another replied.

The gopniks walked off, taking the bugle with them.

The bugler picked himself up, wiped his nose, spat out broken teeth, helped Lyokha to his feet. And, propping each other up, they trudged off towards the sound of angels' voices, to the place where all Soviet people disappear to.

---

* Social delinquents; similar to U.K. "chavs"

YUNA LETTS

Translated by Muireann Maguire

THE SANDBANK

He'd been sitting in the galley for three hours now, his face in his hands. He did not move and only the nervous shudders of his head betrayed that he was awake. That night, the man had lost everything. He had lost his beloved job, and with it he lost the crimson and violet sunsets, the smell of the ocean, his ringside seat to watch performances by amorous whales, and all the manifestations of the sky. He had despoiled the beauty of his own world. He had suffered the greatest indignity that can befall a captain: he had lost the respect of his crew. About once every half-hour a black sailor came to see him, shame-facedly asking for orders, since there was no other commander aboard. Then even this stopped. Shcherbich realized that someone up on deck was now carrying out his duties.

The ship lay on a sandbank, listing slightly to one side. Its blackish-red hull glittered decoratively in the sunlight, attracting a horde of birds. The *Sefean* had beached the evening before. After slicing like a knife through the sandy beach, the ship's metal hulk had lodged squarely in the centre of the national park, a UNESCO world heritage site. The ship had scared off the park's fish and made short work of the coral reefs, which tour guides loved to show to tourists taking them round on boats with transparent bottoms.

Shcherbich sat quite still in the galley. Only his hand moved occasionally, reaching out for the brandy bottle and smoothly decanting it into a glass with a picture of a bee. The contents of the glass splashed into his mouth, his lips smacked exactly twice, and his body once again settled into motionlessness. Pangs of conscience, like hungry piranhas, gnawed mercilessly at his insides; self-pity took possession of the former captain. "It's a tough challenge, fate is trying to break me," Shcherbich thought and dug his nails into the table in panic.

Ecologists, journalists, local officials, and vagrants crowded around the ship, thrilling to the news or the spectacle. What had happened felt like an omen, a portent that could bode good or ill. The ship lay on the sand like a bird that had flown into a window, a plump pigeon that had broken its beak on the glass. Everyone there hated and feared it, everyone wanted to be rid of this huge old tub that had scattered the park's fish.

The journalists blamed the incident on the wind, which had whipped up a storm at sea, and the ocean, obeying the law of emetics, had vomited up foreign organisms. That was what the papers said. In reality, the blame fell elsewhere. The blame belonged to the man now sitting in the galley and drinking brandy from a glass with a picture of a bee; the cause for what had happened lay inside him. The night before, when the boat went off course and the waves swiftly carried it directly onto the national park's precious coral reefs, the captain had been lounging on the couch in the wheel-house, entranced by the sight of extraordinary creatures. He should have seen the coast they were being carried toward, but he looked elsewhere – he was watching wonders.

Shcherbich sent another glass of brandy down the hatch and looked timidly at his mobile phone, jumping in convulsions on the table-top. He recognised the number of the boat's owner who was doubtless beside himself with fury. There was no question what he had to say. This would be about it:

"You son of a bitch, Alexander Petrovich. We've worked together a long time, but now you've really messed it up, you've made a terrible blunder that will cost a lot of people their livelihoods. Natanich won't be able to pay for his daughter's university education, because he won't have a job. Ivan Petrovich will have to kiss his dream of a country cottage and bathhouse goodbye. This isn't just about the old tub getting washed up; the lives of twenty friends have been wrecked. Alexander Petrovich, you've let us all down. Ask your men to forgive you and get lost".

Lulled by the vibrations and his own suffering, Shcherbich leaned his head on the table and grew still. Once again the vast fairytale dream began spinning in his head. The former captain had a vision of gigantic hares with raspberry-flavoured candy floss oozing from holes in their bodies. They walked on water, like gods, collecting curious birds in enormous bags. The birds pecked holes in the bags and flew away to freedom, only to be caught once again in the bag of a giant hole-filled hare. This cycle continued endlessly, allowing no chance of escape, no matter how many times the captain drowned the hares and rescued the birds.

At least one day went by, and a new evening arrived, entirely different from the one before. The boat no longer glittered; it lay peacefully on the sand, merging with the colours of everything around it. And around it were sand, water and also a few multicoloured caps of black sailors who had climbed out for a smoke on the shore. While all of nature filled up with darkness and freshness, in the lighted, stuffy galley of one Russian boat someone's eye rolled open and blinked. Shcherbich wiped spittle from his lip, glanced around and couldn't figure out what he was doing there. A few moments later the stunning knowledge of reality would come back to him, meanwhile he brushed himself down and started munching the sauerkraut which was always there in a glass bowl on the table. He both liked and disliked the sauerkraut: it was nice but honest. As he ate, Shcherbich recalled what had happened to his ship the day before, and his agony recommenced.

The young cook appeared in the galley. He glanced indifferently at the glass bowl, where the sauerkraut had once been, at the brandy, finally at the captain, and said: "I don't know what's going on in your head, but to gobble up all the sauerkraut is pretty rude, Petrovich."

The former captain raised his eyes to the cook and lightning shot from them, as if from the trident of a pagan god. Then he remembered the hares, spooked himself, calmed down and said:

"Oleg, dammit, you'd better get out of here, OK? Go on now."

Shcherbich waved his sleeve at the door and reached for the bottle to pour the last drops of alcohol into his glass. The cook looked on with no intention of leaving.

"Petrovich, now you've really messed it up."

A seagull flew past the window, loudly screeching about some problem of its own. The cook went on standing by the wall with a crafty smile, then he said:

"Okay then, enough kidding around. I have some news for you, Petrovich, happy news, you might call it. There's no sandbank."

For another minute the captain didn't move, but then he raised his head and, naturally, queried:

"No sandbank?"

"No. And there never was one."

Shcherbich sat down and once again covered his face with his hands. The cook let him be. The not-yet-former captain energetically wiped his eyes, flattened his hair, stood up, flung the door open, and was gone. He wasn't seen again anywhere in these parts. Two days later the boat's owner flew in, called the crew together, and asked:

"You all rang me up by turns, but I didn't understand a thing. What collision, what corals? ...And I also want to know, what's happened to Alexander Petrovich? He's not answering his phone."

The young cook rose:

"Two days ago I talked to Shcherbich. He told me he was seeing visions of giant hares dripping candy-floss. But, you know, the way it is at sea, we all have dreams about them."

"Too right", the sailors seconded him.

"The hares attacked us, and then we hit the sand bank, there were some beaches, journalists, corals. That was a bit strange, because we usually have peaceful visions, about singing pumpkins, pickled hats, athletic worms... And now this sandbank. We were very frightened, and Petrovich even ran off somewhere on the shore. I think he'll calm down and come back. Well, because of what's happened, we want to ask a favour... Can you forbid the men to read newspapers and magazines? The ocean is an open space after all, out here any thought can turn into a trance..."

The owner sighed with relief and said loudly:

"So that's what the matter was. Well, we've finally figured it out. Okay then, is everyone listening to me? Reading newspapers is forbidden! Anyone reading them will be fined."

"Understood!" responded the sailors.

The owner shook everyone's hand and left. The sailors chatted among themselves a little longer, and then went to their cabins, bolted their doors and got under their blankets. This was because it was much more interesting when the bug-eyed fairies and big-eared lamps flew into your cabin through the porthole...

THE MISSIONS EXCHANGE

A street. The central square. On the stage, a singer is making an indistinct din; a concert is going on. Children flushed with seasonal colour goggle wide-eyed, jumping up to have a good look. The spice-seller's body bulges out of his tidy stall festooned with garlic braids; on regular days, civilized people who have forgotten how to sneeze greedily snap up his spices. But today is an unusual day; not a single enlightened face is to be found here. Today is an unusual day, and therefore the spices lie on the shelves unsold in their boxes, therefore the singer makes her whining din, and everything around is preparing the audience for an act of spontaneous courage.

People are constantly arriving, by foot and on wheels. The steaming valves of petrol pumps tick loudly. Long-haired onlookers and rectangular muscle-men stride up and down showily, waiting. Their faces show a host of emotions, with half as many again inside, saved for later. As they wait, they shift from foot to foot in time with each other. The overall effect is a sort of dance, but not a ritual one; it is a brand-new, wholly vital creation. At a distance from this enthusiasm some girls are standing: they are tender, smooth-skinned, made of yoghurt and spice and all things nice. Special ionized zones have been provided for them here; in these, they stand in rows, discussing something vitally important:

"I have my own opinion, and I would like to voice it. This is what I say: that kind of person has gone out of fashion. That's my view," says one.

"Of course, but what kind of fashion is this? A straight, elongated pillar with its arms hanging down. Completely tasteless. Why don't we ask for curved, designer body shapes?"

"I agree. This shape has too many straight lines. It won't do. Let's ask for something new!"

"Let's!" they shout in unison, shaking their protruding hairdos firmly in time with the non-ritual dance, which was still captivating the enthusiastic audience.

The soles of thick, strong-toed boots slap precisely on the ground. Dapper Mr Cloak steps up to a free counter.

"I'd like a wonder-shadow", he says, bringing his round head closer to the ear of the *mademoiselle*, who wears an intricate lace headdress.

"They'll bring new ones in the evening. You want one all the same?" the *mademoiselle* asks.

"That'll suit me", announces Cloak in a thick voice and waits as she wraps it up for him.

He smokes cautiously, so as not to scorch himself.

"Here you go," she says, handing him a small parcel, as though it were a baby.

Cloak leaves a voice print and walks away, stamping his boots.

For several more hours nothing changes on the square then the main part of the spectacle suddenly begins. People with glass suitcases of unheard-of sizes come out onstage, they act out all sorts of sketches and distribute envelopes to the audience, checking information about them against their voice prints, stored carefully in their database. The noise becomes indescribable, everyone is laughing and celebrating bawdily. They go on like this for three days without stopping. The envelopes cannot be opened until everyone has received one. And when the suitcases are empty, when everyone has in his hand a parcel with a monogram, the hymn to humanity breaks out. Then everyone tears open their envelopes and discovers their mission for the next thousand days...

Now they are unsealing them:

"I'm going to cultivate rice!"

"I'm an astronomer!"

"I'll be building a ship!"

"I'll have a laboratory!"

"I'll learn to drive!"

Some grin, others grumble, but many are transported by the message written inside, they jump and roar, like fishes. People feel content and reassured. People know where they stand. And if someone is unsatisfied with his lot, he can take himself off immediately to the Missions Exchange and request some new goal for himself, specifying his inclinations and wishes.

The hubbub and singing continue for a long time, and then the fourth night comes, and people wander off to their model houses, in order to get a good night's sleep before the new era. All are soon snoring soundly in their beds; only one of the yoghurt girls is still not asleep and close to her Mr Cloak isn't sleeping either. They don't even want to think about sleep, and instead they are sitting on the edge of the town and inventing love. This was not written in their envelopes, and so one might say that they are breaking the rules. Even though there are no rules at all here, the rules of good behaviour remain.

"You're such a nice girl," says Cloak. "I like to touch you and I like it when you breathe in my ear, when we're lying together."

"You interest me as well, and I love profiteroles too."

"How would it be if we lived in one house, you and me, and always had fresh profiteroles in the fridge?"

"But nobody does that. People sleep in narrow houses, like gods in tombs, and this custom is passed on from generation to generation."

"But we'll be like one person, except that we'll be a Pair. We'll call this Pairanoia, and someday we'll have children and we will be a Family."

"I like the idea. Tomorrow we can go to the Missions Exchange and tell them what we want to do. We'll take some profiteroles with us, and from now on every couple who wishes to live in a narrow house like one person will have to feed each other profiteroles in public. This will be their vow to each other."

"You've come up with a wonderful plan!" said Cloak, drawing his yoghurt girl closer as she tenderly blew in his ear.

The town grew quiet and rolled up into a profiterole lshape. The new people were excitedly inventing a new world for themselves: joyful, good, enduring. Planet Air danced a figure of eight in front of the sun. The planet, like a secret cloud, was fidgeting in anticipation of its discovery. But the people weren't hurrying anywhere. From their earth-born ancestors, they had one inborn memory. If they knew only one thing for sure, they knew there was no need to hurry.

They spent a little longer admiring the concert of lights in the sky, and then Cloak cautiously tucked her into his nighttime wonder-shadow.

"I'd like to propose that you... Let's do it together today."

"I'm willing," she answered shyly.

"Three, four – Atchoo!"

The inventors of love drank their fill of each other's breath and soon fell asleep, happy on the soft shore of air.

THE LITTLE FLOWER FROM THE HOLLOW

S he is a little girl. She lies in her room on her thin little bed and listens to the television through the wall. She would like to be there now, in the next room, watching this funny programme, just to be there, where the light is, and her parents are, and the sound of whispers; but she is lying here on her thin little bed. She is supposed to be asleep. But Mila can't sleep right now, she's a child after all, what kind of child can sleep at nine in the evening, when the television is blaring through the wall? She certainly can't. Mila dreams. She imagines that the wall is super-wide, with a little home for her inside it. But what sort of home? Something like a tree-hollow. Mila thinks about living in this hollow and watching the television in her parents' room through a crack. That's her fantasy.

She would hide there, too, so that nobody could find her. Everyone would hunt high and low, and Mila wouldn't be anywhere. She'd be in the wall. She would sit in her little home and giggle. No-one could find her. And then she'd cautiously come out and hide somewhere in the wardrobe, as though she'd been there all the time. She doesn't want anyone to find out about the hollow in the wall. It's her secret; the others can find their own hollows.

That was what Mila thought, when she was a child of six, and now she is twenty-six and she has just recovered consciousness. She is lying with tangled hair, and around her, just like angels, people in carnival costumes are flying. People in white gowns — apparently doctors. Little has changed since she swallowed that fluid. Mila had thought that she would feel better, that she would fly back to those days when passersby could speak with their facial expressions, when games had a happy ending, and a large sweet could put you in a good mood for an entire day. These days too she has lots of sweets, but they aren't of chocolate and don't have a praline inside. They are made from flesh and conscious thought. These are human sweets, sweets made of people. She sculpts them with her hands, then gobbles them. She loves eating so much. Mila should now be completely content. There are dozens of sweets around her, and she lives in the little wall.

This is just the way she dreamed it. All around her there are walls with only small holes in them through which she can see a large room where a television is switched on. The programmes it shows aren't funny, but at least they're on. This is what she wanted: to be in the little wall. And now here she is. Around the hollow are concrete slabs or dry-faced people — and no-one is able to find her there.

"Here I am!" she calls.

No one can see her. She no longer remembers how to get out. But from time to time she tries to understand. She tried again just now.

"Do you have relatives, friends?" the old man in the white fool's cap asks. "Whom should we phone?"

Mila shrugs. There's no-one. Why should there be? She has spent her whole life in the little wall. No-one ever found her here. She didn't find herself here either.

Hands drag her out of the hollow and carry her off. Mila is driven through the town in a square car. The sun is shining, the radio is playing. She could drive like this forever; she doesn't want to go back into the hollow. But the hollow lures her back every time, every single time. The last time she found herself there completely unexpectedly. She was in a small shop downtown, arranging flowers; they paid her eight dollars an hour. It wasn't much, but she didn't need much. Mila ate rarely, lived in a room on the edge of the town and only spent money on beads. So there she stood among the flowers, wearing beads, and one day that man walked into the shop, precise and even-tempered, wearing a boa-constrictor costume. He fixed his eyes on hers and said: "May I buy this flower?"

"Which one?" Mila queried.

"The most extraordinary one of them all."

The man's gaze was hungry.

"I didn't think boa constrictors ate flowers," Mila remarked, innocently.

"Civilised boa constrictors eat nothing else," said the artist, completing his brilliant performance.

Later, of course, they lay in his bedroom, where the wallpaper was peeling off the walls. He was a sweet in a boa-constrictor wrapper. That was how she thought of him, and she carelessly savoured his flavour for a few years more. And then there was nothing left of him except the wrapper, nothing at all. An empty wrapper. Mila crumpled the wrapper, played with it a little longer and walked out of the flat. She walked and walked through the city, wondering where her favourite sweet had gone, she walked and walked and suddenly found herself in the hollow. She didn't remember exactly how it happened. But at a certain moment she felt there were walls around her and it had become dark, and in the crack there was also darkness, and in the room next door the light was off. So she sat with closed eyes, until they took her for a drive through the town in the square car.

They drive and drive, the sun is shining, the radio is playing, and the colourful face of the man in the doctor's costume is smiling at her. Mila feels peaceful and happy.

"Do you think boa constrictors eat flowers?" she asks.

"Well, usually snakes swallow mammals and other vertebrates."

"But do flowers eat boa constrictors?"

"That's hard to say."

"Well, I'll tell you: flowers do eat boa constrictors, bees, rabbits, tigers, and lions. And guess why? Because flowers eat sweets. All people are sweets. But some of them are flowers, all the same."

"Mila, you ought to sleep now."

She turned on her side, to study his face.

"Could you sing to me?"

"Sing?"

"Yes, something pretty."

"I don't have a good ear for music."

"All right then. I'll sing to you."

"It's a deal."

The sun was shining, the radio was playing, the man in the carnival cap was smiling. Mila drove through town in the square car, singing her favourite song: "I'll dress up like a flower, and I'll go find bees." Unhurriedly, the city flicked over pictures of its buildings; outside the window, trolleybuses hooted and hawkers were bawling; the town was alive. The town was alive, the town is alive, but Mila seems to be leaving this town. Her heart is no longer beating.

But this means nothing. She had wanted to leave for so long. And now she seems to have managed it. She is a small girl and around her are many people. And they're looking at her, waving their hands, calling greetings. They're not welcoming a little flower, they're welcoming Mila.

"Do you know the song I always sing?" she asks.

"Of course," they say, "It's a pretty song, and we all know it."

They started singing the song, and Mila joined in. They made a pleasant choir, harmonic and enduring. They are singing there still. I promise. You can hear them if you put your ear to the wall.

IRINA GLEBOVA

Translated by Carol Yermakova

WHAT HAPPENED TO THE ENGINEER

It is no secret that strange and mysterious incidents occur in our ordinary, everyday lives, and that human reason is powerless to explain them. A ship vanishes in the Bermuda triangle, or a UFO with efficient humanoids on board suddenly flies in out of the blue and then just as suddenly flies off. Incidents like these generally stand out sharply against the regular rhythm of normal daily life, and often are a strong influence on the subsequent fate of both eye witnesses and those directly involved; the door into the Unknown is nudged ajar for an intrigued human race.

One of these remarkably curious incidents occurred one day in the life of Victor Andreyevich N., an engineer turned businessman. This event was utterly inexplicable and certainly flew in the face of all common-sense reasoning.

A mouse appeared in the midst of the former engineer's family. Now how could a mouse appear in a city flat on the sixteenth floor? Certainly it could if mice had already turned up in other flats in the same block, or in the cellar or attic. Or if the people living in the flat were slovenly boozers who came home in the early hours bawling pop songs and staggering around as a result of their immoral lifestyle, and then set about guzzling handfuls of two-day-old buckwheat porridge straight from the pan, dropping half of it on the floor and gazing at the cobwebs festooning the walls, their eyes dull from depravity. It goes without saying that mice, cockroaches, illegitimate children, or heaven knows what else could easily show up in such families. But the fact is that the former engineer's family was the epitome of harmony and what they call correctness: two splendid, exemplary children and an extremely practical yet pretty wife. All the other families living in that block, as well as all the friends of the engineer's family, led equally commendable lives, so the hypothesis that the mouse, doped by an atmosphere of vice, could have been accidentally brought in from some slum in a coat pocket simply didn't hold water as no-one, quite naturally, frequented any slums. The stairway in that block of flats gleamed with cleanliness, the rubbish was taken out on time, yet suddenly against the backdrop of all this cosy, sparkling orderliness, a mouse turned up out of nowhere. And not only turned up, but plopped off the ceiling right onto the lady of the house's head, after which the lady of the house herself promptly plopped onto the kitchen floor in a dead faint.

Coming home that evening from his businessman's business, the former engineer was greeted by the following scene: the engineer's wife was lying on the sofa, her greenish face expressionless as she murmured in a trance: "I go to put the kettle on and suddenly this mouse comes crashing down on me from the ceiling, just comes crashing down, right onto my head, a mouse, from the ceiling, I couldn't believe my eyes, a mouse, falling on my head, from the ceiling, heavens knows why, heaven knows how, right on my head, I go to put the kettle on and suddenly this mouse just comes crashing down..." His son Yurik, top of his class and the pride of his school, was charging round the flat, torch in hand, whooping like a Red Indian and poking a broom handle into every nook and cranny. His daughter Veronika, a student and a

218 / Irina Glebova

beauty, immediately threw herself hysterically into the former engineer's arms, showering his HugoBoss jacket with tears and incoherently babbling some nonsense along the lines of: "such a disgrace... unfit for human habitation... Daddy, I'm scared... it's the end of civilization... right in an urban flat... Sodom and Gomorrah..." and so on and so forth.

It wasn't until way after midnight that the engineer somehow succeeded in stilling the panic in the flat, plying his wife and daughter — now both blue from sobbing — with motherwort, and sending the star pupil Yurik off into the wilds of the Internet.

Sitting at the kitchen table at last, the exhausted engineer was listening to the blissful silence which had finally settled on the flat when what should suddenly land right in his cup of strong, perfectly-brewed tea, but a mouse which came crashing down from somewhere on high. The engineer recoiled, aghast, pushing his cup away and eyeing the mouse with horror and disgust as it scrambled frantically out of the teacup and heavenwards, eyeing the engineer with equal horror and disgust. The noise brought Yurik running from his virtual reality, and father and son spent the rest of the night sitting with their legs drawn up on the sofa, knocking back a whole bottle of cognac to lower their stress levels and drawing up a military campaign.

The next day, for the first time in his life, Yurik, the pride of his school, got a D on a trigonometry test; his mother didn't cook lunch for the first time in her life as she was too terrified to go into the kitchen; the student Veronika swiped her friend's fiancé in a fit of nervous distraction; and the engineer himself stationed splendid new mouse traps throughout the flat, one of which instantly ensnared Barsik the cat. Barsik's cuts were duly treated with iodine, and from that moment on guerrilla warfare broke out in the flat.

Each night without fail some member of the engineer's

household would creep out into the kitchen for a glass of water, and each night without fail the mouse would drop down from the eaves, right on top of that thirsty soul. It would then scuttle off somewhere with a nervous glance, pursued by that same thirst-stricken soul together with the rest of the family, who had been summoned by their screeches. No-one, of course, slept at night; clinging to the edge of their blankets, the family would listen to every tiny rustle, their dry, glassy eyes trained on the ceiling now chequered with the reflections of streetlights; and one windy night, right above Veronika's head, right through one of those reflections, ran the mouse. This incident prompted a number of reactions: Veronika developed a nervous tic and a tendency to hysterical laughter; Yurik fell off a stool and sprained his ankle trying to fix a mousetrap on the ceiling; the engineer's wife began spiking her motherwort with cognac, while the engineer pondered the possibility of exchanging flats.

Of course, everyone knows that changing flats is a long and complicated business, all the more so if you are trying to swap the flat you have lived in for 25 years and where absolutely everything is absolutely perfect — except, of course, for a mouse which has turned up out of the blue — for one just like it, minus the mouse.

The engineer had to make endless phone calls and constantly traipse off to look at prospective flats. In the meantime, the vet had to be called for the cat Barsik who had gorged himself on rat poison, and the psychiatrist for the engineer's wife who was drinking herself into alcoholic delirium from fright. Veronika brought a student named Sasha home as her husband, the proud owner of a Walther pistol, while the mouse developed a penchant for dancing the foxtrot on the ceiling in Yurik's room. "You again, my friggin' false Maya Plisetskaya!" Yurik would hiss nervously. Sasha the student would run in, wrapped in a sheet, and set about firing at the mouse with his pistol, the mousetrap Yurik had fixed on the ceiling would fall down, the father of the house's big toe would get caught in it at once; the neighbours he bumped into in the yard in the morning would turn away and purse their lips; but the treacherous mouse went on strutting around the ceiling as though it were on Broadway. In the face of all this, the flat that finally turned up as a possible exchange seemed nothing short of a godsend.

They managed to find a removal van quite cheaply, the new flat was meticulously checked for cracks and holes, and very soon the whole family could finally sink into a blissfully serene sleep. Until almost six o'clock in the morning, that is. At six o'clock young Sasha was woken by the cries of a panther as the new flat was on Kronverk Prospect right opposite the zoo. Still half asleep, he fired a few quick rounds at the ceiling out of habit, and shattered the stucco. The frightened householders rushed in bearing the traditional motherwort and cognac. Sasha came to his senses somewhat, calmed down and, as it was time to get up anyway, went into the kitchen to make some breakfast. But in the kitchen a mouse fell off the ceiling onto his head, and the six foot four, broad-shouldered Sasha first sobbed like a baby then downed the rest of the motherwort and cognac in one gulp, then filed for divorce from Veronika, screaming that he was bloody sick and tired of it all.

Veronika returned from her court hearing pale but unexpectedly calm and somehow very much together. She changed into Yurik's camouflage trousers, placed Sasha's pistol — which he had left her by way of compensation — in her right hand, and sat down in the kitchen to wait for the marriage-breaking mouse. And there she sat for nigh on two months, saying not a word to anyone, sipping motherwort and cognac from a field flask and refusing lunch. By night she would shoot at the mouse as it pranced over the ceiling, by day she would train her aim, shooting at her mother's empty motherwort and cognac bottles standing on the cupboard.

Meanwhile Yurik had finished school top of his year and passed the university entrance exam with flying colours. He didn't go to university, however. He waltzed off supposedly to Tibet to fathom the fundamentals of phenomena. Which meant that once the engineer had finally managed to send his wife and daughter, who had drunk themselves sick on motherwort, to an "exclusive sanatorium", he was left alone in the flat — not counting Barsik and the mouse.

By that time the former engineer and present businessman had permanently stopped busying himself with any business whatsoever and had quietly retired, devoting his new-found leisure to breading carp from an aquarium which he then tried to fry up for Barsik. But the capricious Barsik turned his nose up at the carp; in fact, he now often refused to eat anything at all except perhaps macaroni and ketchup from his master's plate, but not before one in the morning. Since the engineer's biorhythms had long since been out of sync, he gladly adopted Barsik's timetable, and now cat and master would sup macaroni from the same plate at night, gazing mesmerized at the ceiling where the mouse, inspired, would waltz about like Natasha Rostova at her first grand ball.

Of course, later on there were other events in the life of the family. Yurik returned, supposedly from Tibet, not having fathomed the fundamentals of phenomena, but having learnt how to smoke marijuana; the engineer's wife had a fling with one of the doctors in the sanatorium, the daughter with one of the patients. But they were both soon disenchanted with their chosen and once their alcohol detox was done, they were both only too glad to return home under the engineer's wing.

It is a well-known fact that hardship strengthens family ties and the members of the engineer's household were unspeakably happy to be reunited. Now they pass the long evenings sitting around the kitchen table holding hands, love shining in their eyes — the retired engineer; the engineer's wife, back on motherwort and cognac again; the meditative and supposedly Buddhist pot-head Yurik; the pensive divorcee Veronika; the balding, barmy Barsik — there they all are, with their frozen smiles, immobile as in a picture, just like an old-fashioned photo. Only the mouse breaks the stillness of this composition as it glides across the ceiling in time to a silent tango, never missing a beat and never putting a foot wrong.

The mouse has been dancing the tango on the ceiling every night for many years now and will, no doubt, go on dancing as long as the world goes on turning.

One wonders, of course, why the tango — it's an old dance, after all, and one which went out of fashion long ago. But when all is said and done, the mouse's choice is no stranger than the rest of this tale. Mysterious and puzzling events crop up much more often than would seem at first glance, and logic and reasoning fail before them. A ship unexpectedly vanishes in the Bermuda triangle, or a UFO flies in out of the blue, or suddenly, with no rhyme or reason, a mouse turns up in an urban flat on the sixteenth floor. Where from? Alas, the human mind is far from almighty, and the mouse continues to dance its tango on the ceiling, never missing a beat and never putting a foot wrong, at night, in the family of the former engineer.

THE VOICE OF CONSCIENCE

Once upon a time there lived a pale boy. He lived and lived, then one day he upped and died. Nothing so surprising in that, we all have to die one day, and anyway, this boy was a drug addict, that's why he was pale. But what's worse is that before he died, he managed to fall in love with young Anna, and, hopelessly in love, he began to trail around after her wherever she went and long for her love in return. He would traipse around whining: Anna, I love you. Anna, I long for your love in return. But Anna didn't like the pale boy at all, and she warned him not to set his heart on her loving him in return. But her warning was like water off a duck's back to the pale boy; he kept on whining: Anna, I'll throw myself down the stairs, or Anna, I'll poison myself. But Anna had just graduated from college and had decided to get married, although she hadn't decided who to: to Sergei Sergeyevich the dental technician or to Gosha the artist. Sergei Sergeyevich was past forty, closer to fifty, whereas Gosha was very young, not much more than a boy, talented, with a brilliant future shrouded in mist. And in the midst of all this, not a day goes by without the pale boy showing up round Anna like a bad penny, always whining:

"You know, Anna, if anything happens, I might easily blow my brains out..."

In short, Anna got so fed up with the pale boy she decided she was fed up with all boys. That's why she married Sergei Sergeyevich, who was old enough to be her father; after that, the pale boy upped and died.

The question arises: is there any connection between these two events if the pale boy died of an overdose? Well, clever people wouldn't ask themselves this — the lad kept doing it and doing it, and finally he overdid it, or as they say, he dosed and dosed 'til he finally overdosed. Nothing so surprising in that, really. The police, for instance, didn't have any questions. And the old women sitting by the porch didn't have any questions, either; they somehow knew straight away that the pale boy had killed himself. So Anna walks past those old women, and the old women say: look, there she goes, the one boys die on our porch for. Just look at her skirt, they don't come shorter than that! And her husband's a dentist an' all. We know all about them kinds of dentists! He's probably a killer-dentist an' all. And they live in one flat together. Well, we'll see who bumps the other off first...

Sergei Sergeyevich heard these conversations, too, of course — he wasn't deaf, thank God! — and he obviously didn't like them. Well, who would — you walk past the porch and the old women are sitting there and saying: Your wife's a murderer. And you're a killer-dentist an' all. So we'll never come to *you* to get our teeth fixed.

Sergei Sergeyevich would get very upset. At home he would scold Anna, saying: Because of your short skirts our neighbours the old women won't come to me to get their teeth fixed. Of course not, Anna would agree. They don't have any teeth left. What is there to fix? But joking apart, it won't do at all, of course, all the more so as Sergei Sergeyevich seems to be a bright sort of chap, but he just won't let it drop, always wanting to have his say: What sort of soup do you call that? Trying to poison me, are you? Maybe our neighbours are right after all?

In a word, he turned out not to be much of a husband, nothing but a total disappointment. Just as well Anna hardly ever saw him. But she saw a lot of Gosha the painter. Gosha didn't hint that he might die because of her. Quite the opposite, he was always telling her: Feel free, leave me if you want to, I'll survive somehow. I won't die without you, I'll soldier on. Anna really liked Gosha for that. Gosha really liked Anna, too, mainly because she hadn't insisted he marry her. Gosha really valued his freedom and he suspected all the girls he knew wanted to encroach on it. Usually when he met a girl he would say:

"There's one thing you should know, honey: I'm not about to give up my tiresome freedom."

The girls usually took the huff at first, but then they would get to know Gosha better and would stop being offended. The girls realised this wasn't one of those cases when you got huffy, it was a case for getting happy, for Gosha was a bohemian. A bohemian, in other words, is someone who earns very little, on and off, and at night drinks cheap port at home. Gosha's home comprised an 11 sq. meter room in a communal apartment, one corner of which was damp. Gosha kept empty bottles in the damp corner, for still lifes; in the dry corners he kept nothing at all, since he didn't have anything anyway. Only an easel over by the window and a blanket spread out on the floor. Gosha used the easel for working and the blanket for sleeping. When he woke up, Gosha would drink port straight from the bottle and then set to work. When girls came visiting he would nip to the neighbours to borrow stylish wine glasses. The girls visiting Gosha would sit on the floor on the spread-out blanket, drink port from the neighbours' stylish wine glasses, and secretly rejoice that they would never manage to marry Gosha.

When Anna visited Gosha she would bring her own champagne which she bought with Sergei Sergeyevich's dental technician's stable salary. Sergei Sergeyevich would give her money supposedly for tights, and as he did so he somehow always managed to slip in some comment, something along the lines of: Well, snagging your tights every day, now, that takes skill. If you wore trousers you wouldn't even need any tights, no problem. You'd just darn your socks, pop some trainers on over them, and bob's your uncle. But there you go, wearing such skirts that boys are in danger of going extinct on the porch, and all our money disappears on tights. And by the way, a dental technician's stable salary isn't elastic, you know. Well, it's clear, with a husband like that, the only thing to do is buy champagne and sip it from stylish wine glasses. Luckily for Anna she was able to economize on tights. After all, how do tights usually get snagged? On corners of furniture. But Anna spent most of her time at Gosha's, and he had neither corners, nor furniture to speak of. With all the skill in the world, there was nothing to snag your tights on. So Anna would sit on the floor, her tights intact, and drink first her champagne, then Gosha's port. She drank alone; Gosha worked during the day and he had a golden rule: I never drink when I work. But then afterwards he would get drunk the moment he stepped away from his easel, and immediately start fussing over Anna:

"Darling, you drink too much!" the drunken Gosha would fuss over Anna. "As a friend, I can't bear to see it!"

Gosha had a constant refrain: as a friend, as a friend. At the same time he was always kissing Anna and calling her "darling". But when Anna tried to find out why, if he loved her so much, he considered himself just a friend, Gosha would reply: because there's nothing indecent going on between us. Anna would delicately enquire as to just why there was "nothing indecent" going on between them, and Gosha would think for a while and explain that the process of "indecency" depleted his energy and thus disturbed his work. Anna would get a bit offended and hint that the process of getting drunk also takes certain energy from one's work, yet the port in his house never dried up. But there's no comparison! Gosha would gasp. Getting drunk is a cosmic, metaphysical experience. Far from depleting energy, it connects one to energy, to the Highest Energy. Getting drunk is a lofty process, Gosha would frown. Well then, Anna would venture timidly, so is "indecency", in a way... that is, if there's love... Well yes, if there's love, Gosha would concede. If there's love, then of course. Love, now that's a lofty feeling. Where there's love there's nothing indecent. But you and I are just friends...

In short, you could talk to Gosha for hours about this and not hear anything new. Gosha was like a scratched record. But Anna was extremely fond of spending time at Gosha's even so. At Gosha's her soul was at peace. But no sooner did Anna walk out of Gosha's place than her conscience began to torment her. Anna's conscience manifested in a rather unusual manner; for some reason it appeared to her in the guise of the deceased pale boy. The first time it happened she even got a fright. She had only just left Gosha's and was standing at the top of the stairs when the pale boy's voice suddenly whispered right in her ear: "Aha, just leaving our lover's are we?" Anna had had her fill of that voice when it used to whine for hours: I'll throw myself down the stairs. Now it was the startled Anna herself who nearly fell down the stairs. But the voice went on: "Your marriage put me in the grave and now you're cheating on your husband. That's not nice." Anna walked down the stairs carefully, thinking something along the lines of: I should drink less then I wouldn't hallucinate. And indeed, Anna did try to drink less after this, but things only got worse: far from being silenced, the pale boy's voice even began to draw her into conversation. The result was utter idiocy, as the pale boy would talk to Anna anywhere and everywhere, including public places. What could be more ludicrous than when, for example, Anna was buying some low-fat milk and half a loaf of bread, and the voice was incanting all the while: I did it because of you, and you, you're off getting it on the side... There he goes again, thinks Anna. Getting it on the side! We're just friends. Aha, of course, just friends, the pale boy's voice whinges on. What sort of friendship do you call that? Well, what is it then? Anna says to herself. Of course we're just friends, there's nothing indecent going on between us whatsoever. Aha, the pale boy says doubtfully, really nothing at all? Nothing whatsoever, Anna mutters to herself as she heads for the till. I didn't hear you, the pale boy whispers in her ear. Come on, speak up. How can there be nothing at all? There must be something, for sure. I should know, what with those skirts of yours...

"Why does everyone keep harping about my skirts?!" roars Anna for the whole shop to hear. "There isn't anything indecent going on, got it?!"

The shop assistant was so taken aback that she dropped Anna's bread on the floor. They both apologized to each other for half an hour, but Anna was so embarrassed she couldn't show her face in that shop anymore and had to buy bread elsewhere. An extra half a kilometre of pot-holes every day. And it wasn't as if the pale boy was about to re-heel her pretty shoes afterwards. The cobbler's booth in the arcade was occupied by characters from the Caucasus and they charged — or rather fleeced you for — 150 roubles a time. And then each time you have to go and account for yourself like a little girl: re-heeling... tights... bread... pasta... But Sergei Sergeyevich quickly starts adding it all up in his head, then paces up and down the flat in his stupid striped shirt, bald and bearded, muttering: Well, a dental technician's stable salary isn't elastic, you know... Get him out of my sight! "Seriozha," says Anna. "Seriozha, sweetie, I gave you such a super sweater for Men's Day, you know, the day of the Red Army and the Navy, why don't you ever wear it?" Of course, it was naive to think that just pulling on a super sweater would instantly transform Sergei Sergeyevich into the sweetest man on earth; no, not instantly — it would take more than a super sweet sweater. But, sweater on, clean-shaven, his bald head polished until it shone, and sprinkled with aftershave, Sergei Sergeyevich is already a new man. Not a husband, but a picture portrait. A portrait with hands. And what wonderful hands they were! Those sensitive, skilful, masculine hands of a dental technician. Anna loved Sergei Sergeyevich's hands. At night sometimes, in the early hours, she would take the sleeping Sergei Sergeyevich's hands in her own and gaze at the ceiling, thinking: "I suppose I'm happy after all. Things could be worse. His hands are wonderful and he has a dental technician's stable salary. And Mum likes him. And on the whole we have a harmonious marriage." "For the love of God, Anna. What sort of harmony are you talking about..." a whining voice would suddenly break the silence, and the pale boy's face would slowly begin to ooze through the ceiling.

"What sort of harmony can there be when the wife's always running off for a bit of hanky-panky on the side..."

"What do you mean, on the side?" Anna would hiss, nervously glancing at the sleeping dental technician. "What hanky-panky? I've already told you, nothing happened..."

"Maybe it did, maybe it didn't," the pale boy would raise his eyebrows mysteriously, stretching his right arm through the ceiling as far as his elbow and wagging his finger at Anna. "Maybe it did, maybe it didn't, that's a myth... But you should take a closer look at your darling Gosha..."

"Don't ruin the ceiling, idiot!" Anna would twitch. "We only had it repaired this year!"

"Hey, stop twitching," Sergei Sergeyevich would say sleepily, turning over. "Turned into a lunatic, have you?"

"Sleep, Seriozha, dear!" Anna would say, startled. "Sleep, sweetie! Sleep my sweet gold filling."

The pale boy would throw Anna an ironic look and vanish. Anna was nervous; she couldn't sleep at night and would shout at Sergei Sergeyevich when he was brushing the bits of plaster off the sheet in the mornings: "Well, what did you expect? I told you we should have had a suspended ceiling put in. You're a miser, Sergei. This place is like a cow-shed now. I'm embarrassed to invite guests round."

In fact, it was just Anna's nerves playing up, she had no intention of inviting any guests round. She had more than enough uninvited guests on her hands, and anyway, she preferred to be the guest herself.

"It's so nice at your place!" says Anna the guest, sitting on the floor sipping port from a stylish wine glass.

"And so it should be!" nods Gosha, gazing with satisfaction at the wet canvas. "After all, I'm a chap with a degree in art. I do know a thing or two about interior design! And I have perfect taste, too!"

"Yes, honey!" Anna agrees, gradually growing rosy from

the port. "You're wonderful! Tell me, Gosha, as a friend: will you ever have money?"

"Money?" Gosha asks in surprise, squinting at the canvas. "What's money got to do with anything? Money's a myth! And anyhow, darling" — Gosha sinks to his knees in front of Anna and gazes devotedly into her eyes — "Isn't a dental technician's stable salary enough for us? What do we need money for when there are higher values?"

Anna looks at dashing Gosha, smeared with splendid Phthalo Green oil paint and saturated with the scent of splendid Pine No.4 turps, and rues her base interests.

"You're right, honey," she strokes Gosha's unwashed hair. "Everything is splendid! I don't need anything at all, neither money or 'indecency'. Port and friendship are enough for me!"

"So that's settled, then!" dashing Gosha's face is lit up by a touching boyish smile. "Listen, darling. Don't stop by tomorrow. I have an urgent piece of work to finish. You're a true friend, right, you understand, don't you?"

Anna the true friend sadly finishes her port and nods. Gosha sees her to the door and gives her a fleeting, friendly kiss which lasts half an hour. Smeared with lipstick and green oil paint, Anna floats to the stairs. The pale boy is waiting for her there, hanging like smoke by the window.

"So how was it?" he says. "Allow me to congratulate you on your little 'indecency', my beauty."

"Mind your own business," Anna grunts, striding through the pale boy and going down the stairs.

The pale boy soars overhead muttering:

"Ah, you promiscuous girl. And he doesn't even have an ounce of love for you, we know all about that sort of 'urgent work.' And then there's your poor hubby... A mature man, and a skilled specialist, too. You'll send him to the grave with your goings on. You can't cook, you just go gadding about with your skirts barely covering your bum..."

"Oh, I'm so sick and tired of you!!!" Anna yells, turning round. "Why are you always tailing me? Anyone else would have just died and lain still, but not this one, oh no, he keeps wandering around. 'Laid to rest', they say. Well, they don't give you any rest at all, these restless dead, only unrest!"

"Oh, I do apologize!" The pale boy hovers under the ceiling in a huff. "I do apologize for disturbing your peace. But why, darling, why?" he beseeches, full of pathos, melting into the dark doorway.

Anna glances at her watch, gasps, and forgets about the pale boy at once. Sergei Sergeyevich is due home from work in an hour. Sergei Sergeyevich loves borscht, and once home, Anna bustles about between the beef and the beetroot. The table is littered with greens, the kettle boils nervously on the hob, and the smoke of a half-smoked cigarette hangs over the ashtray. And the pale boy is hanging in there with it. "For Christ's sake! Where have they got to?" cries Anna gazing around in search of the potatoes. "It's hard enough to find anything as it is, without this one hanging about. Aha, there they are. Well, let him hang there, at least he doesn't demand to be fed..."

Anna rushes to peel the potatoes double-quick while the pale boy sways below the ceiling philosophizing:

"Everyone says: drugs are certain death, but in fact drugs are a myth. They said I'd died from drugs. But how could I die from drugs when the only blade that could cut me is your gaze?"

"But you did die!" Anna exclaims, cutting her finger. She tastes the borscht and spits it out. "Yeah, you could poison someone with soup like that!" she admits wearily, perching on the corner of the parsley-strewn table and taking the smoking cigarette butt from the ashtray. "It's some sort of ghastly ghoulish gall, not borscht!"

"Don't talk rot!" The pale boy consoles her as he hovers

in the clouds of smoke. "Your cooking's not bad at all. The chicken bouillon you boiled up yesterday was perfectly edible, and last week you managed to turn out a tasty omelet. And your salads aren't bad..."

"Such compromises with conscience," thinks Anna, distracted and upset, as she waves him away, sniffing and lighting up another cigarette.

"And the cabbage soup you made last time was a success, too..." The pale boy gazes sympathetically at poor Anna. "And this borscht is probably perfectly acceptable... Here, let me taste it!"

The pale boy flies over to the stove and scoops a handful of borscht out of the pan.

"Not with your hands!" Anna cries hysterically, jumping up from the table, but just then the key scrapes in the lock.

"OK then, my beauty, I'll be off!" and with a wink to Anna the pale boy does indeed disappear.

Sergei Sergeivich walks in, changes into his striped shirt and starts criticizing the borscht.

"Such crap borscht!" he says, stirring it gingerly with a spoon. "Trying to poison me or what?"

"Shall I add some sour cream?" Anna suggests guiltily.

"No doubt your sour cream's just as bad!" growls Sergei Sergeyevich the grumbler as he sniffs the sour cream.

"Just as I thought, it's gone off. Stinks like some ghastly ghoulish gall..."

"But it's fresh, today's! I went out to the shop especially for it!" Anna says, getting offended. "Maybe the smell's coming from the neighbours'... Here, I'll close the window..."

"Oh, be quiet," Sergei Sergeyevich raises his voice. "You know how to wear shorter than short skirts all right, but you haven't a clue how to cook..."

Sergei Sergeyevich eats up his borscht with a grimace of disgust and heads off to watch TV. Anna washes up, diluting the dishwashing liquid with her tears. The pale boy watches her mournfully, bobbing near the window in the stream of cigarette smoke.

"Why does he have to be like that with me?!" Anna sobs. "The sour cream was definitely fresh!"

"Um-hmm," the pale boy nods sympathetically. "I noticed it was today's sour cream."

"It's probably the beetroot that was off," Anna sniffs. "But there certainly wasn't any ghoulish gall in it."

"Well, that's obvious!" the pale boy laughs out loud. "How can you put ghoulish gall in a beetroot?"

"Shush!" Anna hisses. "He'll hear and come in!"

"He won't be coming in anywhere anymore!" the pale boy soothes her. "He's been dead for fifteen minutes."

"Dead? What do you mean?!" Anna sinks onto a stool, thunderstruck.

"It was your borscht, of course!" the pale boy shrugs.

"Was it the meat?!" Anna cries out in horror. "I had my doubts, I'm hopeless at buying beef... Mum was always telling me I should learn how to cook..."

"I'm fed up with your moaning..." the pale boy rolls his eyes heavenwards. "It's high time you saw a shrink, that's all. You've got to get a grip on this low self-esteem of yours. Your cooking's absolutely fine. What's the beef got to do with it? Why don't you accuse the parsley? That's your common or garden ghastly ghoulish gall!"

"Good Lord..." Anna says slipping from the stool to the floor. "Where did it come from?"

"Where from?!" says the pale boy wiggling his fingers bashfully.

"What a nightmare..." Anna grows paler than the pale boy. "How many times have I told you: don't touch food with your hands! That's what cutlery's for! You've got no manners!" she yells.

"Look who's talking!" the pale boy says, making a wry face. "You're bawling like a fishwife... Stop screaming, remember the neighbours. People will think someone's being murdered in here..."

"God knows what's going on..." Anna buries her head in her hands. "I've got a migraine; I'll go and fetch a painkiller..."

"You'd better not go in there!" the pale boy declares, looking her in the eye with stern manliness. "Fancy taking a peek at a corpse, do you?"

"It's not as if I'd never seen one before!" Anna says, wearily brushing the pale boy aside.

"Well, yes," the pale boy agrees. "I suppose we could say you're caught between two corpses. You could make a wish..."

"I wish you'd go away!" says Anna, and in a flash the pale boy is sucked out through the window with the smoke. A young paramedic appears in his place:

"Please accept my condolences. A heart attack. He wasn't, how can we put it, in the first flush of youth. This happens all the time now — a person sits down in an armchair, looks at some TV and then — that's it. He watched and watched 'til he finally 'overwatched' as they say. Nothing so surprising in that, really. By the way, what are you doing tomorrow evening?"

The next evening finds Anna hurrying to Gosha's for some sympathy. That evening Gosha is finishing off an important piece of work, as he had said, and is rather at a loss when Anna shows up.

"What a nightmare..." Gosha sympathizes with Anna, stumped. "You're always getting mixed up in something. First one dies, then another..."

"That's just the point," sobs Anna. "It's all rather embarrassing, one right after the other. People will laugh, it's getting awkward..."

"Don't fret," Gosha comforts her. "No more dental technician's stable salary, now that's what I call awkward. But as for what people are saying, that's just nonsense. Public opinion, well, it's a myth. People like to talk about me, too..."

"So they do!" Anna suddenly remembers. "Someone told me I should take a closer look at you... Gosha, honey, why do you have lipstick on your cheek?"

"That's not lipstick!" Gosha hangs his head bashfully. "It's dark red rose madder, oil paint..."

"And what's that naked girl doing sitting on your blanket?" Anna continues to take a closer look at Gosha.

"She's not a girl, she's a model!" Gosha explains primly, pulling the blanket from under the model.

"So why were the two of you doing something indecent when I came in, then?" Anna is perplexed.

"It's not indecent..." Gosha says, covering his nakedness with the blanket, somewhat embarrassed. "There's no such thing as indecency, it's a myth!"

"Impressive!" The jolly widow Anna sends the model packing and pours herself some port. "So tell me, then: in your opinion, what's not a myth?"

"Art!" declares Gosha solemnly, draped in Antic folds. "Hallowed and eternal art! Darling, would you like to see my latest paintings?"

Anna likes looking at Gosha's paintings. She likes looking at Gosha, too. Draped in his blanket, Gosha is striking, like a Roman centurion at the height of the empire. Anna is a cultured young woman, no stranger to art and her interest in it prompts her to move into Gosha's place after Sergei Sergeyevich's funeral. The bench outside Gosha's block of flats is broken so no-one sits on it and no-one says to Anna as she walks by that soon half the town will be dead thanks to her short skirts. Gosha doesn't chide her about her skirts, either, nor does he ask her for financial reports or demand she be home by eight. Admittedly, Gosha doesn't compliment Anna on her legs, either, but lets Anna support him with the money she gets from renting out the late Sergei Sergeyevich's flat. But some evenings he rather too insistently asks her to go out for a walk. This happens when Gosha has models round.

"Gosha," Anna asks timidly. "Your paintings are abstracts, so how come you use models so often?"

"Call that often?" Gosha, stubbly and hung-over, makes light of it. "Darling, if you look at it from the cosmic perspective, it's simply a myth!"

Anna grudgingly goes out for a walk. She really doesn't like leaving the confines of Gosha's studio. When Gosha isn't around, Anna's conscience immediately begins to torment her. Her conscience manifests in the form of the pale boy. When Anna is out for a walk arm-in- arm with Andrei Andreyevich, a retired colonel aged somewhere over fifty, closer to sixty, it seems to her as if the pale boy is always hanging on her other arm.

"You should be ashamed of yourself, Anna!" the little whiner whispers in her ear. "You haven't even worn down the heels of the shoes you wore for the funeral!"

"They re-heeled them properly this time, that's all!" Anna justifies herself under her breath.

Luckily Andrei Andreyevich is slightly hard of hearing and doesn't notice that Anna is always muttering to herself. You could say that Anna had arranged things rather well for herself: Andrei Andreyevich hardly ever hears anything, while Gosha hardly ever says anything. But it has its downsides: Andrei Andreyevich is always having to see doctors, while Gosha is always having models round. So Anna often finds herself left to her own devices. At such times she goes to Sergei Sergeyevich's grave and plants chrysanthemums. The face of the pale boy appears to her amidst their ragged petals.

"Aha," the pale boy nods to her, swaying on a stem.

"Dragged ourselves over here after all, have we? Ah, you promiscuous girl... One right after the other... You could have at least worn a longer skirt in the graveyard..."

Panic-stricken, Anna flees straight to the nearest bar, from where she rings Gosha and Andrei Andreyevich. But Gosha's place is full of models, and Andrei Andreyevich doesn't hear the phone. Instead, it's the pale boy's voice that comes down the line: "Go ahead, hang on the phone," he nags through the crackles and beeps. "You can call all you like, of course, but you won't get through."

"Excuse me, Miss," a curly-haired youth leans over to Anna from an adjacent table. "You can call as much as you like, of course, but you won't get through. Your mobile's switched off. In fact, everything about you seems pretty switched off. Maybe I should walk you home?"

The youth walks Anna to Gosha's block of flats, and then halfway up the stairs; clinging to the banisters, he suddenly starts declaring his undying love for her:

"Anna!" he declares in a voice full of pathos, tossing his curly mane. "Anna, I love you! Anna, I long for your love in return!"

"That's very sweet of you..." Anna smiles in surprise. "I'm quite touched. But don't go getting het up. You've gone rather pale."

"And I shall grow paler still!" vows the spellbound youth. "I would do anything for you! Would you like me to throw myself down the stairs?"

"Oh no, thank you!" Anna declines, and darts into the flat, slamming the door in his paling nose.

That evening Gosha comes home smeared with oil paint the colour of lipstick, and begins telling her the latest gossip:

"Guess what, darling, some young fool was hit by a car, right outside our door. Drunk, most likely..."

"Most likely..." agrees Anna pensively. "Honey, what do you think, could someone kill themselves for love? Could you?"

"Me?" asks Gosha, astonished. "How can you ask such a thing, darling? You should know me better than that. Absolutely not! What do you take me for, a fool? Listen, I have to paint with a model. You couldn't nip out for a while, could you darling, like a true friend?"

Anna hurries out, the pale boy's usual commentary running in her ear all. But then it is as though there is a different voice whispering reproachfully in her other ear. "That's the last thing I need!" Anna gasps, for this new voice is suspiciously similar to that of the curly-haired youth she spurned. "Damn neurotics!" Anna says angrily. "Always getting themselves in trouble and I'm always to blame. Gosha's the only normal, healthy guy around! There's no hysterics with him!"

Anna hurries home to the normal, healthy Gosha. But on her arrival Gosha is far from healthy. Neighbours and the police are milling around him, and he for some reason is lying at the bottom of the stairs.

"Just look at him!" a policeman shows Gosha to Anna. "There you have it, a so-called bohemian. Got himself drunk on port and fell down the stairs. How do you like that?"

"I don't like it at all..." says Anna, sinking into the policeman's arms. "Such a waste. Got himself drunk and fell!"

"Don't you believe it!" The pale boy's voice whispers in her ear. "That's not why he fell!"

"Of course not!" the voice of the curly-haired youth chimes in. "You simply don't understand, Anna, what a femme fatale you are!"

"Yes, darling!" Gosha's voice suddenly joins the chorus, ringing out from on high. "In fact, you were the only one I ever loved. And so I decided to take my own life, for love."

"Well, there's a surprise..." Anna is dumbfounded as she

listens to the chorus of boys. "Fancy, who would have thought it. You, too, Gosha? Well, thanks, I'm flattered, of course... but what am I supposed to do now?!"

"Come now, don't take on so, Miss!" the policeman says sympathetically. "Those drunkards are always falling about here or there, nothing so surprising in that. I gather it wasn't all a bed of roses with him. Ashes to ashes, as they say. Maybe I can help a pretty girl like you in some way?"

VICTOR PUCHKOV
The Sugar Disease

Translated by José Alaniz

The reason I'm walking down the tiled corridor of the local polyclinic is my disease.

Diabetes.

I do this every year. I'm used to the lines, the third-rate doctors, the nurses' feigned concern. I'm used to it all by now.

People have different attitudes toward illness. You can treat it, love it, curse it, suffer from it. You can do lots of things, but none of that's for me. Diabetes is my life. It's as much a part of me as a finger, an arm or an ear. I belong to it, and it belongs to me.

That's how it is.

The polyclinic's not the only place I go. There are lots of offices and organizations, too. The only thing that tells them apart is their function, the seals, the signatures, maybe the people — but not their essence.

The first thing you sense is that characteristic smell of something old. Something almost dead. After the smell comes the picture: a provincial office forever under repair, scuffed-up walls plastered with ads, cheap benches and never enough light: a lone yellow bulb, a single lamp or nothing at all. And people waiting in lines. You're never, ever first; you're always be behind someone. You're in the prison of an unbearable wait.

I hate to complain, but sometimes it all strikes me as so repulsive and nauseating — the old women and old men, their sighs of decrepitude, the shabby corridors — that I want to tear my diabetes out by the roots, toss it onto the ground and stomp on it like a gray snake.

But then I remember that diabetes helped me get into the institute (free). It also puts money on the little card in my left pants pocket. Diabetes gets me around on buses and trains. It got my out of the draft.

Diabetes is a double-edged sword. A lot like you, in fact. Nasty and kind. Generous and cruel.

Diabetes is my William Wilson.

* * *

I'm lying in a bed in the ninth ward. I've been admitted to the Institute of Endocrinology. I'm just lying there staring at another patient. The glucometer is counting off the seconds as he talks:

"The day I got sick, I was walking down the street, not paying attention to anything. Then all of a sudden I was standing in the middle of an intersection. Cars were honking... They found me in an entranceway, sitting on the steps and staring straight ahead. My sugar was at 40. What about yours?"

"Don't know."

I first got sick when I was three. They say that I inherited my illness. My great-grandmother was also a diabetic. But there are other possibilities: chicken-pox, Chernobyl, medical error.

The glucometer signals:

"Pi-pi-pi."

"Well, well," he says, "12.8. A little high. Let's go shoot up."

"Okay."

We diabetics differ from drug addicts in that we don't start daily injections of our own free will. And the needle goes into a muscle, not a vein. The needles are smaller. And the syringes are not disposable — not by a long shot. I remember a time when my mother would boil the glass syringes before every injection. If it's new, a needle won't hurt when it's going in. Sometimes you can feel the insulin flowing into you, and when you pull out the tip, a clear (more rarely, mixed with blood) little drop always squirts out. Just one. Every time.

A diabetic on insulin has lumps. Lipodystrophy. Fatty formations at the spots of injections — on the stomach, arms, hips. These all heal.

Diabetes is a routine, a regimen. Everything you eat, drink, everything you do, feel — it all tells on the disease. And on you.

* * *

"Why are you crying?" she asks, tenderly, like Mama.

What a question. It's perfectly clear why. I've been staying in the hospital alone, no one's come to see me for a week, and so far I've made no friends.

Her name was Elena Vitalyevna. I can't remember what she looked like, but I do know she was young and beautiful. She was my doctor. Elena Vitalyevna.

"Is someone picking on you?"

"No." The tears run down my face like a fast mountain stream, and it's hard for me to look at her. I choke on my tears.

"Well, what is it, then?" Elena Vitalyevna doesn't wait for an answer; she hugs me to her, smoothes my hair and is quiet. I can hear her heart beating. Mine too.

"I won't cry any more."

And to this day I haven't.

* * *

Diabetes is the fourth leading cause of death — after cancer, AIDS and heart diseases.

The most dangerous thing about diabetes is the complications (feet, eyes, kidneys). But what's a lot harder is living with it in the real world. The labyrinth of offices. The prison of the unbearable wait.

At night in the ward almost no one sleeps; they talk.

It's dark. The yellow light in the corridor shines weakly through the glass door. You can't see their faces so you can say whatever you want. You can say who you love, who you hate, what you're afraid of.

"It's good here. At Morozov there are bars on the windows and they take away food brought from home and then give it to you on a schedule. They're always doing searches of the bedside tables.

"I like Nina in the seventh ward..."

"We used to hide food on the ledge outside a little window in the bathroom."

"Diabetes isn't so bad. You can live with it."

"But have you seen a diabetic's foot?"

"No. It's OK here. The doctors are neat and nice. The beds don't creak. Morozov's like a prison."

"Nina's pretty."

"Are we whipping up the sugar tomorrow?"

"Can I go with you, guys?"

"Sure. After breakfast. We'll run up and down the stairs."

"The main thing is not to bring on a seizure, like today."

"Right."

"Hey, Lyokha, where you from?"

"Perm. What about you?"

"Penza. I found a phone under my mattress. It's from Penza, too."

"Call someone."

"They say I'll be discharged in four days."

"Good for you."

* * *

A lot of the kids went home on weekends. In our ward, there was only one kid left. From Ekaterinburg.

The hospital was emptying. Loneliness was seeping out of the walls, it glowed at the nurse's station, emitted the silence of utter desolation.

I was leaving with Papa. As the nurse unlocked the door, I caught sight of the Ekaterinburg kid over my shoulder. He was walking in the hallway, looking at the three of us.

"Bring me something back," he probably wanted to say. But he didn't say anything. I got it.

He didn't know what it meant to get parcels from home. He was all alone there.

I brought him some tangerines and apples. And mineral water.

* * *

From my diary:

Slept well. Remember my dream: I was reading a huge folio with Buddhist doctrines and philosophy on one page, the Gospels on another. They alternated that way. I was reading, and a voice was saying, 'How can you read that?'

I hugged Mom goodbye. Of my own accord. I hugged her and told her not to worry. I know that very soon this solitude will beceome torture. For no reason. I know . But this is good.

I know that loathsome feeling of waiting in vain for someone to come, to sit at a table with you, to say something. That's how the tears start.

I'm listening to Joy Division's Love Will Tear Us Apart.

Love will tear us apart, to pieces. To shreds. Again.

Outside it's hot. The sun spreads out, sliding along the roads, the trees, the houses and puddles, its mischievous fires reflected in them. The yellow of the world. The heat of life. My loneliness in waiting for K.

Love will tear me to pieces. You can't treat it like diabetes. But like diabetes, you can live with it. You get used to it. You take your shots.

If diabetes had a color, it would be yellow.

If love had a color, it would be brownish-green, like K.'s eyes. She will tear me apart.

One piece of me will stay here. Another will move on. Confidently. With a pre-filled syringe in my pocket. Whenever it feels like you're breathing dust, give yourself a shot. Whenever your eyes start to go blurry, give yourself a shot. Whenever you feel alone, give yourself two shots — one short and one long. Humalog and Humulin NHC. If you can exchange the latter for Lantus, that's even better.

Everyone's mission is to dissolve into the world, to dole himself out bit by bit.

Like...

Everyone's mission is to dole himself out, so as to come back. Later.

This is the seed. Our act of sowing. And our harvest.

Come back!

* * *

"We've decided that starting this year we'll put you in Disability Group 3. You'll have to get a job. Group 2 is work-exempt. You might have some problems."

"I'm already working. I haven't had any complaints yet."

"Even so. You'll keep your benefits. Your stipend will decrease by about 200 rubles. This is all for your own good, understand? Your diabetes is under control. You say you don't have any complaints. If there's any deterioration, we'll put you right back in Group 2."

A pawnbroker, with the eyes of Lucifer.

No complaints.

No complaints.

No complaints.

Result?

They cut my stipend by 500 rubles. That's a week out of my life. For a student, that's a lot.

* * *

It's probably even worse for people who get sick at, say, fifteen.

Your first desire is to simply ignore it. This manifests itself when, first, you forget to take the shots, later your vision gets worse, then maybe you have the shivers or your heart really starts to bother you.

Diabetes is you.

Without thinking you eat sweets, candy, cookies. Just like that.

You don't believe in diabetes; you think maybe it's all in your head.

But then...

Your muscles weaken and you can't make a fist. Every movement hurts. Then your stomach starts to ache. Your body is being poisoned by acetone. Your lips are red, your face pale.

You are diabetes.

Your nose can sense the tiniest particles of dust that you're breathing in. It feels like someone's got you by the throat. Your eyes get all blurry, like you're looking through a rainy window. On top of that, you're always having to go to the bathroom.

This is high sugar. Diabetes is taking bites out of you from the inside — because you forgot about it. It demands a shot. You have to stick the needle right into your stomach. So the insulin gets digested faster.

That's when you realize that questions don't mean anything and answers are only good for forms. You're walking with it, hand in hand. You're a pair. Forever.

You belong to it, and it belongs to you.

* * *

When people talk about a disease, they usually tell you not to give up. Like you're at war with it. You can talk that way about the flu, a cold, something like that, about something whose defeat is essentially inevitable. But you don't go to war with diabetes. You live with it.

Though there was a time when my parents refused to give up.

In 1990 (or maybe a bit later) my father and I went to Tajikistan. To see a healer. The newspapers said he could cure just about anything.

I only remember that we drove high up into the mountains. I remember a honey tree, the open door of a lonely house and the warm welcome of the man who lived there. .I remember foxes running across the road.

I remember a precipice and the little stream that dribbled down from it. Next to it was a jerrybuilt latrine and a trash pit.

I also remember a solitary eagle against a blue sky, its wings outspread. My father and I sat on a bench, next to a shed, waiting for the healer. We looked up at the sky. Pure, deep blue. With the eagle.

He didn't ask me anything. He just thrust an aluminum spoon of white powder into my mouth. It tasted bitter. I chewed on it and swallowed it with difficulty. It was some mountain herbs. But their effect was zero. While being treated, I didn't take insulin.

This went on for a week, maybe two.

Then I got really bad: diarrhea, vomiting, a total disconnect from reality. Indifference to everything. Nirvana?

They transported us down from the mountains in an air ambulance, straight to the hospital. I remember its wobbly door: through the crack I could see peaks, cliffs, chasms and clouds.

The only Russian doctor at the hospital told my father,

"You'd better pray." And poured him a glass of pure alcohol.

This state between life and death is the most radiant state I've ever known. I saw my father watching me. I remember he was smiling (though he couldn't have been) and that he had little toy soldiers on his head, in his hair, or rather not soldiers but sailors in their striped shirts. They were also smiling. Someone once told me that a person sees God as his own father. I guess I was seeing God, who loved me, who had created me. I felt light, easy, free and happy. I understood — I'd somehow sniffed it out — that there's nothing hard about dying. And anyway, is there such a thing as death?

?

But I didn't die. The doctors managed to save me. They advised us to stay away from Tajikistan.

Later on, a war started there. People died, but in other ways. Horrible.

* * *

Hypoglycemia.

Hypo.

Low sugar.

It's like fear, or strong anxiety. You shiver, sweat, a green diamond swims before your eyes. It blocks everything out, at first it's all you see. At that moment, hundreds and thousands of blood vessels are bursting in your head.

All you want to do then is eat. Eat whatever you can find, preferably something with glucose.

Sweet tea. Candy. Cookies. Wafers.

A packet of ascorbic acid.

You always have one on you. Just in case. Having a seizure is like being drunk. Your subconscious is unleashed. You might start reciting a poem you saw somewhere, or talking about things you always kept secret. Or you might fall silent. It's like madness.

The green diamond blocks out reality. Everything looks green. You're sweaty, you shake, you stagger.

Your sugar then shoots up. As a rule.

So don't forget to take your shot when you feel a seizure coming on. A paradox. Diabetes.

* * *

The hospital is a community of friends that lasts a few weeks. Sometimes you exchange phone numbers and addresses with them, but you never write or call.

They're discharging Sanya.

The doctor sits with him on his bed, talking softly about something.

His sugars have normalized. Over the course of a day they don't rise more than seven millimoles per liter. The tests are reassuring. Generally speaking, he's fine, so it's time for him to go home. To Oryol.

His mother comes in. She gives an expensive red box of chocolates to the doctor and kisses her on the cheek. Later the two women step out of the room, and Sanya stays behind. We shake hands. Firmly, like friends. We look into each other's eyes.

"Give me a call, write me," I say.

"For sure. Don't you forget either."

"Okay."

We have a warm, close embrace, patting each other on the back.

"Well, 'bye."

"'Bye."

The ward doors slowly close. Through the narrowing crack I see him walking towards the exit.

We never saw each other again. And we never wrote to each other. Though I've held on to his address for some reason.

Diabetics make friends fast, and part easily. But for them love is something else.

I probably did love Elena Vitalyevna. And I definitely loved a girl named Tanya.

The love of diabetics always lies in the shadow of this question: can they be together?

The answer is usually no: someone gets discharged earlier. That's how everything ends.

Tanya had long, straight brown hair.

She would give me massages. Her hands, tender and dry, with thin fingers, would race along my back in circles, tapping, jabbing. Things were good between us.

I was standing by the telephone in the hall dialing my dad's work number. She was waiting her turn. Suddenly she got up, depressed the hook-switch and, having cut off my conversation, ran away. Laughing.

The next day we went to our tests together. That's how we met.

Later on we walked the halls together, rode the elevator, played cards. There aren't many diversions in a hospital. It has no attributes of the outside world: parents, money, movie theaters, cafés. There's you. Only you. And her. And diabetes in both of us.

At night the boys would talk about who liked whom. I stayed quiet. I knew it and they knew it; it was clear enough.

They discharged Tanya a week after we met. I never saw her again. These days I barely remember her.

Diabetic love is brief, but you always want to go back to it.

* * *

It never occurred to me that diabetes would interfere with my choice of profession. Not until someone told me. That's when I realized I'd never get away from it, that no one — not I or anyone else — would ever forget about it. Strange I hadn't realized that sooner.

I walked out of the building with a pink certificate that said Disability Group 3. Minus 500 rubles. But that wasn't the main thing on my mind. I was thinking that diabetes wouldn't let me become a reporter, a person who stays up all night for the sake of "a few lines in the paper," who watches only the news on television.

Fate always has a name. Eternal need. The blind Parcae. Fatum. The Norns. The name of my fate is diabetes, "the sugar disease." No one chooses it and no one changes it. It's your ticket. You live with it.

Diabetes is five shots a day, monthly visits to the endocrinologist, and yearly examinations. It's a limited choice of occupation. It's a stipend of 1,947 rubles, free public transportation and a few other benefits.

It's you.

* * *

Night. I'm reading *Anna Karenina* in an empty room at the sanitarium. A sharp knock at the door, then another.

"Come and look, Chobrek pissed himself. He stunk up the whole floor."

This is Kirik, a guy I know. With him is Lyokha, a huge guy, clumsy and awkward. They call him Medved (the Bear). Or just Med. He's far-sighted, too. Up close he sees almost nothing.

Kirik and Med are looking at me, grinning. I put my index finger to my lips and point to my room-mate Andrei, who is sleeping. "So?"

"What do you mean, 'so'? We can't sleep like this," says Kirik, choking, while Med lowers his gaze. "Don't you smell it?!"

"Get over it," says Andrei's, rubbing his eyes.

"Easy for you to say!"

A minute later we're in their room. The smell of urine has indeed taken over the whole hallway. The balcony's open. Chobrek is sitting there, shivering. He has a white sheet thrown over him. A Roman patrician. Chobrek is crying.

What he's gone through tonight — a year ago I worried I'd go through the same thing. Fear has a name.

Enuresis. Bedwetting.

They say it doesn't only happen to diabetics, but I've only seen it happen to them. For me, this is the far edge of diabetes, its dark side.

Chobrek sobs and looks at the empty courtyard of the sanitarium.

Bedwetting means orange oilcloths underneath you at night, your parents' scolding, the water treatments, and the terror that others will find out.

I put my arms around Chobrek, squeeze his hand. I tell him about me. I had incontinence too; it went away a year ago. This'll pass, brother.

The smell was gone the next day. They moved Chobrek to another ward. He likes boiled eggs, so over breakfast I gave him mine.

Two days later he left. With his mother.

I watched them get on the bus. Chobrek was dragging his things, while his mother — a small, round-shouldered woman with a pale, waxy face — walked ahead of him, saying nothing. They took seats apart from the rest; and the yellow mechanical box carried them away from me forever.

* * *

Life with diabetes is no great feat. It's not heroism. You can get used to it easily.

There are times when diabetes lets go of you. It releases you high into the sky, like a kite. You fly free. Below you everything is so small, inconsequential.

This is diabetes for a 20-year-old. How it goes for others, I don't know. But it seems to me that diabetes grows old right along with you.

With age it grumbles and coughs harder. Someday I'll find out for myself.

* * *

I got here and wrote this down:

I'm standing in line. In front of me is someone's back, every time it's a different one, new and unknown: round-shouldered and bow-backed from the weight of years or something else, or it's wide and thickset, like the trunk of a baobab tree. I see it for the first and last time, just like the faces that replace each other at random behind my back — which for someone else is also making its first and last appearance. I can never remember them, and if I try I always make a mistake and — don't remember them anyway. The faces behind and the backs in front of me are a level array, a series of frames from some amateur film about completely unfamiliar and therefore, to me, superfluous and uninteresting people. They all think the same thing about me. I'm just a copy, a useless photo of someone they don't know. Yet we depend on each other, even if we don't feel the slightest involvement in each other's lives. After all, we're in a line, in an endless chain of ever-changing, self-replacing lines.

Lines irritate us, they drain enormous reserves of our strength, energy and everything else with which loss is associated. A new line is a new loss. Loss of oneself. Every one of us knows this. And every one over and over again loses, leaves behind little pieces of his soul in lines. And every one, over and over again, sooner or later returns to the lines, those dejected troop-trains of line-mates, steadily dissolving into the faceless mass, growing voiceless and gray, like a black and white photograph consigned to an archive.

Each one of us is locked away in the prison of an unbearable wait. The torpor and solidity of a line, its very configuration, perverts us. We're each ready to unload our clips on the back in front of us, and on those we've been trying so long and tediously to see. We become beasts. The moral norms, decorum, rules — they're not for us. Only one law remains for us: the law of the line — dumb, irrefutable, turning us into animals ready to tear each other apart.

What holds us back? What compels us to put up with it and meekly wait our turn?

Hope.

Blind hope.

Hope that...

That all these trials will not have been borne in vain. Not in vain. Not in vain? Not in vain!!!!!!!!!!!!

Now there's a new back in front of me. In an old overcoat. Moths have had a taste of it more than once. It's dark blue. This is an old man. Maybe a veteran, maybe a hero, maybe he shed his blood so that I could now stand in line.

He is hoping for leniency from this line of people. He is expecting the forbearance to which he is entitled. But he'll never get it. Never.

He's tired.

So am I.

We're all as tired as he is.

On the other side of that forbidden door sits some woman in glasses. She already has a double chin. She's not yet old, but she is repulsive. Her voice is shrill and insufferable. In her small hands, she holds our fates. But she hates us all. Me. The old man. Everyone.

We know it. We expect it. Everyone's nerves are strained to the limit. Irritation — eruption — open warfare — we are beasts.

No! No! No!

This has got to stop! A halt, a break, a pause, an easing up — a life without lines...

What should we do? Who's to blame? Those are idiotic, meaningless questions. Everyone of us will point to the person in front of us and say, "He's to blame." He got here before me, he hustled, he's ahead. But everyone who says that knows deep down that he's the guilty one. No one else. That finger I'd just been pointing at those responsible for my misfortunes and woes now turns around and jabs me in the chest. I am responsible. That's why we forsake each other. We're all of us alone. The only thing that unites us is the line. A chain of countless mute, gray snapshots consigned to an archive...

I don't belong to the generation that grew up with lines. But every time, the line tweaks my nose, puts me in my place, and drills me. The line dehumanizes me, deprives me of my voice, leaves me wrung-out like a used teabag.

I know all this. But I don't want to be consigned to an archive. Like hundreds and thousands of others like me.

* * *

There was a time when only the people at the top could afford glucometers. Back then they would take the blood sample by hand, in the hospital. When called, everyone would come out of the ward and form a line. There were no lancets either; the nurse would prick your finger with a needle, then squeeze a drop from a finger that had grown tough and hard from seven such procedures every day.

Then you went for your shots in a cold treatment unit. After that – the cafeteria. All the separate wards came together. Fights would break out over spoons, plates, crusts of bread.

A fun time.

Dozens of diabetics at one table. They're just like you. They don't sweeten their tea with sugar. They count their bread units. They smell of insulin, just like you. You can see the little hillocks of lipodystrophy on their arms. They're all talking about something.

Dozens of faces. Dozens of stories.
One disease.

* * *

Seryozha, my friend, runs ahead and quickly latches the door shut from the other side. Now we can't get back to the pediatric ward. A harmless prank.

I'm left alone with Tanya, and have no idea what to say. I walk up to the locked door, knock and ask him to open up. No answer. I turn around and see Tanya. She's sitting down, her back to the wall, and watching me.

We keep quiet. The silence roars. It's dark.

"Are you afraid?" she asks.

"No. This is weird."

"Yeah. Weird."

We're quiet again. We're sitting next to each other, shoulder to shoulder, saying nothing.

"Want me to sing a song?"

I nod.

She sings *Yesterday*. A great song by a great group. About love.

Back then I didn't understand the words, but I felt something. As if reality had been turned inside out. I sensed the presence of something different, something strange, fundamental.

She sang. And I watched her.

Someday there'll come a time
To believe only in yesterday ...

The light from a streetlamp penetrated the corridor where two people sat in silence, turning their faces green.

Two little green people from another planet.

Seryozha came back later.

"You're singing?"

Two days later Tanya was discharged.

* * *

12:10. I should have seen the neuropathologist at 11:30. But I'm still sitting in the hallway. Soon, soon.

S-o-o-n.

But not right now.

The irony is that I know exactly, word for word, what the doctor will write: *No complaints. Diagnosis: Diabetic polyneuropathy, initial indications.*

This is essentially what they wrote on my discharge slip at the Institute of Endocrinology in 1998. My diagnosis hasn't changed in almost 10 years.

Strange.

She'll tap my knees with a rubber mallet, run a needle in circles over my feet, and ask me to touch my nose with my eyes closed. Then she'll ask if I have any complaints. I know it all by heart.

12:30. The eye doctor.

First a paying patient slipped through (they don't have to wait in line). Next some nurse dropped by for a visit with her daughter. At which point, to top it all off, the bespectacled doctor stuck her head out the door and announced she was taking a break. Half an hour.

12:38. I couldn't take it any more. I burst in without knocking. The doctor swallowed something half-chewed, and turned angrily toward me. Maybe I looked stupid. But I told her just what I thought. In her eyeglasses I could read the words "What nerve!" But from her lips came only a distinct:

"You will kindly leave!"

And then:

"I'll call you."

A young nurse with a lovely figure and blonde hair parades past me, carrying hot tea.

"Get out."

Again I'm in the corridor. I gaze at the scuffed enamel floor. The shadows of patients reflected in it become strange gray figures. Plato's ideal forms were like that, maybe. Salvation lies in memories. And so I see before me Elena Vitalyevna. A splendid brunette, kind, like Mama, caring and tender. My doctor.

"I won't cry any more."

And I don't cry. Ever.

12:45. "Come in, young man."

* * *

My life is an endless corridor with countless doors. A magic theater. Strange journeys along the forks in the road of my own fate, with its mysterious name — diabetes. The sugar disease.

No matter what door I choose, I re-enter myself. Me, a 21-year-old guy with a silent escort, always right behind him.

I'm looking for ... what?

It's as if I left something behind one of those doors.

The mysticism of the line, the prison of the unbearable wait, reflected gray shadows.

I'm behind one of those white wooden rectangles on hinges, with inscriptions in black.

It's so odd.

What's diabetes trying to say to me?

* * *

I've still got the article somewhere. About a woman who cured her diabetes by drinking her own urine.

You hear all sorts of nonsense these days.

I can confirm it: I tried it. One gulp.

It could very well be that with time you get used to it. My parents would grasp at any straw that might help cure their son. Now they're used to it; now this is their fate as much as it is mine. But back then they struggled.

Though at first I resisted, in the end I gave in — out of curiosity, probably.

Urine tastes sweet and salty at the same time.

I raised the pot of straw-colored liquid to my nose and the smell horrified me (it was supposed to be steeped). Screwing up my left eye and grimacing, I swallowed — and rushed off to brush my teeth.

* * *

A fact: diabetics should abstain from sweets.

So that we won't feel it so much, there are lots and lots of different imitations of candy, chocolate, wafers, etc. But these are all just substitutes.

S.U.B.S.T.I.T.U.T.E.S.

Any normal diabetic who's put his time in will simply avoid those in favor of the real thing. With the exception of granulated sugar, of course.

As for me, I like Russian diabetic wafers made with fructose. And some of the chocolates. But the candy — forget it. It's gross.

Forbidden fruit.

I remember once my whole family was staring out the window at a postman struggling across the courtyard with an enormous black-and-yellow box. Who's it for, we wondered. It was for us.

Humanitarian aid from Germany.

It contained everything for a diabetic. Cocoa. Juices. Nuts. Canned goods. Bilberry preserves. Jam. Sugar substitutes. And what not.

The box lasted a week. The whole family partook. Times

were tough: a new country, money problems, and so forth. For a week we lived in paradise out of a black-and-yellow box packed in faraway Germany, where I'd never been.

Diabetics calculate the "bread units" in food. One bread unit is two units of insulin. $1 = 2$: the ratio you need to remember.

It's been a long time since I made any calculations. I've mostly forgotten about diets and regimens. Don't get me wrong, I keep an eye on my glucose levels, etc. I don't miss any shots; I haven't since I was fifteen (at that age everyone blows off their diabetes).

But as for diet, not so much.

Tea: four tablets of Milford and two of Golden Key. This is a classic, I like it a lot.

I love fried potatoes (but not fries).

And sausages.

Meat, by the way, has no bread units, and one piece of candy has two. $1 = 2$. Does this change anything? Not for me.

It's a violation, of course. YES. Very bad.

All the same, diets are not my thing.

Diabetes will forgive me. Or will it?

Oatmeal in the morning, lightly sprinkled with powdered sugar.

Mmmm, *yummy*.

About a kilometer from the sanitarium there was a huge field of garden peas. The guys from our room got into the habit of going there. We'd collect them in bags, and eat them in the evenings. A very particular odor settled into the rooms, and didn't fade until morning. Still, the peas were good.

You could always find alcohol in the ward. The older boys would get it, and drink it on the twelfth floor, in the attic —

and, sometimes, even in the ward. When they did that, they'd ask everyone to look the other way.

Three years later, I went to buy beer in a nearby store with the other older boys. I didn't like it. And nowadays I stay off drink. Diabetes made me that way.

The textbooks say: alcohol lowers sugar levels in the blood.

At first it'll shoot them up pretty high and only later bring them way down. At that point, people often make a mistake: they take a shot. Hypo's unavoidable then. Millions of burst blood vessels in the brain.

With accompanying mental debility.

* * *

"Come in, what're you looking at?"

I show her, with gestures, that there is no way I can undress in front of her.

"Oh, dear light of my heart, I'm not looking."

She looks in her early thirties: dyed blue-black hair; a mole like Marilyn Monroe. She pours the powder into the bath and runs her hands in the water, swirling it.

"When the sand runs out, you get out and call me."

"Okay," I tell her, and the steam, smelling strongly of pine, carries me far away. I turn the hourglass over several times before calling her. It feels great!

Kirik taught me the art of turning seven minutes into twenty. He's now luxuriating in the next tub. I can hear him splashing.

Ah, bliss. Objects go all blurry, as though they're scrubbing themselves clean, revealing something underneath. Splashes of yellow water. Sand rushing out. The time I control. A sensation of my own free will. Only now it's dozing off. Bliss. The pine smell makes my nostrils tingle, lulls me as it fades.

I turn the hour glass over.

It feels so good!

* * *

Diabetes is not something to hide. But sometimes, it's hard to talk to people about it. Not because there's anything shameful about it. No! It's just that they don't get you.

When you discuss diabetes, you're not asking for pity, you're not looking for sympathy, you're not proud of it – you're simply stating a fact. You have an incurable illness. There's no tragedy in this, though everyone thinks just that.

I clearly remember the first time I came clean to these guys I knew. At first they didn't believe me, they laughed. Then their expression changed. The average person needs time to make sense of it. You just can't get it into your head that this normal-sized guy – just like you in every way – can have something wrong with him. After all, he climbed over the wall with you into the neighbor's garden, he played cops and robbers and guessing games with you. He ate candy, for God's sake! How is it possible?

So you show them your lipodystrophy.

And in a few days they've forgotten all about it.

Feigned compassion is another matter. It passes even faster. All those sighs, sad eyes, empty words.

That's why not all diabetics will reveal their secret. Even to their closest friends. You constantly have to come up with all sorts of explanations: for why you have a free travel pass; why before lunch you take out a little wine-colored case and go the bathroom with it; why sometimes you suddenly go all pale and act like you're drunk, whip out some white glucose tablets and gulp them down; why instead of beer you order mineral water. This is diabetes, which they know nothing about.

You always have a choice: to tell or not to tell.

You belong to it, and it belongs to you.

* * *

With the years you get used to giving yourself shots. You pierce your own arm, leg or belly. Everything becomes automatic. You get to the point where you can even tell ahead of time whether you'll be twitching or not after the injection.

Giving a shot to someone else – that's more of a challenge. His skin is more alive, softer.

To inflict pain is a great torture. I don't know what kind of person you'd have to be to endure it calmly.

You uncover the needle – and a strange dread grips you. You feel like holding your breath. You penetrate the muscle too easily. He flinches, just a little. Torture.

A round drop of insulin slithers out of the needle. No blood. Good.

A cotton ball covers up the microscopic little hole. Now you can exhale.

* * *

"In Tajikistan, the healer asked, 'How did you get here?' We said, 'Someone we know brought us, for free.' He said, 'That means you'll leave the same way.' At the time, I didn't pay it any mind. But then I started getting worse and worse. Then I lost consciousness.

"I took you in my arms and walked all over the village, but there were no Russians anywhere. They all threw up their hands. Someone showed me where the hospital was. I shouted, 'It's diabetes!'

"We were lucky. A Ukrainian doctor first injected you with 20 units of insulin. You seemed to be waking up...Then he gave you a shot of glucose. He had no idea what he was doing, but he did it all with such self-assurance. They took us to the hospital in Dushanbe. Several children died there every day. The doctor came in the morning. He examined you, but wouldn't say anything. You seemed to be getting better.

"You were reborn."

This was the first time my father had spoken to me about it like that. I wanted to ask, "Reborn for what?" But I didn't say anything. He sat quietly, too, smoking. Sometimes the smell of cigarettes is very nice.

To inflict pain on someone is torture. I don't know what kind of person you'd have to be to endure it calmly.

Third car of a commuter train.

A test tube crammed full of life. There are students, businessmen, mid-level bureaucrats. Like a pendulum, they go to work in the morning, come home at night. Constants in the equation of fate.

You can meet a future spouse here, or make a friend. The train rushes along, not noticing anything, everyone sits in their seats, talking. This is a well-oiled world, where life outside the window — with its fields and forests flitting past, a life of expanses and freedom — does not penetrate.

A commuter train is that same prison of the unbearable wait, plus the battle for a seat. A strange world. Impassive. Rusted over.

I shattered its calm. Twice. Along with diabetes.

My sugar suddenly shot up. I woke up from a jolt to my left side. Out of the blue a lump rises in my throat. I search for a plastic bag — to no avail. I stagger up from my seat towards the smoke-filled head of the carriage, but before I can say anything — my own vomit cuts me off. The brownish liquid hurtles towards astonished passengers. My stomach explodes with pain.

At the head of the carriage, a bronze-faced man pats me on the shoulder.

"It's okay, it's okay, you'll be fine now."

I want to tell him that I didn't have one too many. Instead I let loose another round.

"Pipe down, pipe down — now it'll be okay."

On the floor I recognize my lunch, along with the spreading stench of acetone.

Only later: home and bed. Insulin.

The ticket-collector looks over my ticket, then asks for my ID and the pink certificate. I've got everything – he won't get any money off me.

He moves on lazily to the head of the carriage. In the window, the next station flickers past.

Dream. Reality.

Dream. Reality.

The terror seeps out of the carriage. After it, the green diamond swims about in front of me. More pain in my stomach. It kills my appetite, but I need to eat. The glucose pills fall onto the filthy floor. I look at my fellow passengers.

Astonishment.

I want to say that I'm not a drunk. But instead, I put the glucose in my mouth. No effect. I need to wait. The pain shrivels up like a dry autumn leaf. I go back out to the front of the carriage. I feel nauseous.

The doors part, people come onboard and the first thing they see is a doubled-up student.

"Drug addict."

"Drunk."

"Nut-case."

Diabetic.

* * *

I well remember the cockroaches. Huge cockroaches crawling out of every crevice in the evening, running along the ceiling, crawling into your bed.

Brown insects the size of half your finger.

They'd exterminate once a week, but after a few days they'd show up again. Fat and well-fed.

I'm in this ward with Shurik because we're both wetting our beds. We already know everything about each other, that's why we say nothing. Shurik isn't afraid of the cockroaches. He catches them with his hands and keeps them in a jar. Then he shows them to the shrieking girls in the next ward.

Once fallen into his hands, a cockroach loses all its prospects for life. What we know of each other, once we've fallen into alien hands, diminishes our lives.

If you see a cockroach running along the blanket — call Shurik. You hear a scratching somewhere by the wall — call Shurik. It's crawling slowly on the ceiling above you — Shurik, where are you?

He was younger than me. One day he burst into tears. I knew why. There was no one in the ward: it was lunchtime. But already you couldn't cover up the smell.

I helped him change: his underwear, the bed sheets, oil cloth, pillowcase and blanket slip. We managed it all before anyone came back.

If you're incontinent — call me.

* * *

There is one incontestable truth, almost an axiom.

A diabetic needs a friend.

Even if that friend doesn't always understand everything. The most important thing is that he be close by. Not only to check up on you (regimen monitoring). Diabetes isn't just high sugar, low insulin, etc.

Diabetes is your view of reality. It's inexplicable fits of panic. Terror. Pessimism.

Sugar depression.

Skepticism and suspiciousness.

Secretiveness.

A friend is your trusted confidant. He may not get everything, but he can feel it, and that's the main thing.

I had a friend like that. He would always ask me: do you feel like you're breathing dust, are you seeing the green diamond, did you forget to bring your shot, how are you feeling?

A friend.

"Had"? Why did I say "had"? I still have him, most likely...

* * *

Strangely enough, everyone wanted to leave the sanitarium. No one wanted to stay there for long. No one except, maybe, for Chobrek – but he had to leave earlier.

Anton, a pudgy, girlish, blond kid cried his whole first night; on the third day they took him away.

Every day someone would leave.

Andrei, my roommate, stayed in the sanitarium a week.

Chobrek – seven days.

Yurik and I – a little more than 12.

We came from the same city, but different parts. In the sanitarium we learnt of each other's existence. Yurik was three years older, though he didn't look it. He was shorter than me and interested only in cars. He would talk about them for hours, and I had to listen. In the evening we'd play cards or talk on the balcony.

After Andrei left, Kirik, Med and I were moved to Yurik's room. Kirik left that same day; he didn't even get to unpack his things.

As a going-away present, he gave me a cassette of Mumiy Troll's *Caviar* and taught me to appreciate Viktor Tsoi of Kino.

One time, the sanitarium's music lovers gathered in our rooms to listen to *Aria*. This was because we had the only tape-player; it belonged to Kirik.

After Kirik left the mood grew somber. We no longer went to collect peas or listened to cassettes.

Med and I loved to play ping pong. In the evenings we'd sneak into a part of the sanitarium that was being renovated (they had set up a table there for the workers) and found the racquets and balls carefully hidden by the previous players.

More and more, Yurik and I wanted to leave. There was absolutely nothing to do there except take pine baths and go to the gym. When they left, everyone always took something with them, as a "souvenir." They took lamps, aluminum forks and spoons from the cafeteria, water glasses.

I took one too.

My parents came to pick me up in a car. While Mama was filling out some forms, I helped Yurik pack. He was leaving with me, without telling anyone. We left Med our deck of cards, some good pillows and our dinner portions. He smiled, though we could see he was really sad to be left alone in an empty room, even with good pillows and a deck of cards...

I slept the whole way home. We dropped Yurik off near the city market, where he lived. And I never saw him again, though I remember perfectly his slick black cowlick, his rather sly merry eyes, and teasing smile. And how he loved cars, too.

* * *

The cabinet held a lot of books.

Soviet poets, mainly. Tvardovsky. Isakovsky. Mayakovsky. Bedny. Poetry of the 1920s and 1940s.

I went to the tutor — she taught all of us while in the hospital, so we didn't fall behind at school — and asked her for something to read. There was positively nothing to do during your free time in that hospital if you didn't have a music player or Tetris. The tutuor gave me Dostoyevsky's *Netochka Nezvanova* — I didn't like it.

Then came Tolstoy's *Childhood*, something by Gorky and some early Chekhov. I read Blok. Verse and poems. I tried *M-Day* by Viktor Suvorov, but couldn't get through it. Back then Suvorov was a top author, a "discoverer of the truth." Hmm... What about now?

Later I read *The Brothers Karamazov*. And to this day I believe there is no book more powerful, because there is none more true.

My hero is Don Quixote. Sometimes I really need his special balsam to repair the body of a knight-errant cut in two. And fat Sancho too. I'll present him with an island. Some day.

* * *

From my diary:

June 11, 2006. Leading the news: Syd Barret, founding member of the great Pink Floyd, has died. Of complications from diabetes. He was 61.

His creative legacy: thirty songs.

The first Pink Floyd album: it's pure hysteria, a blend of mystical psychedelic and artistic dissoluteness. Timeless music.

Syd lived as a recluse in his mother's house and was fond of gardening. Once during a concert Barret is supposed to have suddenly stopped and stared fixedly at a single spot. Many people thought this was the effect of drugs, the accomplice to his madness. But maybe he was seeing the green diamond.

* * *

I have no clue how to tell her about everything, so I just listen, nod, and answer to the point. Her voice sounds ingratiating, with a tinge of artful toadyism.

"So tell me, Vic, can I give him two extra units in the evenings, is that all right?"

"You've checked his sugar. Is it high then?"

"I'll say! Close to 12. We give him a shot for the morning, at six o'clock, one unit, in the mornings he's more or less okay. It was at seven and eight today. So tell me, can I do that, he won't seize up?"

"He shouldn't. Just check his sugar. That should do it. Don't worry about raising the dose."

"Good. Here, look at this."

She's maybe forty-five 45. Thick yellow hair like a funny, wavy crown. Fat hands.

She comes to me with questions fairly often. I'm ashamed that I don't even remember her name. But her son I know well. Andrei, a skinny little guy. Fragile. And very gentle. He's had diabetes for four years.

She hands me an article. Another healer. This time from Altai. She wants to go see him. I tell her:

"It's not worth it. You'll regret it, later."

"Why?"

Coincidences, chance occurrences, repetitions, encounters. Episodes from a strange vision of life.

"I have tried everything there is to try. And I'm still a diabetic. My advice is not to waste your money. Don't worry about raising the dose."

"Uh-huh. A while ago I was took courses in herbal cures. I can give you a book. They say it really helps. Andrei and I drink tea made from hawthorn."

"All right. We'll see."

She has the book with her. She's up on all the latest "innovations". Her son has been taking Lantus shots; my endocrinologist doesn't even know that kind of insulin exists. I accept the brochure happily and say, "Drop by if you have any questions. Goodbye. And don't go to Altai. It's not worth it."

"Goodbye."

* * *

A therapist. The final doctor on my list for today. A small, fat woman with red hair.

"You're so young! And what do you have?"

"Diabetes."

"Diabetes? Wherever did you get that, hmm?"

"My great-grandmother had it."

"Ah, now I get it. Well, any complaints? Do you get colds?"

"No, no complaints."

"Should we just put that down? Can't do it ... Let's check your blood pressure."

She squeezes a black pear. The pulsometer's little arrow marks off the numbers. The air goes out, my veins pulse.

"Your blood pressure is elevated. Have you been worried about something?"

"No."

"Well, it happens. All set..."

"Take care."

"Goodbye. Next!"

Beyond the door awaits the lightness of shuffled-off cares. In the window the streetlamps are on, a light rain is falling. The evening of a hard day.

Cold air rushes over me as I walk out of the dusty polyclinic. I think, or rather I feel, something.

Diabetes perches on the stairs scuffed by people's feet and also says "Goodbye!"

He's tired too. Next to him are some papers; he'll turn them in tomorrow, when I come back to see the endocrinologist. Room № 21.

I step onto the black asphalt. I feel light, free and chilly.

I walk on.

I could take the bus and be home in seven minutes. But I'd rather walk.

In the twilight, people's faces look greenish. I can hear *Yesterday*, coming from somewhere. A great song by a great group. About love.

Sometimes diabetes lets you go. The diabetes of a 20-year-old.

I walk on. Shopping bags, signs in shop-windows, glowing cigarette ends, yellow minivans, the sky's crooked eye blinking from behind blue clouds. The snow will melt soon. Spring will smooth out the gray hillocks of slush, cover everything in green, in joyousness and birdsong.

I walk on. The noise of cars drowns out the silence of the evening. I take out my earphones.

The music unfurls to the pictures of life before me. A car stuck in the snow. The shouts of a mover. The light of streetlamps. Conversations. Figures rushing everywhere. Flashlights.

I walk on. There are moments when you don't need to hurry at all, because these moments will never be repeated. They'll slip away into the substructure of the past. They'll vanish into trifles, transform into the black-and-white dream of the girl artist, who will never come to me again.

I walk on. Schedules, lines, the prison of the unbearable wait, diabetes, the future. It all seems inconsequential compared to what's hidden beneath the black asphalt and behind the blue clouds — where every now and then, the yellow eye of night peeks out.

I walk on.

OLGA YELAGINA

Translated by Andrew Bromfield

THE SECOND LETTER

You know, I thought my first letter might not have reached you. For instance, I dropped the letter in the box, the postman came along, stuck all the letters in his great big huge bag and went off to hand them in at the post office. He's walking along, whistling to himself, and suddenly someone comes round the corner. "Sergeich!" Look at that! An old friend. They haven't seen each other in ages and ages. They hug. Kiss each other on those sagging cheeks that are still so dear. *Long time no see... Come on, let's go celebrate. (Feebly) no, I can't, I'm working. Later, later, Sergeich, what does work matter? Ah, to hell with it!* The postman wakes up in the gutter, with letters scattered all around. He gets up, grunting, looks at his watch, scrabbles together the ones that aren't soaked through. Not all of them...

Or, for instance, the postman came along, stuck all the letters in his great big huge bag and went off to hand them in at the post office. He's walking along, whistling to himself, and suddenly someone comes round the corner: "Sergeich!" Look at that! An old friend. They haven't seen each other in ages and ages. They hug. Kiss each other on those sagging cheeks that are still so dear. *Long time no see... Come on, let's go celebrate. (Feebly) no, I can't, I'm working. Well, if you're working — that's sacred, some other time then, take down my number.* The postman pulls out the first letter he finds in his huge great bag, scribbles the number on the back and stuffs the letter deep in his pocket (mustn't lose it!) — my letter...

Or, let's say... the postman came along, stuck all the letters in his great big huge bag and handed them on to a simple postwoman. And, let's say, the woman is pissed off (there are many factors here, of course — they don't pay her enough, she's not young any longer — cellulite, wrinkles and all the rest — her husband drinks, or left her for another woman, or died, and she has to sit there in the post office, smacking a stamp down on letters (not really very highbrow work)... and she sits there, smacking away with her stamps, and it makes her cry. And suddenly she sees a name on an envelope: "so-and-so" (and your name is so common, it could be the same as the name of her husband, who left her for another woman). Who's it from? From a woman. "Ah, you old goat," she thinks and rips the letter into little pieces without opening it.

Or, for instance, like this... the postman came along, stuck all the letters in his great big huge bag and handed them on to a simple postwoman, who stamps it and sends it to a certain train. The engine driver is blind staggering drunk. His intended died a few days ago. A small, delicate girl who gazed at the world through wide-open eyes in which he saw his reflection. His fault — he slipped up, forgot to kiss her enough, overlooked something, lost her. The engine driver drinks and thinks for the first time in his life that it's all lies, a human being doesn't need lots of money, buildings, men and machines. It's a lie. The only thing a human being needs is another human being. What? What for? Oh God, why this? And how is he going to live now? How can he see himself now, and know what he's like? — his intended, a small delicate girl, has died, and now he has no mirror.

That's what he thinks. And that keeps him drinking without pausing to dry out, with the red-faced, unshaved stoker Uncle Alik. Uncle Alik is a genuine friend, he has an obscure tattoo that has been blurred by life, he looks straight ahead with his cloudy eyes, shakes his head (he understands everything!) and twitches his left eyebrow wisely.

The engine driver drinks, and in the morning he gets into the post train. His head's buzzing, he thinks he sees a pair of eyes outside the window of the locomotive... he passes out, doesn't pull the right switch, loses control. The post train smashes into a passenger train at full speed — an explosion, people hurt, no one has time for letters...

Or maybe even like this... the postman came along, stuck all the letters in his great big huge bag and handed them on to the simple postwoman, who smacks the stamp on it and sends it to a certain train, and the engine driver takes it to the right place, a simple postwoman smacks more stamps on it and sorts it by district-street-building-apartment, another postman sticks the letters in his great big huge bag and, incredibly enough, reaches the right street-building apartment without any trouble, and puts the letter in the letter box... But here's the neighbour's boy. A good boy, all sneakers and dreadlocks, but life's not going well for him today — his parents are fools, he has no money, he's flush out of cigarettes and beer, and in his unbearable childish despair this boy goes up to the neighbour's letter box and clicks his lighter...

So I decided to write you another one.

SYITAR

The morning starts with that damp perfunctory sound: the cleaning lady slapping away furiously with the rag on her mop as it pendulums from one wall to the other in obtuse malevolence. Vshik-vshik. Vshik-vshik. Vshik-vshik...

That's it. The countdown's started. A new day.

The next sound is Lodov's heavy footsteps. Unusual footsteps, with a scraping shuffle: step − and scrape, step − and scrape... And apart from that, with every step he reels from side to side, as if the floor's wired for high voltage. He's well used to it, but it's sheer agony to watch − ICP (infantile cerebral paralysis).

I take my first promenade to the privy. Lodov is shaving, standing at the washbasin, wiggling his face about painfully.

"M-m-morning!" he says, shifting his head as if he wants to but me.

"Morning, how's it going?" I say, and notice that my voice is gruff and gloomy. Apparently I'm adapting to suit his style. See, I'm all twisted too. That way we're on even terms.

Lodov starts shaking his head and going through agony. He has problems with speech as well. Why did I have to ask him how it's going?

"Gyi-gyi-gyiood. Yi-yesterday I bought shyi-shyi-shyioes."

And he starts telling me slowly, at great length, what wonderful shoes they are. He stammers, getting stuck on that explosive guttural "yi", the main link between all the sounds he makes, but he does manage to slip out some words smoothly. And then there is joy in his eyes. Joy at this little victory over himself.

He's a good man, Igor Lodov. Intelligent and talented. It's just a pity no one knows it. People associate physical defects too closely with mental ones. Although when he's not talking or walking, he looks perfectly normal.

"Byi-byi-byirown... with lyi-lyiaces..."

"Good for you," I mutter.

We walk out of the toilet together.

Scrape, scrape, scrape. For some reason I'm hunched over and limping. But it's not deliberate this time, either.

"What's wryi-wryiong with your lyi-lyieg?" Lodov enquires.

"I twisted my ankle," I lie. "I can't walk properly."

"A-ah," Lodov nods understandingly.

And it takes us a long time to walk along the damp corridor. Him going scrape, scrape, and me limping. On even terms.

The long weekend's coming up. Almost all the students are going home. Leaving the ones like me and Lodov — not undergraduates, not postgraduates. Just here, attached to the accommodation. Until they throw us out, or for as long as there are spare rooms. The superintendant's a very kind man, he let us in. But he could have rented the rooms to someone. For money. So he sacrificed his own interests. There's simple human goodness for you, just like that.

You have to work out some kind of cover, though. For instance, I'm listed as a carpenter — I sometimes put locks on doors. And Lodov's an electrician. He hands out electric bulbs to the students and changes sockets. Old ones for new ones. But work doesn't come along very often: our students are the scientific sort, physicists and mathematicians, they don't break down doors. And if they do, they fix them themselves.

At the long weekend you should have a good time. And I'm going go to the shop.

At the desk two people are standing in line for the phone. Lerochka Ivasenko is lisping tenderly into the receiver:

"Mummy! Yes, yes, I hear you... send me a little bit of money... yes... everything's very... what? Everything's very expensive... for textbooks... yes... we have to buy our own textbooks... what?... no, you can't get them at the library."

She's lying there. That's bad, of course. She clutches the phone, and her little nails are all a delicate pink. The money she must spend on them alone. Sweet little girl, "Hail, strange new wondrous youth!"

We're neighbours. And through the thin wall I once heard her opening her heart to a girlfriend about someone.

"You know," she said seriously, "I want to be the sole of his shoe. The mat he walks on. I want to wash his feet in a basin, like a Muslim wife..."

The security guard Sasha holds his hand out to me through his little window.

"Going out?"

There aren't many people around, he's bored because there's no demand for his services — so he clutches at you with words.

In the shop I stand at the glass counter for a long time, choosing between sprats and bread or fortified port wine. I need three roubles more to buy both. It's awkward to ask for credit. I already owe them ten roubles here.

So I stand there, counting my money yet again. Then I ask them to put another three roubles on my slate anyway. As if it's a joke. As if it's not even worth mentioning small things like that.

The salesgirl flings the sprats at me, and they hurtle merrily down the long counter. But they go slightly off course and end up crashing down onto the floor.

"Sorry," the salesgirl says with a smile. That's the way she expresses her superiority over me.

I bend down and pick them up without a word. When you buy on tick, you don't take offence.

When I get back, Sasha's blocking the way in with the full width of his square body and chatting to some girl. The point of the conversation's very simple — she wants to go through, and he won't let her. She tries using her passport, money, entreaties and threats, but it's a boring day for him today, nothing going on. He has to get some kind of satisfaction out of his job, doesn't he?

There'll be hysterics soon. Sasha can sense it. He works with people, after all. A psychologist.

"Sure you won't get drunk and rowdy, now?"

"No, no," she assures him gladly, sniffing to stop the tears from falling.

"Well, I don't really know..."

Keep her just a bit longer. Touch the nerve. Just gently, don't press too hard. That keen sense of measure is professional too.

"All right, your passport," Sasha agrees eventually, giving me a dark look. If there were no witnesses, he'd have chosen the money.

The girl rummages in her little handbag in a hasty, slipshod fashion.

We take the lift together. She turns out to be going to see her friend. Her friend's Nina Ryabova. A large, placid woman. Once when I was drunk I pinned Nina against the windowsill in a dead end of the corridor (the one with the old garden-peas can, filled up to overflowing with cigarette buts). And we kissed. At first she tried to break away (a respectable woman!), then she calmed down and went all limp (weak, can't resist passion). Nina had warm, full lips. Like a horse. But then, I've got nothing against horses.

And I remember she came to me one night, only I was far too drunk, and the desire to sleep outweighed all the others. But Nina started stroking my hair and whispering: "My drunken darling, you just sleep, sleep, don't wake up, and I'll look at you..." I fell asleep to the sound of those words.

She's going to the fifth floor too, Nina's friend, that is.

There are howls coming from number 518. She shudders

and asks: "What's that?" But I just shrug — I don't give away our secrets.

In actual fact, of course, I know that it's Alla, a postgraduate student, beating her jug-eared son. She's probably been to see her ex-husband again, the one who threw her out, supposedly for being unfaithful. But I don't see Alla doing anything like that, I think he just wanted to get rid of her. And she goes to see him every week and takes him new proofs of her innocence, then comes back with no result and lays into her Vic.

(I think about how weak people are and how they almost never rise up against their oppressors. But the desire to hit out is still there and demands an outlet. It doesn't matter who it is. Whoever's nearest.)

But then, they make up quickly and sit there (both in tears) with their arms round each other, and Alla apologizes.

Vic himself takes a philosophical view of the beatings.

"It's no bother to me — it's nothing, she doesn't know how to fight anyway. And it's a relief to her."

He sensibly chooses the tactic of proffering the other cheek.

Nina's friend walks on along the corridor. I watch her as far as the door.

The day passes by as usual: sluggishly and imperceptibly. I run into Vic in the kitchen. We're both cooking potatoes. Only we're at different stages: I'm already boiling, but Vic's still peeling, and for some reason he's biting off the sprouted eyes and spitting them out instead of using a knife. He peels, spits and sums up his day, confiding in me man-to-man.

"It's tough with women. Always crying or fighting."

And he shakes his worldly-wise head.

It gets dark early. It's either evening or night. Pogodin is a lone crimson sail wandering the floors. He's one of the earners, rents his room himself, not a poor relative — not like me and Lodov. (Although he drinks with us, doesn't despise us.) A true democrat. Only he wears a tracksuit that's a poisonous-red colour. The wrong associations.

Now he's looking for some warmth in the night, in somebody's bed. Pogodin has the glittering neck of a green bottle protruding from his pocket. He walks along, knocking on all the doors to see which will open...

I could do with a bit of warmth too. Even without the bed. Just a drink of tea. Out of a flower-pattern mug with a homely, comforting chipped rim.

I knock at Lerochka Ivasenko's door. Lerochka opens the door and takes a step back. As if to say come in, I'm feeling bored anyway.

"Tea?"

I nod.

Lerochka plugs the kettle in and slices a cucumber on a plate. Picks up a piece thoughtfully and starts rubbing her forehead with it. And as she does it, her expression is so intent... Sweet girl...

I put down the bottle of port wine. My contribution, so to speak.

We drink tea. When the moment comes I take hold of her little hand. She doesn't pull it away, and looks into my eyes sinfully. She tests her charm on everyone (it doesn't matter if she likes them or not). Tests the woman in herself.

I pull her close. Quick, quick, before she comes to her senses. Her skin's warm, smooth, alive. Sweet, sweet...

Then suddenly, in a cold voice:

"What are you doing?"

And then, pulling down the blouse that I've violated:

"Why you... you thought that..."

I leave. A defeat. With so many of them, it's not humiliating any more. It just makes you angry. Angry. (And the port wine's still at her place too.)

I'm a pauper — Lerochka can sense it. She'll never want to wash my feet. Girls like that are made for successful men, just one more free gift. But for me — it's Nina Ryabova, with her warm, full lips. Know your place.

There's something quietly boiling up inside me. I go back for the bottle. Lerochka appears in the doorway wearing nothing but her briefs. Laughs when she sees me (how persistent!) Just stands there, not embarrassed at all. Teasing.

I say I've come for the bottle. She sniffs disdainfully. It's boiling up inside me, boiling up... and then I swing round and grab her by the hair. And shake her. The grin immediately disappears from her face. She's afraid. A frightened little girl. I bite her on the neck and run my fingers down her spine, all the way to the end. Don't worry. No need to be afraid of me. And suddenly she reaches for me. (She's realised I'm not just an alcoholic. I'm a man. A savage. A conqueror.) But I pull her off me by the hair and push her away. Lerochka falls onto the bed. Her eyes are half-closed. She's waiting...

But I leave. My little revenge.

We're quits. And I've got the bottle.

All the walls in my room are covered with Lodov's drawings. Nothing but fish. Igor draws them all the time and he gives me a few almost every day. This is the animal he has chosen from all the immense variety of fauna.

I asked him why once, and he said they had a smooth quality. At first I thought Igor liked them because they're slippery and streamlined, but then I realised he meant their smoothness of movement. Fluidity. That was what he found so enchanting. That was his unattainable ideal. They were kind of located at opposite poles: fish, with their slithering grace, and twisted, scraping Lodov. The wave and the zigzag. Ductile silence and stumbling speech.

When he drew, Igor was simply trying to solve the perpetual riddle of movement that nature had set for him.

I sip the port wine slowly and look at these fish. Lodov has definitely achieved perfection. There is something attractive about fish. I'm not sure what it is yet.

When we drink, Lodov often says that no artist has ever captured the movement of a fish. He says it's a thousand times harder than a panther pouncing and antelopes running. I agree. You're a genius, Lodov, I say, a genius. And Igor smiles, he doesn't deny it.

Pogodin arrives with some flat-faced Korean girl. He can smell alcohol from a mile away. He talks for ages about the difficulties of his job. And the Korean girl screws up her eyes, which are narrow enough already. For her, Pogodin is a star. I don't know what tall stories he's been telling her. His ginger moustache sticks out at both sides. He's in TV (such breathtaking heights!). He writes texts for comedy programs on some second-rate channel. After each of his jokes, there's a burst of recorded laughter, supposedly from the audience — to help the viewers at home. So they know where to laugh.

We drink. Pogodin's red clothes offend my eyes. He talks about money, about how he plans to buy an apartment. (How long can you go on living like that?)

Nina and Alla arrive, drawn by the sound of our gathering. Lerochka's hovering behind them.

"There's something wrong with my lock... will you take a look?"

Forget the lock, Lerochka! Later, later, come in...

She came in... Lowered her eyelashes. Even went a bit pink. You wouldn't know her.

Pogodin's making signs at me with his face behind the Korean girl's back. Winking, nodding at Lerochka, wiggling his eyebrows. Where you do get that kind, show me the place. Or else he's asking me to let him have her — I can't tell.

But this isn't about you, Pogodin. Women, in case you didn't know, have very keen intuition. And Lerochka's not reaching out for you, she's not looking at you. She feels things.

The women are waiting for some fun.

Pogodin starts telling us about his job again. This time, apparently, it's for Lerochka.

"The important thing is to toss the viewer a bone right at the very beginning! Steer him, draw him after you through all the obstacles of the adverts... And it's not easy — the viewer's very spoilt nowadays... Fifteen channels, a remote — sit there and click away! That's all it takes! And the viewer's lost forever!"

Pogodin's cheeks redden visibly — he's either afraid of the prospect of defeat or ready for a fight.

Lodov arrives. With a bottle. His eyes are glowing. He tells us someone from the sixth floor gave him an aquarium (they were moving out). All he has to do now is buy the fish, and then he'll solve the problem of piscine motion... Lodov talks for a long time, and very laboriously, because he's so excited. (Pogodin winces as he tries to catch the meaning, and the Korean girl raises her upper lip contemptuously and looks at Pogodin as if she's asking him to translate whatever that muttering is from over there.) But I understand, and I'm delighted too. *This is the start of a completely different life, a new life, not like what came before.* Yes, Lodov, different, of course, different.

We drink to that.

I feel like throwing out the brazen Korean girl, who looks at Lodov as if she isn't sitting on the knees of a comedy-show writer, but on a throne at the very least, and doesn't know a thing about fish, except that you can eat them. But I limit myself to stretching my eyelids back to my temples and twisting the lower part of my face into a moronic expression. The Korean girl doesn't see it. Pogodin smiles apologetically — you know, I didn't choose, just took what came along. Lodov laughs.

The Korean girl hugs Pogodin, inspired by his speech. Nina moves closer to me. We drink.

Igor wants a woman too. He speaks with his "yi". And he reaches out for Lerochka. She doesn't push him away (she's sorry for the poor cripple), just huddles up and pulls her head down into her shoulders. She finds Lodov unpleasant. She looks at me pitifully. Looking for protection. And I suddenly find him unpleasant too.

"Old chap," I say.

I want to say something like she's still a young girl, not used to men yet, ease off, Lodov...

But Lodov (and him such an intelligent man!) forgets he's an ICP case, that he's *different,* and drunk as well. He forgets about his "yi" and he paws at Lerochka, paws at her after I've trained her and groomed her for myself.

I'm not jealous, no. How could I be jealous of Lodov? He just makes me angry. And Lerochka came to give herself up. She came. To me. She might get frightened. The whole night will be wasted. Doesn't he understand, or what?

I take Lodov by the collar of his flannel shirt and chuck him out. Lodov struggles in my arms and bellows. A skinny man with a beard and torment permanently frozen in his eyes... he squirms because he's afraid or he's angry and gives me a painful kick on the knee with his shoe. *Ah, you scumbag, you basket-case!* And suddenly I start to hate him, this living proof of the imperfection of the world, this natural anomaly. Maybe it's your fault my life is all skewed, because when you're always there, you start believing there's no beauty left. And then, as soon as there's the slightest glimmer, you reach out to grab it...

And all my fury focuses on him. I hate him, and I hit him, again and again and again...

They come running out of the room.

"That's enough. Stop it!" Lerochka shouts.

Enough! She's telling me I can stop, that's enough for her, she's avenged... Stupid fool! Thinks it's for her, for her honour!

The security guard Sasha comes running up. He tears me off Lodov. Then for some reason, he hands me to Pogodin, and he (being an intellectual!) doesn't know how to hold me – he hugs me awkwardly from behind, pinning my arms down.

Nina Ryabova is crying and wailing:

"They'll throw us out... they'll throw us out for sure now. Why, why did you let him out?"

Sasha comes back with the superintendant, who's angry because he's been woken up. They talk about something. And Nina babbles something (interceding). Someone else comes to see what the noise is about. I catch a glimpse of Vic in the background, he winks at me – it doesn't matter what happened, I'm on your side anyway... But Lerochka's nowhere to be seen. She's gone. She can't afford to be involved in a scandal.

Sasha politely prods Lodov and me in the direction of the exit.

Night on the brink of morning. Out in the street it's piercingly cold and blue. There's a terrible ache in my knee, little hammers banging away. Lodov's face is battered and bloody. Several drops of blood have stuck in his beard and clotted together.

In the cold we instinctively snuggle up to each other. I want to tell him I'm sorry. Sorry, old chap, don't know what came over me...

Then suddenly he speaks.

He turns toward me, jabs a finger at the sky (up there, look) and forces out the word:

"Syi-yi... syi-yiyi... syitar."

BASYA

Love needs to be nourished constantly. With sacrifices. Terrifying, when you think about it.

That was what Basya said.

And the most important thing is that you have to give everything. It doesn't matter if it's a little or a lot — the point is to give everything. It's midday and devastatingly hot, and I say to you — give me your ice cream. And you give it to me. Unconditionally. You might even die of thirst, who knows. But if you say to me: let's go halves, that's better, that way we'll both survive, then it's over. Over. Do you hear? The End.

How would you like me to cut off my finger? Any one you like, choose. Only make it on the left hand, okay? I use the right hand for writing, it would be awkward...

Basya says.

Kalitin looked at her with that expression in his eyes that Basya called blurred. Kalitin was blurred in general, indistinct. But so what, really? She knew the way he got undressed. Gradually taking everything off himself, even his contact lenses, until he was left naked and blurred. What else? He can't stand anyone making fun of him. In the morning he drinks maroon tea. With hibiscus, called Kar-ka-de. When he rides the Metro, he peeps into other people's newspapers, books and magazines (he likes reading), suggests answers for the crosswords. He never wears shirts. He wears polo necks and sweaters. He has grey hairs. Four. He's proud of them. Wants to look older than he is. Calls it respectability. He hates blondes. Because that's vulgarity. But he likes women with grey hair, skinny. He sings. Well, he purrs, really. That old romance "As I was driving home, I happened to meet you, ta-ta-ta-ta..." A tomcat. He says: "I love you like a thousand devils" (in bed in the morning, between the singing and the Karkade) and also "A swig of cold ale or a bullet in the temple" (to the salesgirl in the shop) — he's very dogmatic.

But Basya's sickly. Always coughing into a hankie. And she doesn't walk so much as creep. Across the bed, for instance. Or sits on the carpet, going through his (Kalitin's) photos, and then creeps across the carpet again to the other end of the room, to put the photo album back in the locker. Sits there till she finds something else interesting, takes it out and creeps back. In fact this creeping's there all the time, in all her movements. From the divan onto Kalitin's knees, from Kalitin back onto the divan. And she says "Seryozhenka, Seryozha..." to him, like it's a question. She's always losing him, can't keep her spatial bearings in life. Once she went to see a girlfriend at the other end of town, and got lost. She came home late, drunk, with a man. As well as Basya, he was carrying a bottle of cognac. "Seryozhenka... I was searching for you everywhere." Kalitin didn't mess about, he punched him. The man hadn't expected to meet him, and he just disappeared. "Don't get the wrong idea, Seryozhenka, we didn't do anything at all really, not really... it's you I love... I was searching for you everywhere, searching ..." After that Kalitin didn't let Basya go out anywhere anymore. But he almost cried, and he tried to worm everything out of her about the man with the cognac — what did he do, where did he touch her, did he kiss her? Basya couldn't remember and she couldn't understand the need for all this, if she loved Kalitin and he was the only one she was thinking about, and he was a kind man — the one with the cognac — he just helped her and gave her a lift home. And that day Kalitin forgot to take his lenses out, and next morning his eyes were red.

And now Basya sits at home, quietly looking through the photos on the carpet. She even tries to drink that tea of his. Kar-ka-de. But it's really sour, tart. And Kalitin comes back late nowadays, he stays on at work. Because he has Basya. The poor thing, poor little lamb. When he gets home, he can take a rest. She should get a bath ready for him. With rose petals. He can lie in it, sweetly perfumed. Her darling. Seryozhenka.

Only there aren't any roses. She'll have to go and buy some. Basya covers her head with a shawl. She buys thirty-four roses (all she had the money for.) Red as blood, as love. She comes home and starts tearing off the petals. My darling. Sweetly and perfumed. Her destiny.

Kalitin arrives. Basya smiles enigmatically and creeps over to him, flows across. Kalitin says: "I'm as hungry as a thousand devils," and starts searching. There's nothing in the frying pans, of course, because Basya's on a diet. He's all set to go to the shop and throw something together quickly — Basya, where's the money? Basya smiles enigmatically and nudges him towards the bathroom, to relax in her rose-scented waters, forget everything that's happened during the day...

But he... he... Well, he didn't get the idea at all.

Basya wept quietly, coughing. Kalitin even closed the door so as not to hear her. He didn't appreciate it, didn't get it all. But all the same she went creeping to him and nestled against him. They made it up. Decided to go to the health spa outside the town.

A big room, cold, on the ground floor. Pine trees outside the window. Basya walking between them, touching them with her hands. She finds a berry, bends down, chews it and spits it out — past its sell-by date. Pale, as pale as a ghost, she was sick on the way here. Kalitin watches her from the window.

Someone comes up to her and asks her a question. Basya stops, sways in the wind and answers the question, nods towards the building, and he takes her by the elbow, smiles, steps into the pine trees, Basya explains something to him — she's very sociable. But meanwhile Kalitin has the face of a murderer premeditating his crime.

The someone, like Basya, also opens his mouth wide, like a fish. And Kalitin hears her exclaiming and exhorting, saying: breathe, breathe! The air! You have to breathe! And he thinks it's very clever of her to say the right thing like that — breathe — that's exactly the right thing. The someone would have died if not for her. But it's still not right, acting like that, with a stranger.

They go to the dining hall for lunch. There are two others at the table — Lilya Makarova and Ilya Petrovich.

Lilya's a blonde. She does everything with gusto: eating, drinking, watching, smelling. She has a red sweater and jeans that she fills to overflowing. Everything about her is taut, stretched, impetuous. Twangy as a bow string. And there's her grin. Lilya's always grinning, just slightly. Seems to know more than she's saying. Or maybe she's not really who she claims to be. It's quite possible.

And it's not clear at all who Ilya Petrovich is. He doesn't talk to them. Stoop-shouldered. In a hand-knitted waistcoat. Stares into his plate. He has the worst room, and there's a gangling consumptive youth living in it as well as him. The youth coughs and cries out in his sleep. Ilya Petrovich is not happy with him. Ilya Petrovich regards his vacation as ruined.

You should go for more walks. Wonderful pine-forest air. Me and Seryozha are going to go out every morning an hour before breakfast. There's a lovely stretch of water just a hundred metres away – a river or a lake – don't you remember, Seryozha? Well, never mind. Anyway, a river or a lake.

Basya says.

Kalitin looks at her and loves her unbearably and nods, says, yes, we're going to walk every morning, that's right, before breakfast. It's very good for them, very healthy.

Suddenly Lilya Makarova grins and turns her head away slightly. As if to say: "Idiots!" But Kalitin (we remember) doesn't like that sort of thing – grins and facetious comments. And they got into a conversation that was kind of small talk, only it was hostile. There now. But why would they do that?

Even Ilya Petrovich felt the tension at the table and looked up from his food.

Is there something between him and her? Kalitin wondered.

But Ilya Petrovich finished his lunch, licked his plate clean, even ate two bread buns more than his quota, from the ones that guests left behind on the tables, then peered around to see what else he could spot. Basya hadn't touched her food yet, and he said: Aren't you going to eat that? Not going to have any more, are you? And she answered nonono, please, take it, although she was just fancying the veggies. And Ilya Petrovich pounced. He freed up his fork first and stuck it in, from a distance, then he dragged it across to himself.

An animal, Kalitin thought.

But Lilya, on the contrary, says in a familiar, approving kind of way, what a wonderful appetite you have, Ilya Petrovich, impressive.

Ilya Petrovich finally finished eating and got up from the table. And so did Lilya, just barely taking hold of his hand and giving Kalitin another glance, with this triumphant snicker, as if I.P. and her were the bee's knees, but Kalitin and Basya were some kind of trash.

There's a draught from the windows. Basya wanders round the room wearing tights and Kalitin's sweater, which comes down to her knees. Looks into all the nightstands and little cupboards. She's put a glass jar with some kind of twisted tree root in it on the TV – beautiful. She shudders. When it's cold, it always makes her feel like eating, she says. They rummaged through everything in the suitcase – the closest thing to food is an electric coil and some tea. They threw the root out of the jar and brewed the tea. Basya found some piece of dry rusk and climbed under the blanket, gnawing on it, happy. She nudges it against Kalitin's lips – want some, want some? So small and skinny. Squeeze her a bit too hard, and something's bound to break. But nothing risked nothing won, and that night Kalitin squeezed her tight too many times to count, risking it – and it was all right.

The morning was sunny and white. As if God was standing outside the door, but not coming in, because he was shy, Basya said. She peeped out from under the blanket and wrinkled her face up at the sun.

They didn't go to the river, or to breakfast either. Because Basya's lips were parted just ever so slightly, and it seemed there was no way to force them to close. Kalitin did try with his fingers, but Basya was laughing too much and it didn't work.

And then lunch was memorable. For the following. A man with a big bushy moustache left one of the tables furthest away and shouted from a distance; Nantseva! And he came over and moved a chair up to Basya. And it took Kalitin a moment to grasp who this Nantseva was, it felt strange to remember that before him Basya had some original surname of her own, as well as an entire period of her life filled with other people instead of Kalitin. Like this guy with the moustache.

Lilya kept trying to needle him too, either about the moustache or something else. But it was useless with him. He was flame-proof, solid as a refractory brick. And he had big ears.

He (the guy with the moustache) kept exclaiming, shaking Basya by the shoulder and twirling his moustache, recalling their student days, talking about things Kalitin didn't know and constantly revealing things that he and Basya had in common. And she seemed to be drifting away from Kalitin. Kalitin started feeling strange again.

When he was done talking, the guy with the moustache dragged Basya (and Kalitin too, naturally) back to his room. Basya kept admiring his moustache and saying of all the things she'd never have expected him to have a huge great moustache like that. And she even touched it with her finger – her perceptions were still fundamentally tactile, hadn't changed since she was little.

They started drinking. The guy with the moustache had only just arrived at the health spa, and his supplies were still intact. They carried on talking about fellow-students, and Kalitin learned that Ivanov had been in a crash and didn't walk too well now, and Veniaminov, for instance, never came out of a hard-drinking binge and now he was... gone... yes, well... And what about Tanechka Komarova, Tanechka? Come on! And she was such a good-looker!... Peltser? He became filthy rich, by the way, he was asking... well, you know... about you... (a pause, a secret glance in Kalitin's direction). And you? Me? The breeze in the tree...

Kalitin suddenly discovered that the guy with the moustache was hard of hearing. When Basya asked him about anything, he nodded and paused and answered off the point, which didn't fit too well with his big ears and Kalitin thought it was funny. He'd already drunk quite a lot himself, and he was feeling a keen attraction to this other Basya, who was drifting further and further away. "Seryozha, just hang on, all right, he's a really old friend of mine..." Kalitin just couldn't bear not getting any attention. He stuck a cigarette in his mouth and stepped out unsteadily into the drowsy silence of the corridor.

The corridor swayed, blew mist into Kalitin's eyes and led him astray, confusing him with its branches. And then he suddenly saw this picture: what if right now Basya and the guy with the moustaches... But Kalitin immediately dismissed this idea as unbearable. He took hold of the wall and set off roughly in the direction of his room.

Lilya Makarova was sitting in front of the TV in the hallway. Smoking. She looked Kalitin straight in the eyes. He walked towards her as if there was a gun trained on him.

"Why weren't you at supper?" she asked, but then, recognising the state he was in, she wiggled her eyebrows knowingly.

Kalitin slouched against the wall and stared angrily at Lilya with that blurred gaze of his. "Don't tell me you're alone?" Lilya asked, looking around in a grotesque parody of amazement, then she asked where's your... hmm-hmm... beloved? And she smiled, and her cunning eyes sparkled as if she knew more than she was saying.

Kalitin said indistinctly that she was his beloved, with no hmm-hmm, and he said what made her, Lilya, so nosy about his love, what was it to her? And Lilya said to him: "Why, tell me, love really does exist after all, does it?" — "Why? Don't you believe in it? Kalitin answered, thinking how good it would be to shake that silly smile off Lilya's face, to teach her a good lesson. "Well, you prove that it does!" Lilya egged him on. "Prove it!"

And he went straight at her. Sullenly, as if she was an enemy. And somehow it happened that he dragged her into his room and knocked her down and shook her and shook her, and he could even remember hitting her on the lips, mostly on that smile — but it didn't go away. And one spring squeaked in a special, sinister, kind of way, like it had never done with Basya. Screer-screer, screer-screer... and Kalitin muttered something basically like what did you say, d'you think I love you? It's her I screer-screer, her... Lilya agreed with everything he said as if he was a mental case... yes-yes, of course, love on, love away... And her face was rigid, with her eyes open, absolutely unchanged by Kalitin's presence.

At the moment when the spring gave its final treacherous squeal, Kalitin started choking Lilya, and she suddenly reached out her hand and patted him on the head as if she was complimenting him and said: "There now, that really is love." Kalitin thought with dull-witted satisfaction that he had won. After that he didn't remember anything.

The next day Ilya Petrovich left, and the guy with the moustache moved to their table. The dark blotches could be seen under Lilya's collar. Basya noticed and whispered to Kalitin that Ilya Petrovich had left his mark, what a fiery little lover. Kalitin nodded gloomily. The guy with the moustache was quiet too, maybe he was hung-over. Only Lilya was the same as ever, ignoring her neck: cheery and smug, constantly making fun of the guy's big ears and big moustache – very brassy.

Basya just trailed her spoon round her plate. And Kalitin suddenly felt irritated. Eat properly. And there's that grin of Lilya's, thinks it's because of her.

And there was Basya still sitting there languidly, poking away sluggishly with her spoon. Maybe if he told her about the blotches, she'd cheer up... But he kept quiet, it wasn't nice to remember.

Basya didn't keep quiet, though. That night she told him all about the guy with the moustache, that he was an old love, and it didn't count that... she said it was the same... the same as with a relative, that he (Kalitin) was so disgustingly drunk as well, and he behaved so badly all evening, disrespectfully, laughing at the moustache. She told him and watched curiously to see what would happen next.

But Kalitin lies there like a corpse. No feelings. Basya was outraged, she said what's happening here, are you deaf or what, last-night-I-was-un-faith... But Kalitin has this sudden absence of love. A total blank.

He looks at Basya. And there's nothing he loves about her. What's happening here?

And she's frightened by his indifference and creeps across the bed — to make up. Doesn't even creep, sort of wallows across. What sort of name is that, anyway — Basya? What's her real name? Ah, who cares?

He turns away to face the wall and lies there without sleeping. As empty-headed as a globe.

AUTHORS' NOTES

ALEKSEI LUKYANOV was born in 1976 near Solikamsk in the Urals. His studies at the Solikamsk Teacher-training College were interrupted by army service. A blacksmith by trade, Lukyanov has written several short novels and a great many short stories. Critics have praised his work for its "ingenious use of the language and intricately woven allusions." (*Book Review*) Two-time Debut finalist. Winner of the New Pushkin Prize "for innovative treatment of Russian literary traditions."

IGOR SAVELYEV was born in 1983 in Ufa (Bashkiria). He holds a degree in Philology from Ufa University and is now at work on his Ph.D. A short novel based on his experiences hitchhiking was a finalist for both the Debut and Belkin prizes in 2004. Critics have noted his "masterful, finely chiseled style based on brilliant counterpoints like a virtuoso music piece." "Here realism is bordering on phantasmagoria ... a striking sample of new-generation psychological prose."

DENIS OSOKIN was born in 1977 in Kazan (Tatarstan). He studied psychology at Warsaw University before enrolling in Kazan University's Department of Philology which he finished in 2002. Winner of the Debut Prize (2001); finalist for the Andrei Bely Prize (2004) and Yuri Kazakov Prize (2005). Osokin's short stories appear regularly in leading literary journals. A book of his miniatures (a mosaic) was published by NLO in 2003.

GULLA KHIRACHEV (pen name of Alisa Ganieva) was born in 1985 in the Dagestani village of Gunib in the Caucasus. The family later moved to Makhachkala, the capital of Dagestan. A graduate of the Moscow Literary Institute, Ganieva works as a literary critic and also writes avant-garde children's tales. "Salam, Dalgat", her first work of fiction for adults, won the Debut Prize in 2009.

POLINA KLYUKINA was born in 1986 in the city of Perm in the Urals. She is currently a student at the Moscow Literary Institute and the Publishing University's Department of Journalism. Her stories have appeared in *Novy Mir*. Debut finalist in 2008.

ALEXANDER GRITSENKO was born in 1980 in Astrakhan on the Volga. He holds degrees from the Moscow Literary Institute and from the Institute of Psychology and Psychoanalysis. Journalist, playwright, scriptwriter, critic, and stage director. Author of two volumes of poetry and two collections of short stories. Winner of the Debut Prize for drama in 2005.

ARSLAN KHASAVOV was born in 1988. A Chechen by nationality, he comes from the village of Braguny near Gudermes, in the Caucasus. Now finishing his studies at the Asia and Africa Institute at Moscow University. He published a cycle of his stories in Yunost. A book of short stories appeared in 2009. Debut finalist in 2009.

OLEG ZOBERN was born in 1980 in Moscow. A graduate of the Moscow Literary Institute, he is the author of numerous short stories in leading literary journals. Winner of the Debut Prize in 2004. Two of his short story collections were published in Holland. Critics have admired him for the "recurrent theme of the road and wandering and his distinctive literary style." (*Ex Libris*)

YUNA LETTS was born in 1985 near Smolensk. She now lives in Maputu, Mozambique, and travels all over Africa as a journalist and photographer. As a travel writer, Letts contributes to the magazine *Telegraph around the World*. In 2009 she published her first book of short stories. Debut finalist in 2009.

IRINA GLEBOVA was born in 1983 in St Petersburg. An artist by training, Glebova specializes in puppet-making. Her short stories have appeared in leading literary journals. Winner of the Debut Prize for fiction in 2007

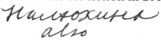

VICTOR PUCHKOV was born in 1985 in Noginsk near Moscow. He has a degree in Philology from the Education University. His work for local newspapers won him the "Nail" Prize. He contributes stories to Moscow periodicals and the radio. "The Sugar Disease" won the Debut Prize in 2006. Puchkov has published two poetry collections, long and short stories, and a novel.

OLGA YELAGINA, was born in 1981 in Ufa (Bashkiria). She is a graduate of the Moscow Literary Institute and the Screenplay Department of the Cinema Institute. She won the prize *Belsk Prostory*, the Bashkirian literary magazine where her early stories appeared. Debut finalist in 2005. Yelagina is now at Moscow University writing her dissertation on contemporary Russian literature.

This collection was compiled by **OLGA SLAVNIKOVA,** the director of the Debut Prize, an internationally known novelist and winner of the Russian Booker and other top prizes, author of several major novels translated into many languages.
Her novel *2017* came out in English in 2010.

COMPLETE GLAS BACKLIST

Mikhail Levitin, *A Jewish God in Paris*, three novellas

Roman Senchin, *Minus*, a novel
an old Siberian town surviving the perestroika dislocation

Maria Galina, *Iramifications*, a novel
adventures of today's Russian traders in the medieval East

Sea Stories. Army Stories
by Alexander Pokrovsky and **Alexander Terekhov**
realities of life inside the army

Andrei Sinyavsky, *Ivan the Fool. Russian Folk Belief*,
a cultural study

Sigizmund Krzhizhanovsky, *Seven Stories*
a rediscovered writer of genius from the 1920s

Leonid Latynin, *The Lair*,
a novel-parable, stories and poems

The Scared Generation, two novels
the grim background of today's ruling class

Alan Cherchesov, *Requiem for the Living*, a novel,
the extraordinary adventures of an Ossetian boy set against
the traditional culture of the Caucasus

Nikolai Klimontovich, *The Road to Rome*,
naughty reminiscences about the late Soviet years

Nina Gabrielyan, *Master of the Grass*,
long and short stories by a leading feminist

Alexander Selin, *The New Romantic*, modern parables

Valery Ronshin, *Living a Life*, *Totally Absurd Tales*

Andrei Sergeev, *Stamp Album*, *A Collection of People,
Things, Relationships and Words*

Lev Rubinstein, *Here I Am*
humorous-philosophical performance poems and essays

Andrei Volos, *Hurramabad*,
national strife in Tajikstan following the collapse of the USSR

Larissa Miller, *Dim and Distant Days*
a Jewish childhood in postwar Moscow recounted
with sober tenderness and insight

Alexander Genis, *Red Bread,* essays
Russian and American civilizations compared
by one of Russia's foremost essayists

Anatoly Mariengof, *A Novel Without Lies*
the turbulent life of a poet in flamboyant
Bohemian Moscow in the 1920s

Irina Muravyova, *The Nomadic Soul,*
a family saga about one more Anna Karenina

The Portable Platonov, a reader
for the centenary of Russia's greatest 20th century writer

Boris Slutsky, *Things That Happened,*
biography of a major mid-20th century poet
interspersed with his poetry

Asar Eppel, *The Grassy Street*
graphic stories from a Moscow suburb in the 1940s

Peter Aleshkovsky, *Skunk: A Life,* a bildungsroman
set in today's Northern Russian countryside

ANTHOLOGIES

War & Peace, army stories versus women's stories:
a compelling portrait of post-post-perestroika Russia

Captives
victors turn out to be captives on conquered territory

NINE of Russia's Foremost Women Writers
collective portrait of women's writing today

Strange Soviet Practices
short stories and documentaries illustrating
some inimitably Soviet phenomena

Childhood, the child is father to the man

Beyond the Looking-Glas, Russian grotesque revisited

A Will & a Way, women's writing of the 1990s

Booker Winners & Others-II
some samplings from the Booker winners

Love Russian Style, Russia tries decadence

Booker Winners & Others, mostly provincial writers

Jews & Strangers, what it means to be a Jew in Russia

Bulgakov & Mandelstam, earlier autobiographical stories

Love and Fear, the two strongest emotions
dominating Russian life

Women's View, Russian women bloodied but unbowed

Soviet Grotesque,
young people's rebellion against the establishment

Revolution, the 1920s versus the 1980s

BOOKS ABOUT RUSSIA

A.J. Perry, *Twelve Stories of Russia: A Novel, I guess*

Contemporary Russian Fiction: A Short List
11 Russian authors interviewed by Kristina Rotkirch

COMING SOON!

The Russian Word's Worth
A humorous and informative guide to
the Russian language, culture and translation
by **Michele A. Berdy**

[handwritten signature]